Fireheart's paws worked furiously, and the river tossed him against the rock, driving the breath out of his body. He scrabbled at the rough surface, bracing himself against the rushing water, and found himself face-to-face with the two kits.

They were crouched on a tangled mat of twigs, leaves, and Twoleg rubbish. The mat lurched and their wails grew louder.

"Here we go," Fireheart muttered. "StarClan help us!" He pushed himself off from the rock, thrusting at the mat with his muzzle to guide it into the current. The two kits whimpered and flattened themselves against the twigs.

Fireheart put every last scrap of energy into pushing the mat ahead of him with his nose and paws. He could feel exhaustion draining the strength from his limbs. Raising his head and blinking water out of his eyes, he realized with horror that he had lost sight of the bank. It seemed as if there was nothing in the world but the churning water, the fragile mat of twigs, and the two terrified kits.

WARRIORS

WARRIORS

FOREST OF
SECRETS

ERIN
HUNTER

AVON BOOKS

An Imprint of HarperCollinsPublishers

Library of Congress Cataloging-in-Publication Data
Hunter, Erin W.
Forest of secrets / Erin Hunter.
    p.   cm. — (Warriors ; bk. 3)
Summary: The warrior cat Fireheart's determination to uncover the
truth about another warrior's death leads him deep into danger, and
reveals secrets that test the strength of Clan loyalties.
    ISBN 0-06-000004-X — ISBN 0-06-052560-6 (lib. bdg.)
    ISBN 0-06-052561-4 (pbk.)
    [1. Cats—Fiction. 2. Fantasy.] I. Title. II. Series: Hunter, Erin W.
Warriors ; bk. 3.
PZ7.H916625Fo 2003
[Fic]—dc21
                                                          2003000445

First Avon edition, 2004

AVON TRADEMARK REG. U.S. PAT. OFF. AND IN OTHER COUNTRIES,
MARCA REGISTRADA, HECHO EN U.S.A.

❖

Visit us on the World Wide Web!
www.harperchildrens.com

To Schrödi, hunting with StarClan,
and to Abbey Cruden,
who has met the real Fireheart

Special thanks to Cherith Baldry

WARRIORS

FOREST OF
SECRETS

ALLEGIANCES

THUNDERCLAN

LEADER

BLUESTAR—blue-gray she-cat, tinged with silver around her muzzle.

DEPUTY

TIGERCLAW—big dark brown tabby tom with unusually long front claws.

MEDICINE CAT

YELLOWFANG—old dark gray she-cat with a broad, flattened face, formerly of ShadowClan.
APPRENTICE, CINDERPELT—dark gray she-cat

WARRIORS

(toms and she-cats without kits)

WHITESTORM—big white tom.
APPRENTICE, BRIGHTPAW

DARKSTRIPE—sleek black-and-gray tabby tom.

LONGTAIL—pale tabby tom with dark black stripes.
APPRENTICE, SWIFTPAW

RUNNINGWIND—swift tabby tom.

WILLOWPELT—very pale gray she-cat with unusual blue eyes.

MOUSEFUR—small dusky brown she-cat.
APPRENTICE, THORNPAW

FIREHEART—handsome ginger tom.
APPRENTICE, CLOUDPAW

GRAYSTRIPE—long-haired solid gray tom.
APPRENTICE, BRACKENPAW

DUSTPELT—dark brown tabby tom.

SANDSTORM—pale ginger she-cat.

APPRENTICES (more than six moons old, in training to become warriors)

SWIFTPAW—black-and-white tom.

BRACKENPAW—golden brown tabby tom.

CLOUDPAW—long-haired white tom.

BRIGHTPAW—she-cat, white with ginger splotches.

THORNPAW—golden brown tabby tom.

QUEENS (she-cats expecting or nursing kits)

FROSTFUR—beautiful white coat and blue eyes.

BRINDLEFACE—pretty tabby.

GOLDENFLOWER—pale ginger coat.

SPECKLETAIL—pale tabby, and the oldest nursery queen.

ELDERS (former warriors and queens, now retired)

HALFTAIL—big dark brown tabby tom with part of his tail missing.

SMALLEAR—gray tom with very small ears; the oldest tom in ThunderClan.

PATCHPELT—small black-and-white tom.

ONE-EYE—pale gray she-cat; the oldest cat in ThunderClan; virtually blind and deaf.

DAPPLETAIL—once-pretty tortoiseshell she-cat with a lovely dappled coat.

BROKENTAIL—long-haired dark brown tabby; blind; formerly ShadowClan leader.

SHADOWCLAN

LEADER   **NIGHTSTAR**—old black tom.

DEPUTY   **CINDERFUR**—thin gray tom.

MEDICINE CAT   **RUNNINGNOSE**—small gray-and-white tom.

WARRIORS   **STUMPYTAIL**—brown tabby tom.
     APPRENTICE, BROWNPAW

     WETFOOT—gray tabby tom.
     APPRENTICE, OAKPAW

     LITTLECLOUD—very small tabby tom.

QUEENS   **DAWNCLOUD**—small tabby.

     DARKFLOWER—black she-cat.

     TALLPOPPY—long-legged light brown tabby she-cat.

WINDCLAN

LEADER   **TALLSTAR**—black-and-white tom with a very long tail.

DEPUTY   **DEADFOOT**—black tom with a twisted paw.

MEDICINE CAT   **BARKFACE**—short-tailed brown tom.

WARRIORS   **MUDCLAW**—mottled dark brown tom.
     APPRENTICE, WEBPAW

     TORNEAR—tabby tom.
     APPRENTICE, RUNNINGPAW

     ONEWHISKER—young brown tabby tom.
     APPRENTICE, WHITEPAW

PRINCESS—light brown tabby with a distinctive white chest and paws—a kittypet.

RAVENPAW—sleek black cat with a white-tipped tail who lives on the farm with Barley.

SMUDGE—plump, friendly black-and-white kitten who lives in a house at the edge of the forest.

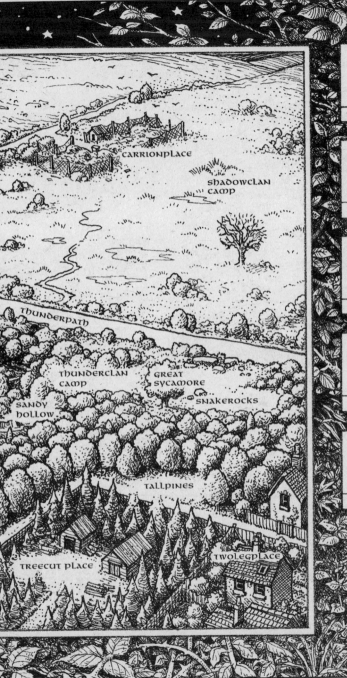

CARRIONPLACE

SHADOWCLAN
CAMP

THUNDERPATH

THUNDERCLAN   GREAT
CAMP   SYCAMORE

SANDY   SNAKEROCKS
HOLLOW

TALLPINES

TREECUT PLACE   TWOLEGPLACE

THUNDERCLAN

RIVERCLAN

SHADOWCLAN

WINDCLAN

STARCLAN

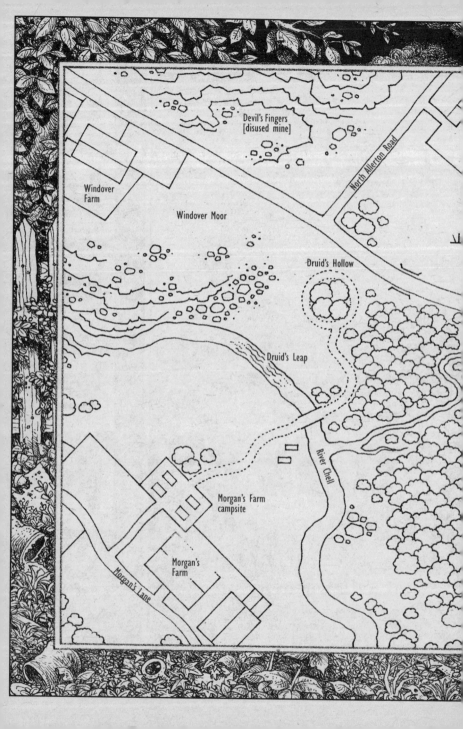

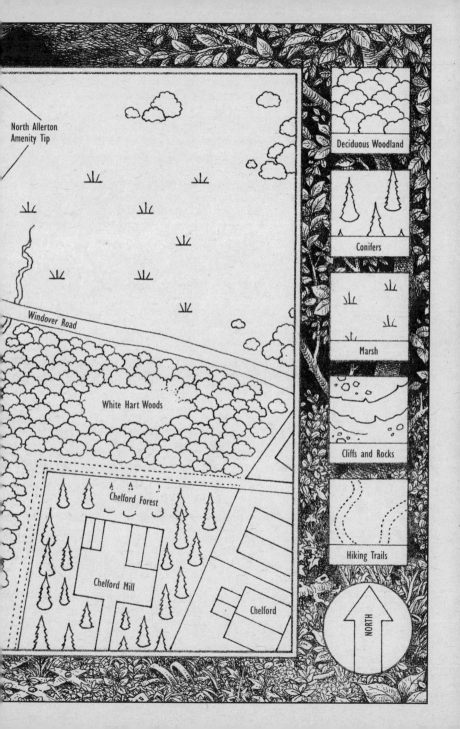

PROLOGUE
❧

Cold gripped the forest, fields, and moorland like an icy claw. Snow covered everything, glittering faintly under a new moon. Nothing broke the silence in the forest except for the occasional soft rush of snow sliding from the branches of trees and the faint rasping of dried reeds when the wind swept through them. Even the murmur of the river was stilled by the ice that stretched from bank to bank.

There was a flicker of movement at the edge of the river. A large tomcat, his bracken-colored fur fluffed up against the cold, emerged from the reeds. He shook snow impatiently from his paws as he sank into the soft drifts with every step.

In front of him, two tiny kits struggled forward with faint mews of distress. They floundered in the powdery snow, the fur on their legs and belly matted into icy clumps, but every time they tried to stop, the tomcat nudged them on.

The three cats trudged along the river until it widened out, and they drew level with a small island not far from the bank. Thick beds of reeds surrounded it, their dry stems poking up through the ice. Stunted, leafless willow trees concealed the center of the island behind snow-covered boughs.

"Almost there," the bracken-colored tom meowed encouragingly. "Follow me."

He slid down the bank into a narrow frozen pathway through the reeds and leaped onto the dry, crisp earth of the island. The bigger of the two kits scrambled after him, but the smaller one collapsed on the ice and crouched there, mewing pitifully. After a moment's pause the tomcat jumped down beside it and tried to nudge it to its paws, but it was too exhausted to move. The tomcat gave its ears a lick, roughly comforting the helpless scrap, and then picked it up by the scruff of the neck and carried it onto the island.

Beyond the willow trees was a stretch of open ground broken by bushes. Snow covered the earth here, crisscrossed by the pawmarks of many cats. The clearing seemed deserted, but bright eyes gleamed from shelter, watching the tomcat as he led the way to the largest clump of bushes and through the outer wall of tangled branches.

The icy chill of the air outside gave way to the warmth of the nursery and the smell of milk. In a deep nest of moss and heather a gray she-cat was suckling a single tabby kit. She raised her head as the tomcat drew closer and gently set down the kit he was carrying. The second kit staggered into the nursery behind him and tried to scrabble its way into the nest.

"Oakheart?" meowed the she-cat. "What have you got there?"

"Kits, Graypool," Oakheart replied. "Will you take them?

They need a mother to look after them."

"But . . ." Graypool's amber eyes were shocked. "Whose kits are they? They're not RiverClan's. Where did you get them?"

"I found them in the forest." Oakheart did not meet the she-cat's eyes as he spoke. "They're lucky a fox didn't find them first."

"In the forest?" meowed the queen, her voice rasping with disbelief. "Oakheart, don't talk to me as if I'm mouse-brained. What cat would abandon her kits in the forest, especially in weather like this?"

Oakheart shrugged. "Rogues, maybe, or Twolegs. How would I know? I couldn't leave them there, could I?" He nosed the smaller kit, which was lying completely still except for the rapid rise and fall of its tiny ribs as it breathed. "Graypool, please . . . Your other kits died, and these will die too, unless you help them."

Graypool's eyes clouded with pain. She looked down at the two kits. Their tiny mouths gaped pink as they mewed piti-fully. "I have plenty of milk," she murmured, half to herself. "Of course I'll take them."

Oakheart puffed out his breath in a sigh of relief. He picked up first one kit and then the other and laid them next to Graypool. She nudged them gently into the curve of her belly next to her own kit, where they began to suckle eagerly.

"I still don't understand," Graypool meowed when they were settled. "Why would two kits be alone in the forest in the middle of leaf-bare? Their mother must be frantic."

The bracken-colored tom prodded a piece of moss with one massive front paw. "I didn't steal them, if that's what you're thinking."

Graypool looked at him for a long moment. "No, I don't think you did," she meowed at last. "But you're not telling me the whole truth, are you?"

"I've told you all you need to know."

"No, you haven't!" Graypool's eyes flashed with anger. "What about their mother? I know what it's like to lose kits, Oakheart. I wouldn't wish that kind of grief on any cat."

Oakheart lifted his head and glared at her, a faint growl coming from the depths of his throat. "Their mother is probably some rogue cat. This is not the weather to go looking for her."

"But Oakheart—"

"Just take care of the kits, please!" The bracken-colored tom sprang to his paws and turned abruptly to push his way out of the nursery. "I'll bring you some fresh-kill," he meowed over his shoulder as he left.

When he had gone, Graypool bent her head over the kits, rasping her tongue over their fur to warm them. The melting snow had washed away most of their scent, though Graypool could still make out the odors of the forest, of dead leaves and frostbitten earth. And there was something beneath that, fainter still. . . .

Graypool paused in her licking. Had she really sensed that, or was she imagining things? Dipping her head again, she opened her mouth to breathe in the kits' scents.

Her eyes grew wider, and she stared unblinking into the dark shadows that edged the nursery. She was not wrong. The fur of these two motherless kits, whose origins Oakheart refused to explain, unmistakably carried the scent of an enemy Clan!

CHAPTER 1

The icy wind whirled snow into Fireheart's face as he struggled down the ravine toward the ThunderClan camp, the mouse he had just killed gripped firmly in his jaws. The flakes were falling so thickly that he could scarcely see where he was going.

His mouth watered as the prey-scent of mouse filled his nostrils. He hadn't eaten since the previous night, a grim sign of how scarce prey was in leaf-bare. Hunger clawed at his belly, but Fireheart would not break the warrior code: The Clan must be fed first.

A glow of pride briefly drove off the chill from the snow that matted his flame-colored coat, as Fireheart remembered the battle that had taken place only three days before. He had joined the other ThunderClan warriors to help support WindClan when the moorland cats were attacked by the other two Clans in the forest. Many cats had been injured in that battle, so it was even more important for those who could still hunt to bring home prey.

As Fireheart pushed his way through the gorse tunnel leading into the camp, he dislodged snow from the spiky branches above, and he flicked his ears as the cold lumps fell on his head. The thorn trees around the camp gave some shelter from the wind, but the clearing in the center of the camp was deserted; all the cats preferred to stay in their dens to keep warm when the snow lay this thick. Broken tree stumps and the branches of a fallen tree poked above the covering of snow. A single line of pawprints crossed from the apprentices' den to the bramble thicket where the kits were cared for. Seeing the trail, Fireheart could not help remembering that he was without an apprentice now, since Cinderpaw had been injured beside the Thunderpath.

Trotting across the snow into the heart of the camp, Fireheart dropped his mouse on the pile of fresh-kill near the bush where the warriors slept. The pile was pitifully small. Such prey as could be found was thin and scrawny, hardly a mouthful for a famished warrior. There would be no more plump mice until newleaf, and that was many moons away.

Fireheart was turning away, ready to go back on hunting duty, when a loud meow sounded behind him. He whirled around.

Shouldering his way out of the warriors' den was the Clan deputy, Tigerclaw. "Fireheart!"

Fireheart padded through the snow toward him, respectfully lowering his head, but conscious that the huge tabby's amber eyes burned into him. All his misgivings about Tigerclaw flooded through him again. The deputy was strong, respected, and an outstanding fighter, but Fireheart knew there was darkness in his heart.

"You don't need to go out hunting again tonight," Tigerclaw growled as Fireheart approached. "Bluestar has chosen you and Graystripe to go to the Gathering."

Fireheart's ears twitched with excitement. It was an honor to accompany the Clan leader to the Gathering, where all four Clans met in peace at full moon.

"You had better eat now," added the dark-coated deputy. "We leave at moonrise." He began to stalk across the clearing toward the Highrock, where Bluestar, the Clan leader, had her den; then he paused and swiveled his massive head to look back at Fireheart. "Just make sure you remember which Clan you belong to at the Gathering," he hissed.

Fireheart felt his fur bristle as anger flared inside him. "What makes you say that?" he demanded boldly. "Do you think I would be disloyal to my own Clan?"

Tigerclaw turned to face him, and Fireheart tried hard not to flinch at the menace in the cat's tensed shoulders. "I saw you in the last battle." The deputy's voice was a low growl, and his ears were flattened against his head as he spat, "I saw you let that RiverClan warrior escape."

Fireheart winced, his mind flashing back to the battle in the WindClan camp. What Tigerclaw said was true. Fireheart had allowed a RiverClan warrior to flee without a scratch, but not out of cowardice or disloyalty. The warrior had been Silverstream. Unknown to the rest of ThunderClan, Fireheart's best friend, Graystripe, was in love with her, and Fireheart could not bring himself to wound her.

Fireheart had done his best to talk his friend out of visiting Silverstream—their relationship went against the warrior code and put both of them in grave danger. But Fireheart also knew that he would never betray Graystripe.

Besides, Tigerclaw had no right to accuse any cat of disloyalty. He had stood on the edge of the battle, watching while Fireheart fought for his life against another RiverClan warrior, and turned away instead of helping him. And that was not the worst accusation Fireheart could make against the deputy. He suspected Tigerclaw of murdering the former ThunderClan deputy, Redtail, and even planning to get rid of their leader herself.

"If you think I'm disloyal, tell Bluestar," he meowed challengingly.

Tigerclaw drew back his lips in a snarl and dropped into a half crouch, sliding out his long claws. "I don't need to bother Bluestar," he hissed. "I can deal with a kittypet like you."

He stared at Fireheart for a moment longer. Fireheart realized with a jolt that there was a trace of fear as well as distrust in the blazing amber eyes. *Tigerclaw wonders how much I know*, he thought suddenly.

Fireheart's friend Ravenpaw, Tigerclaw's own apprentice, had witnessed the murder of Redtail. Tigerclaw had tried to kill him to keep him quiet, so Fireheart had taken him to live with Barley, a loner who lived near a Twoleg farm on the other side of WindClan's territory. Fireheart had tried to tell Ravenpaw's story to Bluestar, but the Clan leader refused to believe that her brave deputy could be guilty of such a thing. As he glared at Tigerclaw, Fireheart's frustration returned; he felt as if a tree had fallen and pinned him to the ground.

Without another word, Tigerclaw swung around and stalked away. As Fireheart watched him go, there was a rustling from inside the warriors' den, and Graystripe poked his head out through the branches.

"What on earth are you doing?" he meowed. "Picking fights with Tigerclaw like that! He'll turn you into crow-food!"

"No cat has the right to call me disloyal," Fireheart argued.

Graystripe bent his head and gave his chest fur a couple of quick licks. "I'm sorry, Fireheart," he muttered. "I know this is all because of me and Silverstream—"

"No, it isn't," Fireheart interrupted, "and you know it. Tigerclaw's the problem, not you." He shook himself, scattering snow from his coat. "Come on; let's eat."

Graystripe pushed the rest of the way out and bounded toward the pile of fresh-kill. Fireheart followed him, picked out a vole, and carried it back to the warriors' den to eat. Graystripe crouched beside him, near the outer curtain of branches.

Whitestorm and a couple of other senior warriors were curled up asleep in the center of the bush, but otherwise the den was empty. Their sleeping bodies warmed the air, and barely any snow had penetrated the thick canopy of branches.

Fireheart took a mouthful of vole. The meat was tough and stringy, but he was so hungry that it tasted delicious. It was gone far too quickly, but it was better than nothing, and it would give him the strength he needed to travel to the Gathering.

When Graystripe had finished his meal in a few ravenous gulps, the two cats lay close together, grooming each other's cold fur. It was a relief to Fireheart to share tongues like this with Graystripe again, after the troubling time when it seemed that Graystripe's love for Silverstream would destroy his friendship with Fireheart. Even though Fireheart still worried about his friend's forbidden affair, since the battle he and Graystripe had rekindled their friendship so it was as close as before. They needed to trust each other if they were to survive the long season of leaf-bare, and even more than that, Fireheart knew he needed Graystripe's support against Tigerclaw's growing hostility.

"I wonder what news we'll hear tonight," he murmured in his friend's gray ear. "I hope RiverClan and ShadowClan have learned their lesson. WindClan won't be driven out of their territory again."

Graystripe shifted uncomfortably. "The battle wasn't just greed for territory," he pointed out. "Prey is even scarcer than usual—RiverClan are starving since the Twolegs moved into their territory."

"I know." Fireheart flicked his ears in reluctant sympathy, understanding that his friend would want to defend Silverstream's Clan. "But forcing another Clan out of their territory isn't the answer."

Graystripe muttered agreement, and then fell silent. Fireheart knew how he must've felt. It was only a few moons since they had crossed the Thunderpath to find WindClan and to bring them home. Yet Graystripe was bound to sympathize with RiverClan too, because of his love for Silverstream. There were no easy answers. The shortage of prey would be a desperate problem for all four Clans, at least until leaf-bare relaxed its cruel grip on the forest.

Growing drowsy under the steady rasp of Graystripe's tongue, Fireheart jumped at the rustle of branches outside the den. Tigerclaw entered, followed by Darkstripe and Longtail. All three of them glowered at Fireheart as they settled in a huddle closer to the center of the bush. Fireheart watched them through slitted eyes, wishing that he could make out their conversation. It was too easy to imagine they were plotting against him. Fireheart's muscles tensed as he realized that he would never be safe within his own Clan while Tigerclaw's treachery remained a secret.

"What's the matter?" asked Graystripe, lifting his head.

Fireheart stretched, trying to relax again. "I don't trust them," he murmured, flicking his ears in the direction of Tigerclaw and the others.

"I don't blame you," meowed Graystripe. "If Tigerclaw ever found out about Silverstream . . ." He shuddered.

Fireheart pressed closer to his side, comforting him, while his ears still strained to catch what Tigerclaw was saying. He thought he heard his own name, and was tempted to creep a little closer, but just then he caught Longtail's eye.

"What are you staring at, *kittypet*?" hissed the tabby warrior. "ThunderClan only wants *loyal* cats." Deliberately he turned his back on Fireheart.

Fireheart sprang to his paws at once. "And who gave *you* the right to question our loyalty?" he spat.

Longtail ignored him.

"That does it!" Fireheart mewed in a fierce undertone to Graystripe. "It's obvious that Tigerclaw is spreading rumors about me."

"But what can you do?" Graystripe sounded resigned to the deputy's hostility.

"I want to talk to Ravenpaw again," Fireheart meowed. "He might remember something else about the battle, something I could use to convince Bluestar."

"But Ravenpaw lives at the Twoleg farm now. You'd have to go all the way across WindClan territory. How would you explain being out of the camp for so long? It would only make Tigerclaw's lies seem like the truth."

Fireheart knew he was willing to take that risk. He had never asked Ravenpaw for any details about how Redtail had died in the battle against RiverClan all those moons ago. At the time it had seemed more important to get the apprentice out of Tigerclaw's way.

Now he knew that he had to find out exactly what Ravenpaw saw. Because he was becoming more and more certain that his friend *must* know something that could prove just how dangerous Tigerclaw was to the Clan.

"I'll go tonight," Fireheart mewed softly. "After the Gathering, I'm going to slip away. If I bring back fresh-kill, I can say I've been hunting."

"You're taking a big risk," mewed Graystripe, giving Fireheart's ear a quick and affectionate lick. "But Tigerclaw is my problem too. If you're determined to go, then I'm coming with you."

The snow had stopped and the clouds had cleared away by the time the ThunderClan cats, Fireheart and Graystripe among them, left the camp and headed through the forest toward Fourtrees. The snow-covered ground seemed to glow in the white light of the full moon, and frost glittered on every twig and stone.

A breeze blew toward them, ruffling the surface of the snow and bearing the scent of many cats. Fireheart shivered with excitement. The territories of all four Clans met in the sacred hollow, and at every full moon a truce was declared for the Clans to gather beneath the four great oaks that stood in the center of the steep-sided clearing.

Fireheart fell in behind Bluestar, who had already dropped into a crouch to creep the last few tail-lengths to the top of the slope and peer down into the glade. A rock reared up in the center of the clearing between the oaks, its jagged outline black against the snow. As Fireheart waited for Bluestar's signal to move, he watched the other Clan cats greeting one another below. He could not help noticing the glares and raised hackles as WindClan faced the cats of RiverClan and ShadowClan. Clearly none of them had forgotten the recent battle; if it weren't for the truce, they would be clawing one another's fur.

Fireheart recognized Tallstar, the leader of WindClan, sitting near the Great Rock, with his deputy, Deadfoot, beside him. Not far away, Runningnose and Mudfur, the medicine cats of ShadowClan and RiverClan, sat side by side, gazing at the other cats with eyes that reflected the moon.

Beside Fireheart, Graystripe's muscles were tense, and his yellow eyes glowed with excitement as he stared down into the glade. Following his gaze, Fireheart saw Silverstream emerge from the shadow, her beautiful black-and-silver coat rippling in the moonlight.

Fireheart suppressed a sigh. "If you're going to talk to her, be careful who sees you," he warned his friend.

"Don't worry," Graystripe meowed. His front paws kneaded the hard ground as he waited for the moment when he could be with the RiverClan cat again.

Fireheart glanced at Bluestar, expecting her to give the signal to descend into the clearing, but instead he saw Whitestorm pad up and crouch beside her in the snow. "Bluestar," Fireheart heard the noble white warrior murmur, "what are you going to say about Brokentail? Will you tell the other Clans that we're sheltering him?"

Fireheart waited tensely for Bluestar's answer. Brokentail had once been Brokenstar, leader of ShadowClan. He had murdered his own father, Raggedstar, and stolen kits from ThunderClan. In retaliation, ThunderClan had helped Brokenstar's own Clan to drive him out into the forest. Not long after, Brokenstar had led a band of rogue cats to attack the ThunderClan camp. In the battle, Yellowfang, the ThunderClan medicine cat, had scratched his eyes, and now Brokentail was a prisoner, blind and defeated. Even though the former leader had been stripped of his StarClan-given name, and was kept under close guard, Fireheart knew that the other Clans would expect ThunderClan to have killed him, or driven him out to die in the forest. They wouldn't welcome the news that Brokentail was still alive.

Bluestar kept her gaze fixed on the cats in the clearing below. "I will say nothing," she replied to Whitestorm. "It doesn't concern the other Clans. Brokentail is ThunderClan's responsibility now."

"Brave words," growled Tigerclaw from where he sat on the other side of Bluestar. "Or are we ashamed to admit what we've done?"

"ThunderClan has no need to be ashamed for showing mercy," Bluestar retorted coolly. "But I see no reason to go looking for trouble." Before Tigerclaw could protest, she sprang to her paws and faced the rest of the ThunderClan cats. "Listen," she meowed. "No cat is to talk about the attack by the rogue cats, or mention Brokentail. These are matters for our Clan alone."

She waited until meows of agreement came from the assembled cats. Then she flicked her tail to signal that the ThunderClan cats could join the other Clans below. She raced down through the bushes, with Tigerclaw just behind her, his huge paws scattering snow.

Fireheart bounded after them. As he slid out of the bushes into the clearing he saw that Tigerclaw had stopped close by, and was giving him a suspicious stare. "Graystripe," Fireheart hissed quietly over his shoulder, "I don't think you should go off with Silverstream tonight. Tigerclaw's already—"

Fireheart suddenly realized that Graystripe was no longer beside him. Looking around, he saw his friend disappearing behind the Great Rock. A heartbeat or two later, Silverstream skirted around a group of ShadowClan cats and followed him.

Fireheart sighed. He glanced at Tigerclaw, wondering if the deputy had seen them go. But Tigerclaw had padded away to join Onewhisker from WindClan, and Fireheart let the fur lie flat on his shoulders again.

Pacing restlessly across the clearing, Fireheart found himself near a group of elders—Patchpelt from ThunderClan, and others he did not know, crouching beneath a glossy-leaved holly bush, where the snow did not lie so thickly. Keeping one eye out for Graystripe, Fireheart settled down to listen to their conversation.

"I remember a leaf-bare even worse than this." It was an old black tom who spoke, his muzzle turned to silver and his flank scarred from many a fight. He had the scent of WindClan on his short, patchy fur. "The river was frozen for more than three moons."

"You're right, Crowfur," a tabby queen agreed. "And prey was scarcer, too, even for RiverClan."

For a heartbeat Fireheart felt surprised that two elders from recently hostile Clans could talk calmly without spitting hatred at each other. But then, they were elders, he reflected. They must have seen many battles in their long lives.

"Young warriors today," the old black cat added with a glance at Fireheart. "They don't know what hardship is."

Fireheart scuffled among the dead leaves under the bush and tried to look respectful. Patchpelt, crouched close to him, gave him a friendly flick with his tail.

"That must have been the season when Bluestar lost her kits," recalled the ThunderClan elder. Fireheart pricked up his ears. He remembered Dappletail saying something once before about Bluestar's kits, which were born just before she became Clan deputy. But he had never learned how many kits she had had, or how old they were when they died.

"And do you remember the thaw that leaf-bare?" Crowfur interrupted Fireheart's thoughts, his eyes unfocused as he lost himself to his memories. "The river in the gorge rose nearly as far as the badger sets."

Patchpelt shivered. "I remember it well. ThunderClan couldn't cross the stream to come here for the Gathering."

"Cats were drowned," the RiverClan queen remembered sadly.

"Prey too," Crowfur added. "The cats who survived nearly starved."

"May StarClan grant it's not so bad this season!" Patchpelt mewed fervently.

Crowfur spat, "These young cats would never cope. We were tougher in those days."

Fireheart could not help protesting. "We have strong warriors now—"

"Who asked your opinion?" growled the cranky old tom. "You're hardly more than a kit!"

"But we—" Fireheart broke off as the air was filled with a shrill yowl and all the cats fell silent. He turned his head to see four cats on top of the Great Rock, silhouettes in the silver moonlight.

"Shh!" hissed Patchpelt. "The meeting's about to start." He twitched his ears at Fireheart and purred softly, "Take no notice of Crowfur. He'd find fault with StarClan."

Fireheart gave Patchpelt a grateful look, tucked his paws under him, and settled down to listen.

Tallstar, the WindClan leader, began by announcing how his cats were recovering after the recent battle against RiverClan and ShadowClan. "One of our elders has died," he meowed, "but all our warriors will live—to fight another day," he added meaningfully.

Nightstar flattened his ears and narrowed his eyes, while Crookedstar let out a threatening growl from deep in his throat.

Fireheart's fur prickled. If the leaders started to fight, their cats would fight too. Had it ever happened at a Gathering? he wondered. Surely not even Nightstar, ShadowClan's bold new leader, would risk the anger of StarClan by breaking the sacred truce!

As Fireheart apprehensively watched the bristling cats, Bluestar stepped forward. "This is good news, Tallstar," she meowed smoothly. "All of us should rejoice to hear that WindClan grows strong again."

Her blue eyes glowed in the moonlight as she glanced at the leaders of ShadowClan and RiverClan. Nightstar turned away from her gaze, and Crookedstar dipped his head, his expression unreadable.

It had been ShadowClan, under Brokenstar's cruel command, who had first driven WindClan away, so that they could extend their own hunting grounds. RiverClan had taken advantage of their exile to hunt in the deserted territory. But after Brokenstar's exile, Bluestar had convinced the other leaders that the life of the forest depended on all four Clans, and that WindClan should return. Fireheart shivered as he remembered the long and difficult journey he had made with Graystripe to find WindClan and bring them home to their bleak upland territory.

That reminded him of how he meant to cross the uplands again to find Ravenpaw, and he shifted uneasily. He was not looking forward to the journey. *At least WindClan are friendly toward ThunderClan*, he thought. *So we shouldn't get attacked on the way.*

"ThunderClan's cats are also recovering," Bluestar went on. "And since the last Gathering two of our apprentices have become warriors. They will now be known as Dustpelt and Sandstorm."

Yowls of approval came up from the mass of cats below the Great Rock—mostly, Fireheart noticed, from ThunderClan and WindClan. He caught a glimpse of Sandstorm, sitting with her pale ginger head raised proudly.

The Gathering proceeded more peacefully now. Fireheart

remembered the previous Gathering, when the leaders had accused one another of hunting outside their own territory, but no cat mentioned this now. A group of rogue cats, led by Brokentail, had been responsible, but the news that these rogues had attacked the ThunderClan camp, and had been soundly defeated, did not seem to have spread. Bluestar's secret about blind Brokentail was safe.

When the meeting was over, Fireheart looked around for Graystripe. If they were going to see Ravenpaw, they needed to leave soon, while the other ThunderClan cats were still in the hollow, and would not notice which way they went.

Fireheart caught the eye of Swiftpaw, Longtail's apprentice, sitting in the middle of a group of young cats from ShadowClan. Swiftpaw looked away guiltily. At any other time Fireheart might have called him over and told him to find his mentor for the journey home, but right now all he cared about was finding Graystripe immediately. He forgot Swiftpaw as soon as he saw his friend weaving his way toward him. There was no sign of Silverstream.

"There you are!" Graystripe called, his yellow eyes shining.

Fireheart could see that he had enjoyed the Gathering, though he doubted that his friend had listened to much of the talk. "Are you ready?" he meowed.

"To go and see Ravenpaw, you mean?"

"Not so loud!" Fireheart hissed, anxiously looking around.

"Yes, I'm ready," Graystripe mewed, more softly. "I can't say I'm looking forward to it. Still, anything to get Tigerclaw out of my fur—unless you've had a better idea?"

Fireheart shook his head. "This is the only way."

The hollow was still full of cats, preparing to leave in four directions. No cat seemed to pay any attention to Fireheart and Graystripe until they had almost reached the slope that led to WindClan's upland territory. Then a meow sounded behind them.

"Hey, Fireheart! Where are you going?"

It was Sandstorm.

"Er . . ." Fireheart shot a desperate glance at Graystripe. "We're going the long way around," he improvised quickly. "Mudclaw from WindClan told us about a warren of young rabbits just inside our territory. We thought we'd bring back some fresh-kill." Suddenly alarmed by the thought that Sandstorm might offer to come with them, he added, "Tell Bluestar, will you, if she asks where we are?"

"Sure." Sandstorm yawned, showing a mouthful of sharp white teeth. "I'll think about you, dashing after rabbits, when I'm curled up in a nice warm nest!" She padded off with a flick of her tail.

Fireheart was relieved; he didn't like lying to her. "Let's go," he meowed to Graystripe. "Before any other cat sees us."

The two young warriors slid into the shelter of the bushes and crept up the slope. At the top, Fireheart paused for a moment, looking back to make sure they had not been followed. Then he and Graystripe bounded over the rim of the hollow and raced toward the moorland and, beyond that, the Twoleg farm.

This is the only way, Fireheart repeated to himself as he ran. He had to find out the truth. Not just for Redtail and Ravenpaw, but for the sake of the whole Clan. Tigerclaw had to be stopped . . . before he had the chance to kill again.

CHAPTER 2

Fireheart sniffed warily at a path where the snow had been trampled down by Twolegs. Lights shone from the Twoleg nest, and somewhere close by he could hear a dog barking. He remembered Barley telling him that the Twolegs let their dogs off the chains at night. He just hoped that he could locate Ravenpaw before he and Graystripe were noticed.

Graystripe slipped through the fence and padded up to him. The icy wind flattened his gray fur against his body. "Smell anything?" he asked.

Fireheart lifted his head to taste the air, and almost at once he caught the scent he was searching for, faint but familiar. Ravenpaw! "This way," he mewed.

He crept along the path, the hard surface icy under his paws. Cautiously he followed the scent to a gap at the bottom of a barn door where the wood had rotted away.

He sniffed, drinking in the smell of hay and the strong, fresh scent of cats. "Ravenpaw?" he whispered. When there was no reply, he repeated, louder, "Ravenpaw?"

"Fireheart, is that you?" A surprised mew came from the darkness on the other side of the door.

"Ravenpaw!" Fireheart squeezed through the gap, thankful to be out of the wind. The scents of the barn flowed around him, and his mouth began to water as he detected the smell of mouse. The barn was dimly lit by moonlight filtering through a small window high under the roof. As his eyes adjusted, Fireheart saw another cat standing a few tail-lengths away.

His friend looked even sleeker and better fed than when Fireheart had seen him last. Fireheart realized how scrawny and bedraggled he must look in comparison.

Ravenpaw purred happily as he padded over to Fireheart and touched noses with him. "Welcome," he mewed. "It's good to see you."

"It's good to see *you*," Graystripe meowed, pushing his way through the gap in the door after Fireheart.

"Did you get WindClan back to their camp safely?" Ravenpaw asked. Fireheart and Graystripe had stayed with him during their journey to bring WindClan home.

"Yes," mewed Fireheart, "but it's a long story. We can't—"

"Well, what's going on here?" Another cat's meow interrupted them.

Fireheart spun around, flattening his ears, ready to fight if this newcomer was a threat. Then he recognized Barley, the black-and-white loner who had willingly shared his home with Ravenpaw. "Hi, Barley," Fireheart meowed, calming down. "We need to talk to Ravenpaw."

"So I see," Barley mewed. "And it must be important, to bring you across the moors in this weather."

"Yes, it is," Fireheart agreed. He glanced at the former

ThunderClan apprentice, the urgency of his mission prickling through his fur. "Ravenpaw, we haven't any time to waste."

Ravenpaw looked puzzled. "You know you can talk to me as much as you want."

"I'll leave you to it, then," Barley offered. "Feel free to hunt. We've plenty of mice here." He gave a friendly nod to the visiting cats, and squeezed out under the door.

"Hunt? Really?" meowed Graystripe. Fireheart felt sharp pangs of hunger grip his belly.

"Of course," mewed Ravenpaw. "Look, why don't you eat first? Then you can tell me why you're here."

"I *know* Tigerclaw killed Redtail," Ravenpaw insisted. "I was there, and I saw him do it."

The three cats were crouched in the hayloft of the Twoleg barn. Hunting had not taken very long. After the desparate struggle to find prey in the snow-covered forest, the barn seemed to the hungry ThunderClan warriors to be overflowing with mice. Now Fireheart was warm, and his stomach felt comfortably full. He would have liked to curl up and sleep in the soft, fragrant hay, but he knew that he had to talk to Ravenpaw right away if he and Graystripe were to get back to camp before their absence was noticed. "Tell us everything you remember," he urged, giving Ravenpaw an encouraging nod.

Ravenpaw stared ahead of him, his eyes dark as he journeyed back in his mind to the battle at the Sunningrocks. Fireheart could see his confidence beginning to ebb. The

black cat was losing himself in his memories, reliving the fear
and the burden of what he knew.

"I'd been wounded in the shoulder," he began, "and
Redtail—he was our deputy then, as you know—told me to
hide in a crack in the rock until it was safe to get away. I was
just going to make a dash for it when I saw Redtail attack a
RiverClan cat. I think it was that gray warrior called Stonefur.
Redtail knocked Stonefur off his paws, and looked as if he was
about to sink in his claws for some serious injury."

"Why didn't he?" Graystripe put in.

"Oakheart came out of nowhere," Ravenpaw explained.
"He sank his teeth into Redtail's scruff and pulled him off
Stonefur." His voice shook as the memories flooded through
his mind's eye. "Stonefur ran away." The cat paused, unconsciously crouching down as if he were scared of something
very close by.

"What next?" Fireheart prompted gently.

"Redtail spat at Oakheart. He asked him if RiverClan warriors were unable to fight their own battles. Redtail was
brave," Ravenpaw added. "The RiverClan deputy was twice
his size. And then . . . then Oakheart said a strange thing.
He told Redtail, 'No ThunderClan cat will ever harm that
warrior.'"

"*What?*" Graystripe narrowed his eyes until they were
yellow slits. "That doesn't make sense. Are you sure you
heard him right?"

"Positive," insisted Ravenpaw.

"But the Clans fight all the time," meowed Fireheart.

"What's so special about Stonefur?"

"I don't know." Ravenpaw shrugged, shying away from their searching questions.

"So what did Redtail do after Oakheart said that?" asked Graystripe.

Ravenpaw's ears pricked up and his eyes widened. "He flew at Oakheart. He bowled him right off his paws and underneath a rocky overhang. I . . . I couldn't see them, though I could hear them snarling. And then I heard a rumbling sound, and the rock collapsed on top of them!" He stopped, shivering.

"Please go on," Fireheart mewed. He hated putting Ravenpaw through this, but he had to know the truth.

"I heard a screech from Oakheart and I saw his tail sticking out from under the rocks." Ravenpaw closed his eyes, as if he wanted to shut out the sight, and then opened them again. "Just then I heard Tigerclaw behind me. He ordered me to go back to the camp, but I'd only gone a little way when I realized I had no idea if Redtail was okay after the rockfall. So I crept back, past all the RiverClan warriors that were running away. And when I got to the rocks, Redtail was charging out of the dust. His tail was straight up and his fur stood on end, but he was all right, not a scratch on him that I could see. And he ran straight into Tigerclaw, who was in the shadows."

"And was that when—" Graystripe began.

"Yes." Ravenpaw's claws flexed as if he was imagining himself back in the battle. "Tigerclaw grabbed Redtail and pinned him down. Redtail struggled, but he couldn't break free. And . . ." Ravenpaw swallowed, and stared at the floor. "Tigerclaw sank his teeth into Redtail's throat, and it was all over." He dropped his chin onto his paws.

Fireheart moved closer to him, and pressed his body against Ravenpaw's flank. "So Oakheart died when the rocks fell on him. It was an accident," he murmured. "No cat killed him."

"That still doesn't *prove* that Tigerclaw killed Redtail," Graystripe pointed out. "I don't see that any of this helps us at all."

For a heartbeat Fireheart stared at him, discouraged. Then his eyes widened and he sat up, paws tingling with excitement. "Yes, it does. If we can prove the rockfall story, it shows that Tigerclaw was lying when he said Oakheart killed Redtail, and when he claimed to have killed Oakheart in revenge."

"Just a minute," Graystripe interrupted. "Ravenpaw, at the Gathering you didn't say anything about falling rocks. You made it sound as if Redtail killed Oakheart."

"Did I?" Ravenpaw blinked, and struggled to focus on Graystripe. "I didn't mean to. This is what really happened, I promise."

"And that's why Bluestar wouldn't listen to us," Fireheart went on excitedly. "She couldn't believe that Redtail would have killed another deputy. But Redtail *didn't* kill him. Bluestar will *have* to take us seriously now!"

Fireheart's brain was whirling with everything they had discovered. He wanted to ask Ravenpaw more questions, but he could smell the fear-scent on his friend, and saw the old haunted look in his eyes, as if telling his story had brought back all his unhappy memories of ThunderClan. "Is there any more you can tell us, Ravenpaw?" he mewed gently.

Ravenpaw shook his head.

"This means so much to the Clan," Fireheart told him. "Hopefully now we stand a chance of convincing Bluestar that Tigerclaw is dangerous."

"If she listens," Graystripe pointed out. "It's a pity you told her Ravenpaw's first story," he added to Fireheart. "Now he's changed everything, she won't know what to believe."

"But he hasn't changed everything," Fireheart protested, as Ravenpaw flinched at Graystripe's irritable tone. "We misunderstood, that's all. I'll convince Bluestar somehow," he added. "At least we know the truth now."

The black cat looked a little happier, but Fireheart could see that he didn't want to think about the past anymore. He settled beside Ravenpaw, purring encouragement, and for a short while the three cats shared tongues.

Then Fireheart pushed himself to his paws. "It's time we were on our way," he meowed.

"Take care," Ravenpaw mewed. "And watch out for Tigerclaw."

"Don't worry," Fireheart assured him. "You've given us what we need to deal with him." With Graystripe behind him, he slid under the door and ventured out into the snow.

"It's freezing out here!" Graystripe grumbled as they bounded down to the fence at the edge of the Twoleg farm.

"We should have taken a couple more of those mice to feed the Clan," he added.

"Yeah, right," Fireheart retorted. "And what would you tell Tigerclaw when he asked you where you found such fat mice in this weather?"

The moon was close to setting, and soon the sky would begin to pale toward dawn. The chill of the snow soon penetrated Fireheart's winter-thick fur, even colder after the warmth of the barn. His legs were aching with weariness; it had been a long night, and they still had to cross WindClan's territory before they could rest in their own camp. Fireheart could not stop thinking about what Ravenpaw had told them. He was sure that his friend was telling the truth, but it would be hard to convince the rest of the Clan. Bluestar had already refused to believe Ravenpaw's original story.

Yet that was when Fireheart thought Redtail had killed Oakheart. Bluestar could not accept that Redtail would kill another warrior unnecessarily. Now Fireheart understood the real story, that Oakheart had died by accident. . . . But how could Fireheart accuse Tigerclaw again unless he had something to back up what Ravenpaw had told him?

"The RiverClan cats would know," he realized aloud, pausing under a rocky outcrop on the moorland slope, where the snow was not so thick.

"What?" meowed Graystripe, padding up to him to share the shelter. "Know what?"

"How Oakheart died," Fireheart replied. "They must have seen Oakheart's body. They would be able to tell us whether he died from a rockfall, and not a death blow from a warrior."

"Yes, the marks on his body would prove it," agreed Graystripe.

"And they might know what Oakheart meant when he said that no ThunderClan cat should attack Stonefur," Fireheart added. "We need to speak to a RiverClan warrior who took part in the battle, maybe Stonefur himself."

"But you can't just walk into the RiverClan camp and ask," Graystripe protested. "Think of how tense it was at the Gathering—it's too soon after the battle."

"I know one RiverClan warrior who would welcome you," Fireheart murmured.

"If you mean Silverstream, yes, I could ask her," Graystripe agreed. "Now, can we please get back to the camp before my paws freeze completely?"

The two cats padded onward, more slowly now as weariness made their limbs heavy. They were within sight of Fourtrees when they spotted three other cats climbing the hillside. The breeze carried the scent of a WindClan patrol to Fireheart. Not wanting to explain their presence in WindClan territory, he looked swiftly around for cover, but the snow stretched smoothly on all sides, with no rocks or bushes nearby. And it was clear that the WindClan cats had already seen them, as they changed direction to meet them.

Fireheart recognized the familiar uneven gait of the Clan deputy, Deadfoot, with the tabby warrior Tornear, and his apprentice, Runningpaw.

"Hello, Fireheart," called Deadfoot, limping up with a

puzzled look in his eyes. "You're a long way from home."

"Er . . . yes," Fireheart admitted, dipping his head respect-fully. "We just . . . we picked up a ShadowClan scent trail, and it led us up here."

"ShadowClan on our territory!" Deadfoot's fur began to bristle.

"I reckon it was an old scent," Graystripe put in hastily. "Nothing to worry about. We're sorry we crossed your border."

"You're welcome here," meowed Tornear. "The other Clans would have destroyed us in the last battle if your Clan hadn't helped. Now we're sure they'll keep away. They know they have ThunderClan to reckon with."

Fireheart felt embarrassed at Tornear's praise. He and Graystripe had helped the WindClan cats in the past, but this time he was uncomfortable with the thought that any cats from WindClan had seen them on their territory. "We'd best be getting back," he muttered. "Everything seems quiet enough up here."

"May StarClan light your path," meowed Deadfoot grate-fully.

The other WindClan cats wished Fireheart and Graystripe good hunting, and went on toward their own camp.

"That was bad luck," Fireheart growled as he and Graystripe padded down to Fourtrees.

"Why?" asked Graystripe. "The WindClan cats didn't mind us on their territory. We're all friends now."

"Use your brains, Graystripe," Fireheart mewed. "What if Deadfoot mentions that he saw us to Bluestar at the next

Gathering? She's bound to wonder what we were doing out here!"

Graystripe stopped. "Mousedung!" he spat. "I never thought of that." His eyes met Fireheart's, and Fireheart saw his own uneasy feelings reflected there. "Bluestar won't like it if she finds out we're sneaking around investigating Tigerclaw."

Fireheart shrugged. "Let's just hope we can settle all this before the next Gathering. Now come on; we ought to try to catch something to take back with us."

He set off again, picking up the pace until the two cats were racing over the snow. As they skirted the hollow at Fourtrees and entered their own forest territory, he relaxed a little, pausing to drink the air in the hope of picking up the scent of prey. Graystripe sniffed hopefully among the roots of a nearby tree, and came back looking disappointed.

"Nothing," he grumbled. "Not a single mouse—not even a whisker!"

"We haven't got time to keep looking," Fireheart decided. He saw that the sky was already growing lighter above the trees. Time was running out, and their absence from camp was more likely to be noticed with every heartbeat.

The dawn light was growing stronger as they reached the ravine. Limbs aching with weariness, muscles stiff with cold, Fireheart led the way silently between the boulders toward the gorse tunnel. Thankful to be home at last, he bounded into the tunnel's dark mouth. As he emerged into the camp, he skidded to a halt so abruptly that Graystripe cannoned into him from behind.

"Move, you big furball!" Graystripe gave a muffled mew.

Fireheart didn't reply. Sitting a few tail-lengths away, in the middle of the clearing, was Tigerclaw. His head was sunk below his massive shoulders, and his yellow eyes were gleaming with triumph.

"Maybe you'd like to tell me where you've been?" he growled. "And why it took you so long to get back from the Gathering?"

CHAPTER 3

"Well?" Tigerclaw challenged.

"We thought we'd hunt." Fireheart raised his head to hold the deputy's amber gaze. "The Clan needs fresh-kill."

"But we couldn't find anything," Graystripe added, coming to stand beside Fireheart.

"Was the prey all curled up in their nests, eh?" Tigerclaw hissed. He padded forward until he stood nose to nose with Fireheart, sniffed him, and then did the same to Graystripe. "So how is it the pair of you smell of mouse?"

Fireheart exchanged a glance with Graystripe. It seemed a long time since they had hunted in the Twoleg barn, and he had forgotten that they might still be carrying the scent of the mice they ate.

Graystripe looked back at him helplessly, anxiety making his eyes wide.

"Bluestar should hear about this," the deputy growled. "Follow me."

Fireheart and Graystripe had no choice but to obey. Tigerclaw led them across the clearing to Bluestar's den at the foot of the Highrock. Beyond the curtain of lichen that covered the entrance, Fireheart could see the Clan leader curled up, apparently asleep, but as Tigerclaw shouldered his way into the den she raised her head at once and sat up.

"What is it, Tigerclaw?" she meowed, sounding puzzled.

"These two brave warriors have been out hunting." Tigerclaw's voice was thick with contempt. "They're full-fed, but they haven't brought home a single piece of fresh-kill for the Clan."

"Is this true?" Bluestar turned her ice-blue eyes on the young warriors.

"We weren't on a hunting patrol," Graystripe mumbled.

That was true, thought Fireheart. Strictly speaking, they hadn't broken the warrior code by not bringing back any prey, but he knew it was no real excuse.

"We ate the first prey we caught, to keep our strength up," he meowed. "And then we couldn't find anything else. We meant to bring back fresh-kill, but our luck was out."

Tigerclaw gave a snort of disgust, as if he didn't believe a word Fireheart had said.

"Even so," Bluestar meowed, "with prey so scarce, every cat should think of the Clan before himself, and share what they have. I'm disappointed in you both."

Fireheart couldn't help feeling ashamed. Bluestar had brought him into the Clan when he was a kittypet, and he wanted to show her that he deserved her trust. If he had been alone with Bluestar, he might have tried to explain his real reason for being so late back to camp. But with Tigerclaw glaring at him, it was impossible.

Besides, Fireheart wasn't ready to tell Bluestar about Ravenpaw's latest version of the Sunningrocks battle. He wanted to speak to cats from RiverClan first, to confirm how Oakheart had really died.

"I'm sorry, Bluestar," he murmured.

"'Sorry' fills no bellies," Bluestar warned him. "You must understand that the needs of the Clan come first, especially in leaf-bare. Until next sunrise, you'll hunt for the Clan, not for yourselves. When the rest of the Clan have eaten, then you can take food for yourself." Her gaze softened. "You both look exhausted," she observed. "Go and sleep now. But I shall expect to see you out hunting before sunhigh."

"Yes, Bluestar." Fireheart dipped his head and backed out of the den.

Graystripe followed him, his fur fluffed up in a mixture of fear and embarrassment. "I thought she'd have our tails off for sure!" he meowed as the two cats turned toward the warriors' den.

"Then you should think yourselves lucky." The low growl came from behind them; Fireheart glanced over his shoulder to see that Tigerclaw was padding after them. "If I were Clan leader, I'd have punished you properly."

Fireheart felt his fur prickle with anger. His lips drew back in the beginnings of a snarl. Then he heard a warning hiss from Graystripe, and bit back what he wanted to say, turning away from Tigerclaw again.

"That's right, kittypet," Tigerclaw jeered. "Slink back to your nest. Bluestar may trust you, but I don't. I saw you at the

WindClan battle, don't forget." He bounded past the two younger cats and pushed his way into the warriors' den ahead of them.

Graystripe let out a long, shivering breath. "Fireheart," he meowed solemnly, "you're either the bravest cat in all the Clans, or raving mad! For StarClan's sake, don't wind Tigerclaw up any more."

"I didn't ask for him to hate me," Fireheart pointed out angrily. He slid through the branches to see Tigerclaw settling himself into his place near the center. The dark tabby ignored Fireheart, turning himself around two or three times before curling up to sleep.

Fireheart made for his own sleeping place. Nearby, Sandstorm and Dustpelt were stretched out together.

Sandstorm sat up as Fireheart approached. "Tigerclaw has been watching for you ever since we got back from the Gathering," she whispered. "I gave him your message, but I don't think he believed me. What did you do to tweak his tail?"

Fireheart felt comforted by the sympathetic look in her eyes, but he couldn't stop his jaws from gaping in a massive yawn. "I'm sorry, Sandstorm," he mumbled. "I've got to get some sleep. I'll talk to you later."

He half expected Sandstorm to be offended, but instead she got up and padded over to him. As he settled into the soft moss that lined the floor of the den she crouched down beside him and pressed her side against his.

Dustpelt opened one eye and glared at Fireheart. He let

out a snort and pointedly turned his back.

But Fireheart was too tired to worry about Dustpelt's jealousy. He was already drifting into sleep. As his eyes closed, his last sensation was of Sandstorm's fur warm against his flank.

Fireheart paced along the hunting trail. His body felt full of energy, and he opened his jaws to taste the scent of prey. He knew he was dreaming, but he felt his belly growl in anticipation of fresh-kill.

Bracken arched over his head. A bright, pearly light poured down on him, as if the moon was full in a cloudless sky. Every fern frond, every blade of grass glowed, and the pale shapes of primroses, clustering thickly beside the path, seemed to shine with a light of their own. All around him Fireheart could feel the damp warmth of newleaf. The icy, snow-covered camp seemed nine lives away.

As the path began to lead upward, another cat stepped out in front of him. Fireheart halted, his heart thudding as he recognized Spottedleaf. The tortoiseshell cat padded forward until she could touch her soft pink nose to his.

Fireheart rubbed his face against hers, a purr rising from deep inside him. When Fireheart first came to the forest, Spottedleaf had been the ThunderClan medicine cat. She had been killed in cold blood by an invading ShadowClan warrior. Fireheart missed her still, but her spirit had returned to him in dreams more than once.

Spottedleaf took a pace back. "Come, Fireheart," she mewed. "I want to show you something." She turned and padded softly away, glancing around from time to time to make sure he was following.

Fireheart bounded after her, admiring the dapple of moonlight on her fur. Soon they came to the top of the hill. Spottedleaf led him out of the bracken tunnel and onto a high, grassy ridge. "Look," she meowed, raising her muzzle to point.

Fireheart blinked. Instead of the familiar span of trees and fields ahead of him, a shining expanse of water stretched as far as he could see. The reflected light dazzled him, and he closed his eyes. Where had all this water come from? He couldn't even tell if this was Clan territory—the silver sheen flattened everything and hid the usual landmarks.

Spottedleaf's sweet scent filled the air around him. Her voice sounded close to his ear. "Remember, Fireheart," she murmured, "water can quench fire."

Startled, Fireheart opened his eyes again. A chill breeze fluttered the surface of the water, penetrating his fur. Spottedleaf was gone. As Fireheart turned in every direction, searching for her, the light began to fade. The warmth went with it, and the feeling of grass under his paws. In less than a heartbeat he was plunged into cold and darkness.

"Fireheart! Fireheart!"

A cat was nudging him. Fireheart tried to duck away, and heard his name called again. It was Graystripe's voice. Fireheart forced his eyes open to see the big gray cat crouched anxiously over him.

"Fireheart," he repeated. "Wake up. It's nearly sunhigh."

Grunting with the effort, Fireheart hauled himself out of his nest and sat up. Pale, cold light was filtering through the branches of the den. Willowpelt and Darkstripe still slept closer to the center of the bush, but Sandstorm and Dustpelt had left already.

"You were muttering in your sleep," Graystripe told him. "Are you okay?"

"What?" Fireheart had not yet shaken off the dream. It was always a bitter waking, to realize that Spottedleaf was dead, and he would never speak to her again except in his dreams.

"It's nearly sunhigh," repeated Graystripe. "We should be out hunting."

"I know," Fireheart mewed, fighting to wake up properly.

"Hurry up, then." His friend gave him a final nudge before heading out of the den. "Meet you at the gorse tunnel."

Fireheart licked one paw and rubbed it over his face. As his head cleared, he suddenly remembered Spottedleaf's warning: "Water can quench fire." What was she trying to tell him? Fireheart thought back to Spottedleaf's earlier prophecy, that fire would save the Clan. As he followed Graystripe out of the den, Fireheart found himself shivering, and not from cold. He could feel trouble gathering like rain-heavy storm clouds. If the water that was coming quenched fire, then what would save the Clan? Did Spottedleaf's words mean that ThunderClan was doomed?

CHAPTER 4

Fireheart bounded up the ravine, the snow crisp under his paws. The sun shone in a pale blue sky, and though there was little warmth in its rays the sight of it cheered Fireheart and made him hopeful that newleaf was not far away.

Just behind him, Graystripe echoed Fireheart's thoughts. "With any luck, the sun will bring some prey out."

"Not if they hear you stomping along!" Sandstorm teased as she scrambled past him.

Brackenpaw, Graystripe's apprentice, protested loyally, "He doesn't stomp!" but Graystripe only responded with a good-natured growl. Fireheart felt new energy flow into his limbs. Even though their duties today were meant as punishment, no cat had told them they had to hunt alone, and it was good to be with friends.

Fireheart winced at the memory of Bluestar's ice-cold gaze when she had rebuked him and Graystripe for apparently hunting for themselves. He would make up for lying to her by bringing back as much fresh-kill as he could. The Clan needed it badly. By the time he and Graystripe left the den that morning, the store of prey in the camp had almost gone, and most of the cats had already left to hunt. Fireheart had spotted Tigerclaw on his way back down the ravine with the morning patrol. A squirrel was clamped in his jaws, its long tail brushing the snow. The deputy's eyes narrowed menacingly as he passed Fireheart, but he did not put his prey down to speak.

At the top of the slope, Sandstorm ran on ahead, while Graystripe began showing Brackenpaw where to search for mice among the tree roots. Watching them, Fireheart couldn't suppress a pang of loss as he thought of Cinderpaw, who had been his own apprentice. She would be with them now if it hadn't been for her accident. Instead, her crippled leg, the result of an accident on the Thunderpath, kept her in the den with Yellowfang, the ThunderClan medicine cat.

Pushing away these heavy thoughts, he crept forward, his jaws parted as he examined the forest smells. A faint breeze stirred the surface of the snow and brought a familiar scent. Rabbit!

Lifting his head, Fireheart could see the brown-furred creature snuffling under a clump of bracken, where a few green spikes of grass poked through the snow. He dropped into a hunting crouch, and delicately, pawstep by pawstep, drew closer. At the last moment the rabbit sensed him and sprang up, but it was too late. Before it could even squeal, Fireheart pounced.

Triumphantly, Fireheart headed back to the camp, dragging the rabbit along with him. As soon as he entered the clearing, he saw with relief that the pile of fresh-kill was swelling again after the morning patrols. Bluestar was standing beside it. "Well done, Fireheart," she meowed as he brought the rabbit to the pile. "Will you take that straight to Yellowfang in her den?"

Warmed by his leader's approval, Fireheart hauled the rabbit across the clearing. A tunnel of ferns, brown and brittle now, led to the secluded corner of the camp where the ThunderClan medicine cat had her den inside a split rock.

Ducking under the ferns, Fireheart saw Yellowfang lying in the mouth of her den with her paws tucked under her chest. Cinderpaw sat in front of her, her smoky gray fur fluffed up and her blue eyes focused on the medicine cat's broad face.

"Now, Cinderpaw," came the old cat's rasping mew. "One-eye's paw pads are cracked because of the cold. What are we going to do for her?"

"Marigold leaves in case of infection," Cinderpaw replied promptly. "Ointment of yarrow to soften the pads and help them heal. Poppy seed if she's in pain."

"Well done," purred Yellowfang.

Cinderpaw sat up even straighter, and her eyes shone with pride. As Fireheart knew only too well, the medicine cat didn't give praise lightly.

"Right, you can take her the leaves and the ointment," meowed Yellowfang. "She won't need the poppy seed unless the cuts get worse."

Cinderpaw stood up and was on her way into the den

when she caught sight of Fireheart standing by the tunnel. Mewing in delight, she hurried over to him with an awkward, lurching gait.

Regret stabbed at Fireheart, sharp as a claw. Cinderpaw had been a ceaseless bundle of energy before the Thunderpath accident that crushed her leg. Now she would never run properly again, and had had to give up her dreams of becoming a ThunderClan warrior.

But the Thunderpath monster had not crushed her bright spirit. Her eyes were dancing as she reached Fireheart. "Fresh-kill!" she exclaimed. "Is that for us? Great!"

"About time too!" grumbled Yellowfang, still sitting inside her den. "Mind you, the rabbit's very welcome," she added. "We've had half the Clan in here since sunrise, complaining about some ache or other."

Fireheart carried the rabbit across the clearing and dropped it in front of the medicine cat.

Yellowfang poked it with one paw. "It might have a bit of flesh on its bones for once," she remarked grudgingly. "All right, Cinderpaw, take the marigold leaves and the yarrow to One-eye, and hurry back. If you're quick there might be some rabbit left."

Cinderpaw purred and brushed Yellowfang's shoulder with the tip of her tail as she went past her into the den.

Softly, Fireheart mewed, "How's she doing? Is she settling down?"

"She's fine," snapped Yellowfang. "Stop worrying about her."

Fireheart wished he could. Cinderpaw had been his apprentice. He could not help feeling that he had been partly responsible for her accident. He should have stopped her from going to the Thunderpath alone.

Then he brought himself up short, remembering exactly how the accident had happened. Tigerclaw had asked Bluestar to meet him by the Thunderpath, but Bluestar had been too ill to go. Few warriors were in the camp; Fireheart himself had been about to leave on an urgent mission for catnip to treat Bluestar's greencough. He had told Cinderpaw not to go meet Tigerclaw instead of him, but Cinderpaw had ignored his order. The accident had happened because Tigerclaw had placed his scent marker too close to the edge of the Thunderpath. Fireheart suspected that it was meant as a trap for Bluestar, and Tigerclaw was responsible.

As Fireheart said good-bye to Yellowfang and went back to hunting, he felt a new surge of determination to bring Tigerclaw's guilt into the open. For the sake of Redtail, murdered; for Ravenpaw, driven from the Clan; for Cinderpaw, crippled. And for all the Clan cats, both now and to come, who were in danger from Tigerclaw's greed for power.

It was the day after their hunting punishment. Fireheart had decided there was no time to lose before visiting RiverClan territory, to discover how Oakheart had really died. He crouched at the edge of the forest and looked out toward the frozen river. The wind made a rustling sound in the dry reeds that poked up through the ice and snow.

Beside him, Graystripe sniffed the breeze, alert for the scent of other cats. "I can smell RiverClan cats," he whispered. "But the scent's old. I think we can cross safely."

Fireheart realized he was more worried about cats from his own Clan seeing them than meeting an enemy patrol. Already Tigerclaw suspected him of treachery. If the deputy found out what they were doing now, they'd be crowfood. "All right," he whispered back. "Let's go."

Graystripe led the way confidently across the ice, keeping his weight low over his paws so that he didn't slip. At first Fireheart was impressed; then he realized that Graystripe had been crossing the river secretly for moons now, to go and meet Silverstream. He followed more cautiously, half expecting the ice to crack under his weight and plunge him into the freezing dark water below. Here, downstream of the Sunningrocks, the river itself was the boundary between the two Clans. Fireheart's fur prickled as he crossed, and he kept glancing back to make sure that no cat from his Clan was watching.

Once they reached the far bank, they crept into the shelter of a reed bed and sniffed the air again for signs of RiverClan cats. Fireheart was conscious of Graystripe's unspoken fear; every muscle of the gray warrior's body was tense as he peered through the reed stems. "We must both be mad," he hissed to Fireheart. "You made me promise to meet Silverstream at Fourtrees whenever I wanted to see her, and now here we are, in RiverClan territory again."

"I know," Fireheart answered. "But there's no other way.

We need to talk to a RiverClan cat, and Silverstream's more likely to help us than any of the others."

He was just as apprehensive as his friend. They were surrounded by scents of RiverClan, though none of them were fresh. To Fireheart, it felt as if he were a kittypet in the forest for the first time again, lost in a frightening and unfamiliar place.

Using the reeds for cover, the two cats began to work their way upstream. Fireheart tried to step lightly, as if he were stalking prey, his belly skimming the snow. He was uncomfortably aware of how his flame-colored coat stood out against the white surface. The scent of RiverClan cats was growing more powerful, and he guessed the camp must be nearby. "How much farther?" he mewed softly to Graystripe.

"Not far. See that island up ahead?"

They had come to a place where the river curved away from ThunderClan territory and grew wider. Not far ahead a small island surrounded by reed beds showed above the frozen surface. Willow trees stooped low from the banks of the island, the tips of their overhanging branches trapped in the ice.

"An island?" Fireheart echoed in amazement. "But what happens when the river isn't frozen? Do they swim across?"

"Silverstream says the water's very shallow there," Graystripe explained. "But I've never been right into the camp myself."

Beside them, the ground sloped gently upward, away from the reedy shore. At the top, gorse and hawthorn grew thickly, with the occasional holly showing green and shiny under its coating of snow. But there was a bare expanse of shore between the reeds and the sheltering bushes, with no cover for prey or cats.

Graystripe had been moving forward in a low crouch; now he lifted his head, scenting the air and looking warily around. Then, without warning, he sprang away from the reeds and dashed up the slope.

Fireheart raced after him, his paws skidding in the snow. Reaching the bushes, they plunged between the branches and stopped, gasping for breath. Fireheart listened for the yowling of an alerted patrol, but no sound came up from the camp. He flopped down on the dead leaves and puffed out a sigh of relief.

"We can see the entrance of the camp from here," Graystripe told him. "I used to wait here for Silverstream."

Fireheart hoped she would come soon. Every moment they spent here increased their chances of discovery. Shifting his position so he had a good view of the slope and the island camp, he could just make out the silhouettes of cats moving around. He was so intent on trying to peer into the thick bushes that screened the island that he didn't see the tabby who was padding past their hiding place until she was barely a tail-length away. She carried a small squirrel in her jaws, and her gaze was fixed on the frozen ground.

Fireheart froze into a crouch, ready to spring out if the cat spotted them, and tracked her with his gaze as she passed. Luckily, he thought, the scent of the prey she was carrying must have masked the scent of ThunderClan intruders.

Suddenly he realized that a group of four cats, led by Leopardfur, the RiverClan deputy, had emerged from the camp. Leopardfur was fiercely hostile toward ThunderClan, ever since her patrol had come upon Fireheart and Graystripe trespassing on RiverClan territory as they returned from bringing WindClan home. A RiverClan cat had died in the ensuing fight, and Leopardfur did not forgive easily. If she discovered Fireheart and Graystripe now, she wouldn't even give them a chance to explain what they were doing on this side of the river.

To Fireheart's relief, the patrol didn't come their way. Instead they set off across the frozen river toward the Sunningrocks—off to patrol the border, Fireheart guessed.

At last a familiar silver-gray shape appeared.

"Silverstream!" purred Graystripe.

Fireheart watched the RiverClan she-cat stepping delicately across the ice toward the bank. She was certainly beautiful, he realized, with a finely shaped head and thick, sleek fur. No wonder Graystripe was captivated by her.

Graystripe rose to his paws, ready to call out to her, when two other cats emerged from the camp and ran to catch up with Silverstream. One of them was the smoky black warrior Blackclaw, recognizable from Gatherings by his long legs and lean body, and a smaller cat Fireheart guessed must have been Blackclaw's apprentice.

"Hunting patrol," Graystripe murmured.

All three cats began to climb the slope. Fireheart let out a hiss, half impatience, half fear. He had hoped they would be able to speak to Silverstream alone. How could they separate her from her companions? What if Blackclaw scented the intruders? After all, he wasn't carrying a helpful mouthful of prey to block his scent glands.

Blackclaw took the lead with his apprentice, and Silverstream followed a tail-length or two behind. As the patrol reached the bushes, Silverstream paused, her ears pricked warily as if she had detected a familiar but unexpected scent. Graystripe let out a short, sharp hiss, and Silverstream's ears swiveled toward the sound.

"Silverstream!" Graystripe mewed softly.

The she-cat flicked her ears, and Fireheart let out the breath he had been holding. She had heard.

"Blackclaw!" she called to the warrior ahead of her. "I'll try for a mouse in the bushes here. Don't wait for me."

Fireheart heard an answering mew from Blackclaw. Moments later Silverstream slipped through the branches until she reached the space where the young ThunderClan warriors were crouching. She pressed herself against Graystripe, purring loudly, and the two cats rubbed their faces together with obvious delight.

"I thought you only wanted us to meet at Fourtrees," Silverstream meowed when the two cats had finished greeting each other. "What are you doing here?"

"I brought Fireheart to see you," Graystripe explained. "He needs to ask you something."

Fireheart had not spoken to Silverstream since he had let her escape in the battle. He guessed she was remembering that, too, for she dipped her head graciously toward him, with no trace of the defensive hostility she had shown when he had tried to discourage her from seeing Graystripe at the start of their relationship. "Yes, Fireheart?"

"What do you know about the battle at the Sunningrocks, where Oakheart died?" Fireheart launched straight in. "Were you there?"

"No," Silverstream replied. She looked thoughtful. "Is it very important?"

"Yes, it is. Could you ask some cat who was? I need—"

"I'll do better than that," Silverstream interrupted him. "I'll bring Mistyfoot to talk to you herself."

Fireheart exchanged a glance with Graystripe. Was that a good idea?

"It's okay," meowed Silverstream, as if she guessed what was worrying him. "Mistyfoot knows about me and Graystripe. She doesn't like it, but she won't give me away. She'll come now if I ask her."

Fireheart hesitated, then dipped his head in assent. "All right. Thanks."

He had hardly finished speaking before Silverstream turned and slid out of the bushes again. Fireheart watched her bounding through the snow toward the camp.

"Isn't she *great*?" Graystripe murmured.

Fireheart said nothing, but settled down to wait. He was getting more nervous with every moment that passed. If he and Graystripe stayed in RiverClan territory for much longer, some of the RiverClan cats were bound to find them. They would be lucky to escape with their fur intact. "Graystripe," he began. "If Silverstream can't—"

Just then he saw the silver-gray tabby crossing the ice from the camp again, with another cat behind her. They raced up the slope, and Silverstream led the way into the bushes. The cat she brought with her was a slender queen with thick gray fur and blue eyes. For a heartbeat, Fireheart thought she seemed familiar. He decided he must have seen her at a Gathering.

When the queen saw Fireheart and Graystripe she stopped dead. Her fur began to rise suspiciously and she flattened her ears against her head.

"Mistyfoot," meowed Silverstream quietly, "these are—"

"ThunderClan cats!" hissed Mistyfoot. "What are they doing here? This is RiverClan territory!"

"Mistyfoot, listen . . ." Silverstream went over to her friend, and tried to nudge her toward Fireheart and Graystripe.

Mistyfoot stood her ground; Fireheart couldn't help feeling daunted by the look of blank hostility in her eyes. Had he been stupid to think that RiverClan would help him?

"I kept your secret about *him*," Mistyfoot reminded Silverstream, jerking her chin at Graystripe. "But I'm not going to keep quiet if you start bringing the whole of ThunderClan here."

"Don't be ridiculous," Silverstream retorted.

"It's all right, Mistyfoot," Fireheart put in quickly. "We

haven't taken any of your prey, and we're not here to spy. We need to speak to a cat who fought in the battle at Sunningrocks, where Oakheart died."

"Why?" Mistyfoot narrowed her eyes.

"It's . . . hard to explain," Fireheart mewed. "But it's nothing that could harm RiverClan. I swear that by StarClan," he added.

The young queen seemed to relax, and this time she let Silverstream urge her forward until she was sitting beside Fireheart.

Graystripe stood up, ducking his head to avoid the low-hanging branches. "If you two are going to talk, Silverstream and I will leave you to it."

Fireheart opened his mouth to protest, alarmed at the idea of being left alone in enemy territory. But Graystripe and Silverstream were already slipping out of the bushes.

Just before they vanished among the tough hawthorn branches, Graystripe looked back. "Oh, Fireheart," he meowed quietly, "before you go back, make sure you roll in something strong, to hide the RiverClan scent." He blinked in embarrassment. "Fox dung is good."

"Wait, Graystripe—" Fireheart jumped to his paws. But it was no use. Graystripe and Silverstream were gone.

"Don't worry," meowed Mistyfoot behind him. "I won't eat you. You'd give me bellyache." Fireheart turned back to see her blue eyes sparkling with amusement. "You're Fireheart, aren't you?" she went on. "I've seen you at Gatherings. They say you used to be a kittypet." Her voice was cool, with thinly veiled suspicion.

"That's true," Fireheart admitted heavily, feeling the familiar sting at the contempt of Clanborn cats for his past. "But I'm a warrior now."

Mistyfoot licked her paw and drew it slowly over one ear, keeping her eyes fixed on his face. "All right," she meowed at last. "I fought in the battle. What do you want to know?"

Fireheart paused for a moment, putting his thoughts in order. He would have only one chance to find out the truth; he mustn't make any mistakes.

"Get on with it," growled Mistyfoot. "I've left my kits to come and talk to you."

"It won't take long," Fireheart promised. "What can you tell me about the way Oakheart died?"

"Oakheart?" Mistyfoot looked down at her paws. After a deep breath, she lifted her eyes to Fireheart again. "Oakheart was my father; did you know that?"

"No, I didn't," mewed Fireheart. "I'm sorry. I never met him, but they say he was a brave warrior."

"He was the best and the bravest," Mistyfoot agreed. "And he should never have died. It was an accident."

Fireheart felt his heart begin to race. This was exactly what he needed to know! "Are you sure?" he asked. "No cat killed him?"

"He was wounded in the battle, but not enough to kill him,"

meowed Mistyfoot. "Afterward, we found his body under some fallen rocks. Our medicine cat said that was what killed him."

"So no cat was responsible . . ." Fireheart muttered. "Ravenpaw was right."

"What?" The blue-gray queen frowned.

"Nothing," Fireheart meowed hastily. "Nothing important. Thank you, Mistyfoot. That's just what I wanted to know."

"Then if that's all—"

"No, Mistyfoot, wait! There's one more thing. In the battle, one of our cats heard Oakheart say that no ThunderClan cat should harm Stonefur. Do you know what he meant by that?"

The RiverClan queen was silent for a while, her blue eyes gazing into the distance. Then she shook her head firmly, as if she were flicking water off it. "Stonefur is my brother," she mewed.

"Then Oakheart was his father, too," Fireheart realized. "Is that why he wanted to protect him from ThunderClan cats?"

"No!" Mistyfoot's eyes flashed blue fire. "Oakheart never tried to protect either of us. He wanted us to be warriors like him, and bring honor to the Clan."

"Then why . . . ?"

"I don't know." She sounded as if she was genuinely puzzled.

Fireheart tried not to feel disappointed. At least he knew for certain now how Oakheart had died. But he couldn't shake off the feeling that what Oakheart had said about

Stonefur was important, if only he could understand it.

"My mother might know," Mistyfoot meowed unexpectedly. Fireheart turned back to her, his ears pricked. "Graypool," she added. "If she can't explain it, no cat can."

"Could you ask her?"

"Maybe . . ." Mistyfoot's expression was still guarded, but Fireheart guessed that she was as curious about the meaning of Oakheart's words as he was himself. "But it might be better for you to speak to her yourself."

Fireheart blinked in surprise that Mistyfoot should suggest such a thing, when she had seemed so hostile at first. "Can I?" he asked. "Now?"

"No," Mistyfoot decided after a pause. "It's too risky for you to stay here any longer. Leopardfur's patrol will be back soon. Besides, Graypool is an elder now, and hardly ever leaves the camp. She'll take some persuading before she'll come out. But don't worry; I'll think of a reason."

Fireheart bowed his head in reluctant agreement. Part of him was wildly impatient to hear what Graypool had to say, but the rest of him knew that Mistyfoot was right. "How will I know where to meet her?"

"I'll send a message with Silverstream," Mistyfoot promised. "Now go. If Leopardfur finds you here, I won't be able to help you."

Fireheart blinked at her. He would have liked to give the young queen a lick of gratitude, but he was afraid of getting a clawed ear in return. Mistyfoot seemed to have gotten over the worst of her hostility, but she wasn't going to let him forget that they came from two different Clans.

"Thank you, Mistyfoot," he meowed. "I won't forget this. And if ever I can do anything for you—"

"Just *go*!" Mistyfoot hissed. As Fireheart slipped past her toward the gap in the bushes, she added with a purr of amusement, "And don't forget the fox dung."

CHAPTER 5

"I can't believe I'm doing this," Fireheart muttered as he pushed through the gorse tunnel into his own camp.

He had found some fresh fox dung in the forest, and rolled in it until he reeked. No cat would ever guess he had been into RiverClan territory now. Whether they would let him into the warriors' den was another matter. At least he had managed to catch a squirrel on his way back, so he wasn't returning empty-pawed.

As he emerged from the gorse tunnel, Fireheart saw Bluestar standing on top of the Highrock. He realized he had just missed hearing her call the Clan together, because other cats were appearing from their dens to gather below her.

Fireheart left his squirrel on the pile of fresh-kill and padded over to join them. Across the clearing, Brindleface's kits tumbled out of the nursery, followed by Brindleface herself. Fireheart could easily pick out his sister's son, Cloudkit, by his gleaming white fur. Princess, Fireheart's sister who still lived in Twolegplace, had no wish to leave the comfortable life of a kittypet, but Fireheart's tales of Clan life had captivated her, and she had given her eldest son to the Clan.

So far the Clan cats were finding it hard to accept another kittypet among them even though Brindleface treated him like one of her own kits. Fireheart knew from experience how much determination Cloudkit would need to make a place for himself.

As he drew closer, Fireheart heard the white kit complaining loudly to Brindleface. "Why can't I be an apprentice? I'm nearly as big as that dumb ginger kit of Frostfur's!"

Fireheart's interest quickened. Bluestar must be about to perform the apprentice-naming ceremony for Frostfur's two remaining kits. Their brother and sister, Brackenpaw and Cinderpaw, had been named apprentices a few moons ago, and Fireheart could guess that these two must be desperate for their own naming. He was glad that he had returned in time to witness it.

"Shh!" Brindleface whispered to Cloudkit, as she gathered her kits around her and found them a place to sit. "You can't be an apprentice until you're six moons old."

"But I want to be an apprentice *now!*"

Fireheart left Brindleface trying to explain Clan customs to the insistent Cloudkit and went to sit near the front of the gathering, next to Sandstorm.

Her head whipped around in alarm as he took his place. "Fireheart! Where have you been? You smell like a fox that's been dead for a moon!"

"Sorry," Fireheart mumbled. "It was an accident." He hated the stench as much as any cat, and he didn't like having to lie to Sandstorm about how he came to smell like that.

"Well, stay away from me till it wears off!" Though Sandstorm's words were firm, there was laughter in her eyes as she shifted a tail-length away from him.

"And clean yourself up before you come into the den," growled a familiar voice. Fireheart turned to see Tigerclaw standing behind him. "I'm not going to sleep with that stink in my nose!"

Fireheart dipped his head in embarrassment as Tigerclaw stalked away, then looked up as Bluestar began to speak.

"We are gathered here to give two Clan kits their apprentice names." She glanced down to where Frostfur was sitting proudly, with her tail curled neatly over her paws. The two kits sat one on each side of her, and as Bluestar spoke, the bigger of them, a ginger kit like his brother Brackenpaw, sprang impatiently to his paws.

"Yes, come forward, both of you," Bluestar invited warmly.

The ginger kit dashed forward and skidded to a stop at the foot of the Highrock. His sister followed more sedately. She was white like her mother, except for ginger patches along her back, and a ginger tail.

Fireheart closed his eyes for a moment. Not long ago, he had been given Cinderpaw as his apprentice. He half wished that he could be mentor to one of these kits, but he knew that if Bluestar had chosen him for this honor, she would have already told him to expect it.

Perhaps she would never choose him again, he thought with

a pang that chilled his heart, after he had failed Cinderpaw so badly.

"Mousefur," meowed Bluestar, "you have told me that you are ready to take on an apprentice. You will be mentor to Thornpaw."

Fireheart watched as Mousefur, a wiry, compact she-cat with brown fur, stepped forward and went to stand beside the ginger kit, who scampered up to meet her.

"Mousefur," Bluestar went on, "you have shown yourself a brave and intelligent warrior. See that you pass on your courage and wisdom to your new apprentice."

While Bluestar spoke, Mousefur looked just as proud as the newly named Thornpaw. The two of them touched noses and withdrew to the edge of the clearing. Fireheart could hear Thornpaw meowing eagerly, as if he was already plying his mentor with questions.

The ginger-and-white kit was still standing beneath the Highrock, looking up at Bluestar. Fireheart was close enough to see her whiskers quivering with anticipation.

"Whitestorm," Bluestar announced, "you are free to take a new apprentice now that Sandstorm has become a warrior. You will be mentor to Brightpaw."

The big white cat, who had been stretched out at the front of the gathering, stood up and padded over to Brightpaw. She waited for him with her eyes shining.

"Whitestorm," meowed Bluestar, "you are a warrior of great skill and experience. I know that you will pass on all you know to this young apprentice."

"Certainly," Whitestorm purred. "Welcome, Brightpaw." He bent to touch noses with her, and escorted her back to the assembled cats.

The other cats began to gather around, congratulating the two new apprentices and calling them by their new names. As he went to join them, Fireheart caught sight of Graystripe at the back of the crowd, beside the tunnel. His friend must have returned to camp unseen while the rest of the Clan were listening to Bluestar.

"It's all arranged," Graystripe mewed softly, padding over to Fireheart. "If it's sunny tomorrow, Silverstream and Mistyfoot will persuade Graypool to leave the camp for some exercise. They'll meet us at sunhigh."

"Where?" Fireheart asked, not sure that he wanted to go far into RiverClan territory two days running. It was dangerous to leave so much fresh ThunderClan scent there.

"There's a quiet glade just over the border, not far from the Twoleg bridge," Graystripe explained. "Silverstream and I used to meet there, before, you know . . ."

Fireheart understood. Graystripe had been keeping his promise about meeting Silverstream only at Fourtrees, and it was only because of his desire to find out about the Sunningrocks battle that they were taking an extra risk. "Thank you," he murmured sincerely.

As he padded over to the pile of fresh-kill to choose a piece for himself, his paws twitched in anticipation of the next sunhigh, when he would discover what Graypool knew of this mystery.

✠   ✠   ✠

"This is the place," Graystripe whispered.

He and Fireheart were only a few rabbit-hops over the RiverClan border, on their own side of the river. The ground gave way to a deep hollow, sheltered by thornbushes. Snow had drifted there, and a tiny stream, frozen now into icicles, carved a deep channel between two rocks. Fireheart guessed that when newleaf came and the snow melted, this would be a beautiful and well-hidden place.

The two cats squeezed under one of the thornbushes and scrabbled among the dead leaves to make comfortable nests while they waited. Fireheart had caught a mouse on the way and brought it as a gift for Graypool. He dropped it where the leaves were driest, trying to forget his own hunger, and settled down with his paws tucked under him. He knew he was putting himself and his friends in danger with this meeting, not to mention the fact that he was breaking the warrior code and lying to his Clan—yet he believed that this was all for the sake of his Clan. Fireheart only wished he could be sure that the path he had chosen was the right one.

The weak leaf-bare sunlight glittered on the snow in the hollow. Sunhigh had come and gone, and Fireheart was beginning to think the other cats weren't coming when he caught a RiverClan scent and heard a thin, elderly voice raised in complaint from the direction of the river.

"This is too far for my old bones. I'm going to freeze to death."

"Nonsense, Graypool, it's a beautiful day." That was

Silverstream. "The exercise will do you good."

Fireheart heard a snort of contempt in response. Three cats came into view, picking their way down the side of the hollow. Two of them were Silverstream and Mistyfoot. The third was an elder he had never seen before, a skinny she-cat with patchy fur and a scarred muzzle turning white with age.

Halfway down the hollow she paused, stiffening as she sniffed the air. "There are ThunderClan cats here!" she hissed.

Fireheart saw Silverstream and Mistyfoot exchange a worried glance. "Yes, I know," Mistyfoot soothed the elderly she-cat. "It's all right."

Graypool gave her a suspicious look. "What do you mean, all right? What are they doing here?"

"They just want to talk to you," Mistyfoot said gently. "Trust me."

For a heartbeat Fireheart was afraid the elder would turn back, yowling, to raise the alarm, but to his relief Graypool's curiosity was too much for her. She padded after Mistyfoot, shaking her paws with disgust as they sank into the soft snow.

"Graystripe?" Silverstream mewed warily.

Graystripe stuck his head out of the bush. "We're here."

The three RiverClan cats pushed their way into the prickly shelter. Graypool tensed as she came face to face with Fireheart and Graystripe, and her yellow eyes flared with hostility.

"This is Fireheart, and this is Graystripe," meowed Silverstream. "They—"

"Two of them," Graypool interrupted. "There had better be a good explanation for this."

"There is," Mistyfoot assured her. "They're decent cats—for ThunderClan, anyway. Give them a chance to explain."

Both she and Silverstream looked expectantly at Fireheart.

"We need to talk to you," Fireheart began, feeling his whiskers twitch nervously. He pushed the piece of fresh-kill toward her with one paw. "Here, I brought you this."

Graypool eyed the mouse. "Well, at least you remember your manners, ThunderClan or not." She crouched down and began to crunch the fresh-kill, showing teeth broken with age. "Stringy, but it'll do," she rasped, gulping.

While she was still eating, Fireheart tried to find the right words for what he needed to say. "I want to ask you about something Oakheart said before he died," he ventured.

Graypool's ears twitched.

"I heard what happened in the battle at the Sunningrocks," Fireheart continued. "Before he died, Oakheart told one of our warriors that no ThunderClan cat should ever harm Stonefur. Do you know what he might have meant?"

Graypool did not reply until she had swallowed the last morsel of mouse and swiped a remarkably pink tongue around her muzzle. Then she sat up and curled her tail around her paws. She fixed a thoughtful gaze on Fireheart for several long moments, until he felt that she could see everything that was in his mind.

"I think you should go," she mewed at last to the two young RiverClan cats. "Go on, out. You too," she added to Graystripe.

"I'll talk to Fireheart alone. I can see he's the one who needs to know."

Fireheart bit back a protest. If he insisted that Graystripe should stay, the RiverClan elder might refuse to talk at all. He looked at his friend and saw his own puzzled expression reflected in Graystripe's yellow eyes. What did Graypool have to say that she didn't want her own Clan to hear? Fireheart shivered, and not from the cold. Some instinct told him there was a secret here, dark as the shadow of a crow's wing. But if it was a RiverClan secret, he couldn't imagine what it could have to do with ThunderClan.

From the glances they exchanged, Silverstream and Mistyfoot were just as confused, but they started to back out from the bush without protest.

"We'll wait for you near the Twoleg bridge," Silverstream mewed.

"There's no need," Graypool hissed impatiently. "I may be old, but I'm not helpless. I'll find my own way back."

Silverstream shrugged and the two RiverClan cats withdrew, with Graystripe following them.

Graypool sat in silence until the scents of the cats who had left began to fade. "Now," she began, "Mistyfoot has told you that I'm her mother, and Stonefur's?"

"Yes." Fireheart's initial nervousness was ebbing away, to be replaced with respect for this ancient enemy queen, as he sensed the wisdom beneath her apparent short temper.

"Well," growled the old cat, "I'm not." As Fireheart opened his mouth to speak, she went on. "I brought the pair of them up as kits, but I didn't give birth to them. Oakheart brought them to me in the middle of leaf-bare, when they were just a few days old."

"But where did Oakheart get the kits?" Fireheart blurted out.

Graypool's eyes narrowed. "He *told* me he found them in the forest, as if they'd been abandoned by rogue cats or Twolegs," she meowed. "But I'm not stupid, and my nose has always worked just fine. The kits smelled of the forest all right, but there was another scent underneath. The scent of ThunderClan."

CHAPTER 6

✿

"What?" Fireheart was so astonished he could hardly speak. "Are you saying that Mistyfoot and Stonefur came from ThunderClan?"

"Yes." Graypool gave her chest fur a couple of licks. "That's exactly what I'm telling you."

Fireheart was stunned. "Did Oakheart steal them?" he asked.

Graypool's fur bristled, and she drew her lips back in a snarl. "Oakheart was a noble warrior. He would never stoop to stealing kits!"

"I'm sorry." Alarmed, Fireheart crouched and flattened his ears. "I didn't mean . . . It's just so hard to believe!"

Graypool sniffed, and her fur gradually lay flat again. Fireheart was still struggling with what she had just told him. If Oakheart hadn't stolen the kits, perhaps rogue cats had taken them from the ThunderClan camp—but why? And why abandon them so quickly, when the scent of their Clan was still on their fur?

"Then . . . if they were ThunderClan kits, why did you look after them?" he stammered. What Clan would willingly take

70

in enemy kits, and in a season when prey was already scarce?

Graypool shrugged. "Because Oakheart asked me to. He may not have been deputy back then, but he was a fine young warrior. I'd recently given birth to kits of my own, but all except one died in the bitter cold. I had plenty of milk to spare, and the poor little scraps would never have lived to see the sunrise if some cat hadn't cared for them. Their ThunderClan scent soon faded," she went on. "And even if Oakheart hadn't told the truth about where they came from, I respected him enough not to ask any more questions. Thanks to Oakheart, and to me, they grew into strong kits, and now they're good warriors—a credit to their Clan."

"Do Mistyfoot and Stonefur know all this?" Fireheart asked.

"Now listen to me," rasped Graypool. "Mistyfoot and Stonefur know nothing, and if you tell them what I've just told you, I'll rip your liver out and feed it to the crows." She thrust her head forward and drew her lips back as she spoke, baring her teeth. In spite of her age, Fireheart flinched.

"They never doubted that I'm their real mother," Graypool growled. "I like to think they even look a bit like me."

As she spoke, Fireheart felt something stir in his mind, like the twitch of a fallen leaf that betrayed the mouse sheltering beneath it. He thought that what Graypool had just said should mean something to him, but when he tried to capture the thought it scuttled away.

"They have always been loyal to RiverClan," Graypool insisted. "I don't want that loyalty to be divided now. I've heard the gossip about you, Fireheart—I know you were once a kittypet—so you should understand more than any cat what it means to have a paw in two places."

Fireheart knew he would never make any cat go through the uncertainties that he suffered himself about not fully belonging to his Clan. "I promise I'll never tell them," he meowed solemnly. "I swear it by StarClan."

The old cat relaxed and stretched, her front paws extended and her rump in the air. "I accept your word, Fireheart," she replied. "I don't know if this has helped you at all. But it might explain why Oakheart would never let a ThunderClan cat harm Mistyfoot or Stonefur. Even if he claimed to know nothing about where they came from, he would have smelled the ThunderClan scent on them as clearly as I did. As far as they're concerned, they are loyal only to RiverClan, but it would seem that Oakheart's loyalties were divided on their behalf."

"I'm very grateful to you," Fireheart purred, trying to sound as respectful as he could. "I don't know what this means in relation to what I have to find out, but I really think it's important, for both our Clans."

"That's as may be," mewed Graypool. She frowned. "But now that I've told you everything, you must leave our territory."

"Of course," Fireheart meowed. "You won't even know I've been here. And Graypool . . ." He paused before thrusting his way out of the bush and held her pale yellow gaze for a moment. "Thank you."

❈   ❈   ❈

Fireheart's mind was spinning as he returned to the camp. Mistyfoot and Stonefur had ThunderClan blood! But they belonged entirely to RiverClan now, with no idea of their divided heritage. Blood loyalty and Clan loyalty were not always the same, Fireheart reflected. His own kittypet roots did not make his commitment to ThunderClan any less strong.

And perhaps now that Mistyfoot had confirmed how Oakheart had died, Bluestar would be willing to accept that Tigerclaw had killed Redtail. Fireheart decided to ask her about Graypool's latest revelation too; Bluestar might be able to tell him if a pair of kits had ever been stolen from the ThunderClan camp.

When he reached the clearing, Fireheart made straight for the Highrock. As he approached Bluestar's den, he heard two cats meowing together, and picked up Tigerclaw's scent along with Bluestar's. Quickly he pressed himself against the rock, hoping to stay out of sight, as the deputy shouldered his way out past the curtain of lichen that screened the mouth of the den.

"I'll try a hunting patrol toward the Snakerocks," the dark tabby called over his shoulder. "No cat has hunted there for a few days."

"Good idea," agreed Bluestar, following him out. "Prey is still scarce. May StarClan grant the thaw comes soon."

Tigerclaw grunted agreement and loped off toward the warriors' den, not noticing Fireheart where he crouched by the rock.

When he had gone, Fireheart padded up to the mouth of

the den. "Bluestar," he called, as the Clan leader turned to go back inside. "I'd like to talk to you."

"Very well," Bluestar meowed calmly. "Come in."

Fireheart followed her into the den. The curtain of lichen swung back into place, cutting off the bright snow-light. In the dim interior, Bluestar sat facing him. "What is it?" she asked.

Fireheart took a deep breath. "You remember the story that Ravenpaw told, that Redtail killed Oakheart at the battle of the Sunningrocks?"

Bluestar stiffened. "Fireheart, that is *over*," she growled. "I told you before, I have reasons enough to be satisfied that this isn't true."

"I know." Fireheart bowed his head respectfully. "But I've found out something new."

Bluestar waited in silence. Fireheart couldn't tell what she was thinking. "No cat killed Oakheart—not Redtail, not Tigerclaw," he went on, nervously aware that it was too late now to change his mind. "Oakheart died when a rock collapsed on top of him."

Bluestar frowned. "How do you know this?"

"I . . . I went to see Ravenpaw again," Fireheart admitted. "After the last Gathering." He was ready for anger as he made his confession, but the Clan leader remained calm.

"So that's why you were late," she observed.

"I had to find out the truth," Fireheart meowed quickly. "And I—"

"Wait a moment," Bluestar interrupted. "Ravenpaw told

you at first that Redtail killed Oakheart. Is he changing his story now?"

"No, not at all," Fireheart promised. "I misunderstood him. Redtail was partly responsible for Oakheart's death, because he drove him under the overhanging rock that collapsed on top of him. But he didn't mean to kill him. And that's what you couldn't believe," he reminded Bluestar. "That Redtail would deliberately kill another cat. Besides . . ."

"Well?" Bluestar sounded as calm as ever.

"I went across the river and spoke to a RiverClan cat," Fireheart confessed. "Just to be sure. She told me that it's true: Oakheart died from the rockfall." He looked at his paws, bracing himself for Bluestar's fury that he had been trespassing on enemy territory, but when he looked up again, there was nothing in the leader's eyes except for intense interest.

She gave him a slight nod, and Fireheart went on. "So we know for a fact that Tigerclaw was lying about how Oakheart died—he didn't kill him himself, in revenge for Redtail. The rockfall killed him. Isn't it possible that he is lying about Redtail's death as well?"

As he spoke, Bluestar began to look troubled, narrowing her eyes so that only the faintest sliver of blue showed in the dim light of the den. She let out a long sigh. "Tigerclaw is a fine deputy," she murmured. "And these are serious charges."

"I know," Fireheart agreed quietly. "But can't you see, Bluestar, how dangerous he is?"

Bluestar sank her head onto her chest. She was silent for

so long that Fireheart wondered if he should leave, but she had not dismissed him.

"There's something else," he ventured. "Something strange about two of the RiverClan warriors."

Bluestar looked up at that; her ears flicked forward. For a heartbeat Fireheart hesitated to spread the rumors of a temperamental RiverClan elder, but his need to know the truth gave him the courage to go on. "Ravenpaw told me that in the Sunningrocks battle Oakheart stopped Redtail from attacking a warrior named Stonefur. Oakheart said that no ThunderClan cat should ever harm Stonefur. I . . . I had the chance to speak to one of the RiverClan elders. She told me that Oakheart brought Mistyfoot and Stonefur to her when they were tiny kits. It was leaf-bare, and she said that the kits would have died with no one to take care of them. Graypool—the elder—suckled them. She said that . . . that they had the scent of ThunderClan kits. Could that be true? Were kits ever stolen from our camp?"

For a few heartbeats he thought Bluestar had not heard him, she was so still. Then she rose to her paws and padded forward a couple of paces until she stood almost nose to nose with him. "And you listened to this nonsense?" she hissed.

"I just thought I should—"

"This isn't what I expect from you, Fireheart," Bluestar growled. Her eyes glittered like ice, and her hackles were raised. "To go into enemy territory and listen to idle gossip? To believe what a RiverClan cat tells you? You would do better to think about your own duties than to come here telling tales about Tigerclaw." She studied him for a long moment. "Maybe Tigerclaw is right to doubt your loyalty."

"I—I'm sorry," Fireheart stammered. "But I thought Graypool was telling the truth."

Bluestar let out a long breath. All the interest she had shown before had vanished, leaving her expression cold and remote. "Go," she ordered. "Find yourself something useful to do—something that befits a warrior. And never—*never*—mention this to me again. Do you understand?"

"Yes, Bluestar." Fireheart began backing out of the den. "But what about Tigerclaw? He—"

"Go!" Bluestar spat the command.

Fireheart's paws scrabbled in the sand in his haste to obey. Once out of the den he turned and hurtled across the clearing, only coming to rest when he had put several fox-lengths between himself and Bluestar. He felt utterly bewildered. At first Bluestar had seemed prepared to listen to him, but as soon as he mentioned the stolen ThunderClan kits, she had refused to hear any more.

A sudden chill swept through Fireheart. What if Bluestar began to wonder how he had managed to speak with the RiverClan cats? What if she found out about Graystripe and Silverstream? And what about Tigerclaw? For a short time, Fireheart had let himself hope that he could make Bluestar understand how dangerous the deputy was.

Thistles and thorns, he thought. *Now she won't hear another word against Tigerclaw. I blew it!*

CHAPTER 7

❧

Confused and unhappy, Fireheart made for the warriors' den. Before he reached it he hesitated. He did not want to risk meeting Tigerclaw, and he wasn't in the mood for sharing tongues with his friends.

Instead, almost unconsciously, he headed for the tunnel of ferns that led to Yellowfang's den. Cinderpaw limped out and almost collided with him. Fireheart fell back on his haunches with a thump, and Cinderpaw skidded to a halt, spraying him with snow.

"Sorry, Fireheart," she puffed. "I didn't see you there."

Fireheart shook the snow off his coat. His heart felt suddenly lighter at the sight of Cinderpaw, her blue eyes sparkling with mischief, and fur sticking out in all directions. This was how she used to look, when she was his apprentice; for a while, after the accident, Fireheart had been afraid that this Cinderpaw had vanished forever. "What's the hurry?" he asked.

"I'm going out to look for herbs for Yellowfang," Cinderpaw explained. "So many cats have been ill, what with all this snow, that her stocks are getting very low. I want to find as much as I can before it gets dark."

"I'll come and help you," Fireheart offered. Bluestar had told him to do something useful, and not even Tigerclaw could find fault if he went to collect herbs for the medicine cat.

"Great!" Cinderpaw meowed happily.

Side by side, they headed across the clearing toward the gorse tunnel. Fireheart had to slow his pace to match Cinderpaw's, but if she was aware of it she didn't seem to mind.

Just before they reached the tunnel, Fireheart heard the shrill voices of kits. He turned and stared at the branches of a fallen tree, close to the elders' den. A group of kits had surrounded Brokentail, who had been given a nest among the branches.

Ever since Bluestar had offered shelter to Brokentail, he had lived alone in his den, with warriors to guard him. Not many cats passed that way, and the kits had no reason to be anywhere near him.

"Rogue! Traitor!" That was Cloudkit's voice raised in a jeering meow. Fireheart watched in alarm as the white kit darted forward, jabbed Brokentail in the ribs with one paw, and scrambled back out of range. One of the other kits copied him, squealing, "Can't catch me!"

Darkstripe, whose turn it was to guard the blind cat, made no attempt to send the kits away. He sat a fox-length away, watching with his paws tucked under him and a gleam of amusement in his eyes.

Brokentail swung his head from side to side in frustration,

but with his cloudy, unseeing eyes he could not retaliate. His dark tabby fur looked dull and patchy, and his broad face was scored with scars, some of them from the clawing that had ruined his eyes. There was no trace of the former arrogant and bloodthirsty leader now.

Fireheart exchanged a worried glance with Cinderpaw. Many cats, he knew, thought Brokentail deserved to suffer, but seeing the former leader so old and helpless, he could not help feeling a scrap of pity. Anger began to burn inside him as the taunting went on. "Wait for me," he mewed to Cinderpaw, and hurried over toward the edge of the clearing.

He saw Cloudkit pounce on the blind tom's tail, worrying it with needle-sharp teeth. Brokentail scrabbled away from him on unsteady legs and swiped one paw in his direction.

In an instant, Darkstripe jumped to his paws, hissing, "Touch that kit, traitor, and I'll flay your skin in strips!"

Fireheart was too angry to speak. Leaping toward Cloudkit, he grabbed him by the scruff of the neck and swung him around, away from Brokentail.

Cloudkit wailed in protest. "Stop it! That *hurts*!"

Fireheart dropped him roughly into the snow and let out a low growl through bared teeth. "Go home!" he ordered the other kits. "Go home to your mothers. *Now*!"

The kits stared at him, wide-eyed with fear, and then scuttled off, to disappear into the nursery.

"As for you—" Fireheart hissed to Cloudkit.

"Leave the kit alone," Darkstripe interrupted, padding up to stand beside Cloudkit. "He's not doing any harm."

"Keep out of this, Darkstripe," growled Fireheart.

Darkstripe shouldered past him, almost knocking him over, before stalking back to his prisoner. "Kittypet!" he sneered over his shoulder.

Fireheart's muscles tensed. He wanted to leap at Darkstripe and force the insult back down his throat, but he stopped himself. This was no time for Clan warriors to start fighting each other. Besides, he had to deal with Cloudkit.

"Did you hear that?" he demanded, glaring down at the white kit. "Kittypet?"

"So?" Cloudkit muttered mutinously. "What's a kittypet?"

Fireheart gulped as he realized that Cloudkit had not yet learned what his origins meant to the Clan. "Well, a kittypet is a cat who lives with Twolegs," he began carefully. "Some Clan cats don't believe that a cat who's born a kittypet will ever make a good warrior. And that includes me, because like you, I was born in Twolegplace."

As Fireheart spoke, Cloudkit's eyes grew wider and wider. "What do you mean?" he meowed. "I was born *here!*"

Fireheart stared at him. "No, you weren't," he meowed. "Your mother is my sister, Princess. She lives in a Twoleg nest. She gave you to the Clan when you were very young, so you could be a warrior."

For a few moments Cloudkit stood rigid, as if he were a kit made of snow and ice. "Why didn't you *tell* me?" he demanded.

"I'm sorry," Fireheart meowed. "I . . . I thought you knew. I thought Brindleface would have told you."

Cloudkit backed away a couple of tail-lengths. The shock

in his blue eyes was slowly replaced with cold understanding. "So that's why the other cats hate me," he spat. "They think I'll never be any good because I wasn't born in this dump of a forest. It's stupid!"

Fireheart struggled to find the right words to reassure him. He couldn't help remembering how excited Princess had been when she gave her son to the Clan, and how he had promised her that Cloudkit would have a wonderful life ahead of him. Now he was forcing Cloudkit to think about his past, and the difficulties he would have before being accepted by the Clan. What if the kit began to think that Fireheart and Princess had made the wrong decision?

Fireheart sighed. "It may be stupid, but that's the way it is. I should know. Listen," he explained patiently. "Warriors like Darkstripe think being a kittypet is something bad. It just means we have to work twice as hard to make them see that kittypet blood is nothing to be ashamed of."

Cloudkit straightened up. "I don't care!" he mewed. "I'm going to be the best warrior in the Clan. I'll fight any cat who says I'm not. I'll be brave enough to kill outlaws like old Brokentail."

Fireheart was relieved to see Cloudkit's spirit overcoming the shock of his discovery. But he wasn't sure that the kit really understood the meaning of the warrior code. "There's more to being a warrior than killing," he warned Cloudkit. "A true warrior—the best warrior—isn't cruel or mean. He doesn't claw an enemy who can't fight back. Where's the honor in that?"

Cloudkit ducked his head, not meeting Fireheart's eyes. Fireheart hoped he had said the right thing. Looking around for Cinderpaw, he saw that she had gone up to Brokentail and was checking his tail where Cloudkit had worried it. "There's no damage," she mewed to the blinded tom.

Brokentail crouched motionless, his ruined eyes fixed on his paws, and did not respond. Reluctantly Fireheart went over and nudged the old cat to his paws. "Come on," he meowed. "Let's get you back to your den."

Brokentail turned in silence and let Fireheart guide him back to the leaf-lined hollow under the dead branches. Darkstripe watched them shuffle past with a contemptuous flick of his tail.

"Right, Cinderpaw," Fireheart meowed when Brokentail was settled. "Let's go and find those herbs."

"Where are you going?" Cloudkit piped up, bouncing over to them with all his energy restored. "Can I come?"

When Fireheart hesitated, Cinderpaw mewed, "Oh, let him come, Fireheart. He only gets into trouble because he's bored. And we could do with some more help."

Cloudkit's eyes gleamed with pleasure, and a loud purr rose from his throat, an enormous sound to come from his small, fluffy body.

Fireheart shrugged. "All right. But put one paw wrong, and you'll be back in the nursery before you can say 'mouse'!"

Limping steadily, Cinderpaw led the way along the ravine to the hollow where the apprentices had their training sessions. Already the sun was beginning to go down, casting long blue shadows across the snow. Cloudkit scampered ahead of them, peering into holes in the rock and stalking imaginary prey.

"How can you find herbs with snow on the ground?" Fireheart asked. "Won't everything be frozen?"

"There'll still be berries," Cinderpaw pointed out. "Yellowfang told me to look for juniper—that's good for coughs and bellyaches—and broom to make poultices for broken legs and wounds. Oh, and alder bark for toothache."

"Berries!" Cloudkit skittered sideways toward them. "I'll find lots for you!" He dashed away again in the direction of a clump of bushes growing up the side of the hollow.

Cinderpaw flicked her tail in amusement. "He's keen," she remarked. "Once he's apprenticed, he'll learn quickly."

Fireheart made a noncommittal noise in his throat. Cloudkit's energy reminded him of Cinderpaw when she was first made apprentice. Except Cinderpaw would never have taunted a helpless cat like blind Brokentail.

"Well, if he's *my* apprentice, he'd better start listening to me," he muttered.

"Oh, yes?" Cinderpaw gave Fireheart a teasing look. "You're a really tough mentor—all your apprentices will be trembling in their fur!"

Fireheart met her laughing eyes and felt himself relaxing. As usual, being with Cinderpaw was lifting his spirits. He would stop worrying about Cloudkit and get on with the job they had come to do.

"Cinderpaw!" Cloudkit called from farther along the

hollow. "There are berries here—come and look!"

Fireheart craned his neck and saw the white kit crouching beneath a small, dark-leaved bush that pushed its way up between two rocks. Bright scarlet berries grew close to the stems.

"They look tasty," Cloudkit mewed as the two cats drew nearer. He stretched his jaws wide to take a hungry mouthful.

At the same moment a gasp came from Cinderpaw. To Fireheart's amazement she shot forward, propelling herself over the snow as fast as her injured leg would allow. "No, Cloudkit!" she yowled.

She barreled into the kit, bowling him over. Cloudkit squealed in shock and the two cats scuffled together on the ground. Fireheart bounded over, anxious that Cloudkit might hurt the injured Cinderpaw, but as he reached them she pushed the kit off her and sat up, panting. "Did you touch one?" she demanded.

"N-No," Cloudkit stammered, puzzled. "I was only—"

"Look." Cinderpaw shoved him around until his nose was a mouse-length from the bush. Fireheart had never heard her sound so fierce. "Look but don't touch. That's yew. The berries are so poisonous they are called deathberries. Even one could kill you."

Cloudkit's eyes were round as the full moon. Speechless for once, he gazed, horrified, at Cinderpaw.

"All right," she mewed more gently, giving his shoulder a couple of comforting licks. "It didn't happen this time. But take a good look now, so you don't make that mistake again.

And never—do you hear me, *never*—eat anything if you don't know what it is."

"Yes, Cinderpaw," Cloudkit promised.

"Go on looking for berries, then." Cinderpaw nudged the kit to his paws. "And call me as soon as you find anything."

Cloudkit padded off, glancing back over his shoulder once or twice as he went. Fireheart couldn't remember seeing him so subdued. Bold as the kit was, he had received a real shock. "It's a good thing you were here, Cinderpaw," he meowed, feeling a pang of guilt that he hadn't known enough to warn Cloudkit. "You've learned such a lot from Yellowfang."

"She's a good teacher," Cinderpaw replied. She shook several clumps of snow off her fur and began padding up the hollow after Cloudkit. Fireheart walked beside her, once more slowing his pace to match hers.

This time Cinderpaw noticed. "You know, my leg has healed as much as it ever will," she meowed quietly. "I'll be sorry to leave Yellowfang's den, but I can't stay there forever." She turned to look at Fireheart. All the mischief had faded from her eyes; instead, there was pain and uncertainty in the blue depths. "I don't know what I'll do."

Fireheart stretched over to her and rubbed his face comfortingly against hers. "Bluestar will know."

"Maybe." Cinderpaw shrugged. "Ever since I was a tiny kit, I wanted to be just like Bluestar. She's so noble, and she's given her whole life to the Clan. But Fireheart, what can I give now?"

"I don't know," Fireheart admitted.

The life of a cat could be followed clearly through the Clan, from kit to apprentice to warrior, sometimes to queen, and then retired to an honorable old age among the elders. Fireheart had no idea what happened to a cat who was injured too badly for the warrior life, for the long patrols, the hunting and fighting that were required of a warrior. Even the queens who cared for the kits in the nursery had all been warriors once, with skills that enabled them to feed and defend their little ones.

Cinderpaw was brave and intelligent, and before her accident she had shown endless energy and commitment to the Clan. Surely that couldn't all be thrown away? *This is Tigerclaw's fault*, Fireheart thought darkly. *He laid the trail that led to her accident.* "You should go to Bluestar," he suggested out loud. "Ask her what she thinks."

"Perhaps I will." Cinderpaw shrugged.

"Cinderpaw!" A shrill meow from Cloudkit interrupted them. "Come and see what I've found!"

"Coming, Cloudkit!" Cinderpaw limped away, mewing good-humoredly to Fireheart as she went, "Maybe it's deadly nightshade this time."

Fireheart watched her go. He hoped that Bluestar would be able to find a way to give Cinderpaw a worthwhile life within the Clan. Cinderpaw was right: Bluestar was a great leader, and not just in battle. She truly cared for all her cats.

Knowing that, Fireheart felt even more confused when he remembered her reaction to Graypool's news. Why had Bluestar acted so strangely when he told her that two

RiverClan warriors had been ThunderClan kits? The story had outraged her so much that she was closing her eyes to the danger from Tigerclaw.

Fireheart shook his head as he padded slowly after Cinderpaw. There was a deeply buried mystery surrounding those cats, and he was beginning to feel that it might be beyond his power to ever understand it.

CHAPTER 8

Fireheart crouched in the nursery, watching a litter of kits suckling their mother. For a moment he was filled with excitement to see the tiny creatures who were the future of the Clan.

Then something stirred in his mind. ThunderClan had no kits as young as these. Where had they come from? He let his gaze travel from the kits to their mother, and saw nothing but a rippling pelt of silver-gray. The queen had no face.

Fireheart choked back a cry of horror. As he stared, the silvery shape of the queen began to fade, leaving nothing but darkness. The kits squirmed and let out squeals of terror and loss. A bitterly cold wind rose and swept away the warm scents of the nursery. Fireheart leaped to his paws and tried to follow the sound of the helpless kits, lost in the windblown darkness. "I can't find you!" he wailed. "Where are you?"

Then a light appeared, soft and golden. Fireheart could see another cat sitting in front of him with the tiny kits sheltered between her paws. It was Spottedleaf.

Fireheart opened his mouth to speak to her. She gave him a look of infinite kindness before the image vanished, and Fireheart found himself scrabbling among the mossy bedding in the warriors' den.

"Do you have to make so much racket?" Dustpelt was grumbling. "No cat can get a wink of sleep."

Fireheart sat up. "Sorry," he mumbled. He couldn't help glancing toward the center of the den, where Tigerclaw slept. The deputy had complained before about the noise Fireheart made when he was dreaming.

To his relief, Tigerclaw wasn't there. Fireheart could see from the light that filtered through the branches that the sun was already above the trees. He gave himself a quick wash, trying to hide from Dustpelt how much the dream had shaken him. Frightened, lonely kits . . . kits whose mother faded away. Was it a prophecy? And if so, what could it mean? There were no kits that young in the Clan now. Or was it about the former ThunderClan kits—Mistyfoot and Stonefur? Had their real mother disappeared somehow?

While he was washing, Dustpelt gave him a final glare and pushed his way out through the branches, leaving Fireheart alone except for Longtail and Runningwind, sleeping in their usual places.

There was no sign of Graystripe, Fireheart noticed, and his bedding was cold, as if he had been out since dawn. *Gone to meet Silverstream*, he guessed. He tried to understand his friend's strength of feeling, but he couldn't help worrying, and longing for the old uncomplicated days when they were apprentices together. Fireheart poked his head out of the branches to see the snow-covered camp glittering under the cold winter sun. No sign of a thaw yet.

Beside the nettle patch, Sandstorm was crouching over a piece of fresh-kill. "Good morning, Fireheart," she greeted him cheerfully. "If you want to eat, you'd better do it quickly, while there's still some prey left."

Fireheart realized that his belly was aching with hunger. It felt as if he hadn't eaten for a moon. He bounded over to the pile of fresh-kill and saw that Sandstorm was right. Only a few pieces remained. He chose a starling and took it back to the nettle patch to eat with Sandstorm. "We'll have to hunt today," he meowed between mouthfuls.

"Whitestorm and Mousefur have already gone out with their new apprentices," Sandstorm told him. "Brightpaw and Thornpaw couldn't wait!"

Fireheart wondered if Graystripe had taken his apprentice out, too, but a moment later Brackenpaw emerged alone from the apprentices' den. The light brown tabby looked around before trotting over to Fireheart.

"Have you seen Graystripe?" he called.

"Sorry." Fireheart shrugged. "He was gone when I woke up."

"He's never here," Brackenpaw mewed sadly. "If this goes on, Swiftpaw will be a warrior before me—Brightpaw and Thornpaw too."

"Rubbish," Fireheart meowed. He suddenly felt angry with Graystripe and his obsession with the RiverClan she-cat. No warrior had the right to neglect his apprentice like this. "You're doing fine, Brackenpaw. You can come out hunting with me, if you like."

"Thanks," purred Brackenpaw, beginning to look happier.

"I'll come too," offered Sandstorm, gulping down the last of her meal and running her tongue around her jaws. She took the lead as the three cats made their way along the gorse tunnel.

"Now, Brackenpaw," Fireheart meowed when they had reached the edge of the training hollow. "Where's a good place to look for prey?"

"Under the trees," replied Brackenpaw, pointing with a flick of his tail. "That's where mice and squirrels come for nuts and seeds."

"Good," meowed Fireheart. "Let's see if you're right."

They headed farther around the hollow; on the way they passed Brindleface, watching fondly as her kits scrambled about in the snow. "They needed to stretch their legs," she explained. "All this snow has made them restless."

Cloudkit was sitting under the yew bush with a couple of his littermates, explaining importantly that those were deathberries, and they must never, *never* eat them. Feeling amused by the young kit's seriousness, Fireheart meowed a greeting as he went by.

Beneath the trees at the top of the hollow the snow was not so thick, and streaks of brown earth showed amid the white. As the three cats crept forward, Fireheart heard the scuttering of tiny paws, and scented mouse. Automatically he dropped into a hunting crouch and slid forward, barely putting any weight on his paws so as not to alarm his prey. The mouse remained unaware of the danger, its back to him as it nibbled on a fallen seed. When Fireheart was a tail-length away, he sprang, and turned back triumphantly to his friends with the prey in his jaws.

"Good catch," called Sandstorm.

Fireheart scraped earth over his kill so he could collect it later. "The next one's yours, Brackenpaw," he meowed.

Brackenpaw raised his head proudly and began to stalk forward, his eyes darting from side to side. Fireheart spotted a blackbird pecking among the berries at the foot of a holly bush, but this time he held back.

The apprentice noticed the bird almost as soon as Fireheart did. Stealthily, paw by paw, he crept up on it. His haunches rocked from side to side as he readied himself to pounce. Watching, Fireheart thought he held back a heartbeat too long. The blackbird sensed him and fluttered upward, but Brackenpaw hurled himself after it with a mighty leap and batted it out of the air.

Keeping one paw on his prey, he turned to look at Fireheart. "I got the timing wrong," he admitted. "I waited too long, didn't I?"

"Maybe," Fireheart replied. "But don't look so upset. You *caught* it, and that's what counts."

"When you get back, you can take it to the elders," meowed Sandstorm.

Brackenpaw brightened up at that. "Yes, I—" he began. He was interrupted by a shrill, terrified wailing that came from the direction of the hollow.

Fireheart spun around. "That sounds like a kit!"

With Sandstorm and Brackenpaw at his side, he raced

toward the sound. Bursting out of the trees, he launched himself toward the crest of the hollow and looked down.

"Great StarClan!" Sandstorm gasped.

Just below the three cats loomed a bulky black-and-white animal; Fireheart picked up the rank scent of a badger. He had never seen one out in the open before, although he had often heard them shuffling noisily in the bushes. With one massive, hook-clawed paw, it was reaching into a gap between two rocks, where Cloudkit was cowering.

"Fireheart!" he wailed. "Help me!"

Fireheart felt as if every hair on his body was bristling. He launched himself down into the hollow, his front paws outstretched for the attack. He was dimly aware of Sandstorm and Brackenpaw at his heels. Fireheart raked his claws down the badger's side, and the huge beast rounded on him with a roar, jaws snapping. It was fast; it might even have caught Fireheart if Brackenpaw hadn't leaped from the side, clawing for its eyes.

The badger whipped its head around to where Sandstorm had sunk her teeth into one of its back legs. Kicking out strongly, it threw her off, and she rolled into the snow.

Fireheart dashed in again to claw the badger's flank. Drops of scarlet blood fell onto the snow. The badger growled, but it was backing away now, and as Sandstorm got to her paws and advanced, spitting, it turned and lumbered off up the ravine.

Fireheart spun around to Cloudkit. "Are you hurt?"

Cloudkit crept out from the cleft in the rock, trembling

uncontrollably. "N-No."

Fireheart felt shaky with relief. "What happened? Where's Brindleface?"

"I don't know. We were all playing, and then I turned around and I couldn't see any of the others. I thought I'd come and find you, and then there was the badger. . . ." He let out a terrified mew, and crouched down with his head on his paws.

Fireheart was stretching his neck to give him a comforting lick when he heard Sandstorm say, "Fireheart, look."

Fireheart turned. Brackenpaw was lying on his side, blood seeping from his hind leg into the snow.

"It's nothing," he grunted, bravely trying to get to his paws.

"Stay still while we look," Sandstorm ordered.

Fireheart rushed over and examined the wound. To his relief, the slash on Brackenpaw's leg was long but not deep, and the bleeding had nearly stopped. "You were lucky, thank StarClan," he meowed. "And you saved me from a nasty bite. It was a brave thing to do, Brackenpaw."

The apprentice's eyes shone at Fireheart's praise. "It wasn't really brave," he mewed shakily. "I didn't have time to think."

"A warrior couldn't have done better," meowed Sandstorm. "But what's a badger doing out in daylight? They always hunt by night."

"It must be hungry, like us," Fireheart guessed. "Otherwise it wouldn't attack something as big as Cloudkit." He turned back to the kit and nudged him gently to his paws. "Come on;

let's get you back to camp."

Sandstorm helped Brackenpaw to get up and padded beside him as he limped to the top of the hollow and toward the ravine. Fireheart followed with Cloudkit, who kept very close to him.

As they reached the ravine, Brindleface burst out of it, frantically calling Cloudkit's name. Other cats came hurrying behind her, drawn out of the camp by her panic-stricken wailing. Fireheart spotted Runningwind and Dustpelt; then his heart sank as Tigerclaw followed them out of the tunnel.

Brindleface sprang at Cloudkit and covered him with anxious licks. "Where have you *been?*" she scolded. "I've been looking for you *everywhere*! You shouldn't run away like that."

"I didn't!" Cloudkit protested.

"What's going on?" Tigerclaw shouldered his way to the front of the group of cats.

Fireheart explained, while Brindleface continued to smooth down Cloudkit's ruffled fur. "We drove the badger off," he told the deputy. "Brackenpaw was very brave."

All the while he was speaking, Tigerclaw stared at him with fierce amber eyes, but Fireheart held his head high; this time he had no reason to feel guilty.

"You'd better go to Yellowfang and have that leg seen to," the deputy grunted to Brackenpaw. "As for you . . ." He swung around and loomed threateningly over Cloudkit. "What were you doing, putting yourself in danger like that? Do you think that warriors have nothing better to do than rescue you?"

Cloudkit flattened his ears. "I'm sorry, Tigerclaw. I didn't mean to get into danger."

"Didn't mean to! Has no cat taught you any better than to go wandering away like that?"

"He's only a kit," Brindleface protested mildly, turning her gentle green gaze on the deputy.

Tigerclaw drew his lips back in a snarl. "He's caused more trouble already than all the rest of the kits put together," he growled. "It's time he learned a lesson. He can do some real work for a change."

Fireheart opened his mouth to object. For once Cloudkit hadn't meant to cause trouble; his bad fright had been punishment enough for straying away from Brindleface.

But Tigerclaw was still talking. "You can go and look after the elders," he ordered. "Clear out their dirty bedding and fetch clean moss. Make sure they have enough fresh-kill, and go over their coats for ticks."

"Ticks!" exclaimed Cloudkit, losing the last of his fear in outrage. "I'm not doing that! Why can't they see to their own ticks?"

"Because they're elders," Tigerclaw hissed. "You need to start understanding a lot more about the ways of the Clan, if you ever want to be an apprentice." He glared at Cloudkit. "Go on. And keep at it until I tell you to stop."

Cloudkit looked mutinous for a moment longer, but not even he would defy Tigerclaw twice. He met the deputy's glare with hot blue eyes, and then ran off toward the tunnel. Brindleface let out a mew of distress and followed him.

"I always said bringing kittypets into the Clan was a bad

idea," Tigerclaw growled to Dustpelt. He glared at Fireheart as he spoke, as if he was daring the young warrior to protest.

Fireheart looked away. "Come on, Brackenpaw," he mewed, swallowing his anger. There was no point getting into a fight. "Let's get you to Yellowfang."

"I'll go back and see if I can find our prey," offered Sandstorm. "We don't want that badger to get it!" She started to scramble back up the ravine. Fireheart meowed his thanks after her and set off for the camp with Brackenpaw. The apprentice was limping quite badly, and looked tired.

As they approached the gorse tunnel, Fireheart was surprised to see Brokentail stumbling out with Yellowfang at his side. Two guards, Darkstripe and Longtail, followed closely.

"We must be mad, taking him out like this," Longtail grumbled. "What if he runs off?"

"Runs off?" rasped Yellowfang. "And I suppose you think hedgehogs can fly? He's not running anywhere, you stupid furball." Carefully she cleared the snow from a smooth rock and guided Brokentail to it. He settled down with his blind face raised to the sun and sniffed the air.

"It's a fine day," Yellowfang murmured, curling her scrawny gray body close to his. Fireheart had never heard her sound so gentle. "Soon the snow will melt, and new-leaf will be here. Prey will be good and fat. You'll feel better then."

Listening, Fireheart recalled what no other cat knew—that Yellowfang was Brokentail's mother. Even Brokentail himself didn't know, and now he gave no sign that he had heard Yellowfang's kind words. Fireheart winced at the pain in the medicine cat's eyes. She had been forced to give Brokentail up when he was born because medicine cats were forbidden to have kits. And later she had blinded him to save her adopted Clan from the rogue cats' attack.

But she still loved him, although she meant no more to him than any other cat in ThunderClan. Fireheart could almost have yowled in sympathy with her.

"I'll have to tell Tigerclaw about this," Darkstripe meowed fussily, pacing at the foot of the rock where the cats sat. "He didn't give any orders to let the prisoner leave the camp."

Stalking up to him, Fireheart pushed his muzzle into Darkstripe's face. "*Bluestar* was Clan leader last time I looked," he spat. "And who do you think she's going to listen to—you or the medicine cat?"

Darkstripe reared up on his back legs, his lips drawn back to show his fangs. Behind him, Fireheart heard Brackenpaw hiss in alarm. He tensed, ready for the older warrior to strike, but before a fight could break out Yellowfang interrupted them with a furious growl.

"Stop this nonsense! What's happened to Brackenpaw?" Her flattened face appeared over the edge of the rock, creased with worry.

"He was clawed by a badger," Fireheart told her, with a last glare at Darkstripe.

The old medicine cat jumped down stiffly and inspected Brackenpaw's leg, sniffing all along the wound. "You'll live," she grunted. "Go to my den. Cinderpaw's there, and she'll give you some herbs to press on that."

"Thank you, Yellowfang," Brackenpaw meowed, and limped off.

Fireheart followed, but before he entered the gorse tunnel he looked back. Yellowfang had climbed back onto the rock and was sitting with her flank pressed close against Brokentail, gently licking his fur. Fireheart could just hear her rasping the soft noises that a queen would make to her kits.

But Brokentail was as unresponsive as ever. He would not even turn to the she-cat and share tongues with her.

Sadly, Fireheart padded into the tunnel. There were few bonds stronger than the one between a mother and her kits. Yellowfang clearly still felt that bond, even after all the grief that Brokentail had caused—killing his father, destroying his own Clan with his bloodthirsty leadership, attacking ThunderClan with a band of rogue cats. But in one part of Yellowfang's mind, he was still her kit.

So how, Fireheart wondered, had Mistyfoot and Stonefur been separated from their mother? Why had Oakheart brought them to RiverClan? And most of all, why had no ThunderClan cats tried to find them?

CHAPTER 9

❧

In Yellowfang's den, Fireheart explained what had happened while Cinderpaw inspected the gash on Brackenpaw's leg and brought him a poultice to put on it.

"You'd better rest here tonight," the gray she-cat told the apprentice. "But I'm pretty sure your leg will be good as new in a day or two." She spoke cheerfully, without any bitterness that her own leg would never recover so well. Turning to Fireheart, she added, "I just had Cloudkit in here. He told me he had to go over the elders' coats for ticks, so I gave him some mouse bile."

"What's that for?" asked Brackenpaw.

"If you put some on the ticks, they soon drop off," Cinderpaw told him. Her blue eyes glimmered with amusement. "But don't lick your paws afterward. It's foul stuff."

"I'm sure Cloudkit will enjoy doing that." Fireheart grimaced. "It's a pity that Tigerclaw had to punish him, though, because I don't think it was his fault that the badger attacked him."

Cinderpaw shrugged. "There's no arguing with Tigerclaw."

"That's true," Fireheart agreed. "Anyway, I think I'll go and make sure that Cloudkit's okay."

As soon as he set paw in the elders' den, his nose wrinkled against the reek of the mouse bile. Smallear was lying on one side while Cloudkit searched his gray fur for ticks. The elder twitched as Cloudkit dabbed some of the bile inside his hind leg. "Watch it, young kit! Keep your claws sheathed."

"They are sheathed," muttered Cloudkit, his face screwed up with disgust. "There, that's got it. You're done, Smallear."

Dappletail, who had been watching intently, glanced around at Fireheart. "Your kin is very efficient, Fireheart," she rasped. "No, Cloudkit," she added as the kit started toward her, carrying the bile-soaked moss. "I'm sure I've no ticks. And I wouldn't wake One-eye if I were you." She nodded to where the old cat was sleeping, curled up beside the trunk of the fallen tree. "She won't thank you for disturbing her."

Cloudkit looked around hopefully. None of the other elders was there. "Can I go then?" he asked.

"You can see to One-eye later," Fireheart meowed. "Meanwhile, you'd better get the dirty bedding out of here. Come on; I'll help you."

"And make sure the new lot's dry!" growled Smallear.

Together Fireheart and Cloudkit raked out the old moss and heather and made several trips to carry it out of the camp. Fireheart showed Cloudkit how to clean the mouse bile from his paws by rubbing them in the snow. "Now we'll go and fetch some fresh moss," he meowed. "Come on. I know a good place."

"I'm tired," Cloudkit complained as he trailed after

Fireheart. "I don't want to do this."

"Well, too bad, you have to," Fireheart retorted. "Cheer up; it could be worse. Did I tell you that when I was an apprentice I had to look after Yellowfang all on my own?"

"Yellowfang!" Cloudkit's eyes widened. "Phew, I bet she was a grump! Did she claw you?"

"Only with her tongue," Fireheart replied. "And that's sharp enough!"

Cloudkit let out a short purr of laughter. To Fireheart's relief, he stopped complaining, and when they came to the patch of deep moss he did his share of digging it out of the snow, and copied Fireheart as he showed him how to shake the worst of the moisture off.

They were returning to the camp, their jaws laden with moss, when Fireheart saw a cat slip out of the gorse tunnel and bound up the side of the ravine. The massive body and striped pelt were unmistakable. It was Tigerclaw.

Fireheart narrowed his eyes. The deputy had looked almost furtive, peering around before he left the tunnel and disappearing over the lip of the ravine as fast as possible. Fireheart felt uneasy. Something wasn't quite right.

"Cloudkit," he meowed, dropping his wad of moss on the ground, "take your load of bedding in to the elders, and then come back for mine. There's something I've got to do."

Cloudkit mewed in agreement through his mouthful of moss and carried on toward the tunnel. Fireheart turned and raced back up the slope to the place where Tigerclaw had disappeared.

The Clan deputy was out of sight, but between his scent trail and the massive pawprints in the snow, Fireheart had no difficulty following him. He took care not to catch up, in case Tigerclaw saw or smelled him.

The trail led unwaveringly through Tallpines, past Treecutplace. Fireheart realized with a jolt that Tigerclaw had to be heading for Twolegplace. His heart lurched with fear. Was the deputy on his way to find Princess, Fireheart's sister? Maybe he was so angry with Cloudkit that he wanted to hurt the kit's mother. Fireheart had never told the Clan exactly where Princess lived, but it wouldn't be impossible for Tigerclaw to pick up her scent from his knowledge of Cloudkit's. He kept low, careful to move silently. As the trail wound through a clump of gorse, movement in the corner of his eye caught his attention. It was a mouse, scuffling under one of the bushes.

Fireheart did not want to stop and hunt, but this mouse was practically begging to be caught. Instinctively his body dropped into a hunting crouch as he crept up on the prey. His pounce landed him squarely on top of it, and he took a moment longer to bury it in the snow before he began to follow Tigerclaw again. Fireheart moved more quickly now, afraid of what the deputy might have done in the time he had delayed.

As he rounded the stump of a fallen tree, he practically collided with Tigerclaw himself, loping along in the opposite direction.

The deputy reared back in surprise. "Mouse-brain!" he hissed. "What are you doing here?"

Fireheart's first reaction was one of relief. Tigerclaw hadn't possibly had time to reach Twolegplace and harm Princess already. Then he realized that the deputy was glaring at him with a look of deep suspicion in his amber eyes. *He mustn't know I was following him*, Fireheart thought desperately.

"I . . . I came out to show Cloudkit a good place to find bedding," he stammered. "And then I thought I might as well hunt for a bit."

"I don't see any prey," growled Tigerclaw.

"It's buried just back there." Fireheart jerked his head in the direction he had come.

The warrior narrowed his eyes. "Show me."

Furious that Tigerclaw didn't believe him, but also deeply relieved at the luck that had led him to catch prey, Fireheart led the way back along the trail and scraped the snow away from the mouse he had just buried. "Satisfied?"

The Clan deputy frowned at him. Fireheart could almost read his thoughts; he was dying to blame Fireheart for something, but couldn't manage it this time.

At last he grunted, "Get on with it, then." He dipped his head to pick up Fireheart's mouse and marched off in the direction of the camp.

Fireheart watched him go, and then started running along the trail again, toward Twolegplace. He could at least find out where Tigerclaw had been. He swiveled his ears backward from time to time; he wouldn't put it past Tigerclaw to turn back and follow him, but he heard nothing, and gradually he began to relax.

Tigerclaw's scent trail came to an end near the fences that enclosed the Twoleg territory. Fireheart walked back and forth under the trees, studying the ground. The snow was churned up by the marks of many paws—too many for him to read. There were many strange scents, too. Several cats had been here, and recently.

Fireheart wrinkled his nose in disgust. The cat scents were muddled up with those of long-dead prey and the stink of Twoleg rubbish. Except for Tigerclaw's own scent, it was impossible to identify any of them. Thinking deeply, Fireheart sat washing his paws. There was no way of telling whether Tigerclaw had met these unknown cats, or whether he had just crossed their trail. He was about to set off for camp again when he heard a meow from behind him.

"Fireheart! Fireheart!"

Springing to his paws, he whirled around. Sitting on the fence at the end of her Twoleg garden was his sister, Princess. Instantly Fireheart raced across to the fence and leaped up beside her.

Princess broke into a deep, throaty purr and rubbed the side of her face against his. "Fireheart, you're so thin!" she exclaimed, pulling away from him. "Are you getting enough to eat?"

"No, nor is any cat in the Clan," Fireheart admitted. "Prey is scarce in this weather."

"Are you hungry now?" his sister asked. "There's a bowl of food in my Twolegs' nest. You can have it if you like."

For a couple of heartbeats Fireheart was tempted. His

mouth watered at the thought of filling his belly with food he hadn't had to catch first. But common sense won. He couldn't possibly return to camp with Twoleg scents all over him, and the warrior code forbade him to eat before feeding the rest of the Clan. "Thanks, Princess, but I can't," he meowed.

"I hope you're feeding Cloudkit," Princess mewed anxiously. "I've been watching for you for days, so you can tell me how he is."

"He's doing well," Fireheart replied. "He'll be made an apprentice soon."

Princess's eyes shone with pride, and Fireheart felt a prickle of uncertainty in his fur. He knew how much it meant to his sister to have given her firstborn to the Clan. There was no way he could let her have any doubts about how the kit was settling into Clan life. "Cloudkit's strong and brave," he told her. "And intelligent." *And nosey, spoiled, disrespectful*, he added to himself. But surely Cloudkit would learn soon enough, when he grew used to Clan ways. "I'm sure he'll make a fine warrior," he meowed.

Princess purred. "Of course he will, with you to teach him."

Fireheart's ears twitched with embarrassment. Princess thought he found it easy being a warrior. She didn't know the problems he had inside the Clan, or how difficult it was to decide what was the right thing to do when he discovered things that affected the Clan.

"I'd better go," he mewed. "I'll come to visit you again soon. And when newleaf comes, I'll bring Cloudkit with me."

He gave Princess an affectionate lick in farewell and left her purring even harder at the thought of seeing her beloved kit again.

Fireheart padded back along Tigerclaw's scent trail, keeping a lookout for prey as he went. After telling Tigerclaw he was hunting, he knew he had better return to camp with a respectable catch. Gradually he became aware of an unfamiliar sound. He had to pause and think before he realized what it was. Somewhere, water was dripping. Glancing around, he saw a silver globule bulging at the end of a thorn twig. The droplet swelled and glittered in the sunlight before falling to melt a tiny hole in the snow.

Fireheart raised his head. The patter of water was all around him now, and a warm breeze ruffled his fur. With a surge of joy he realized that the harsh season of leaf-bare was drawing to an end. Soon newleaf would come, and prey would be plentiful again. The thaw had begun!

CHAPTER 10

❧

Back in the camp, Fireheart spotted Bluestar leaving the nursery. Quickly he dropped his catch on the pile of fresh-kill and padded over to her.

"Yes, Fireheart, what is it?" the leader asked. Her voice was calm, but with a sinking feeling, Fireheart knew that the lack of warmth meant she had not forgiven him for asking about the missing ThunderClan kits.

He lowered his head respectfully. "Bluestar, I was hunting near Twolegplace, and—"

"Why there?" Bluestar interrupted. "Sometimes I think you spend too much time near Twolegplace, Fireheart."

"I—I just thought there might be prey there," Fireheart stammered. "Anyway, while I was there, I smelled some strange cats."

At once Bluestar was alert; her ears flicked up and she fixed her eyes intently on Fireheart. "How many cats? What Clan were they from?"

"I'm not sure how many," Fireheart admitted. "Five or six at least. But they didn't have the scent of any Clan." He wrinkled his nose as he remembered. "They smelled of crowfood, which made me sure they weren't kittypets."

Bluestar looked thoughtful, and to Fireheart's relief her hostility toward him seemed to ebb away. "How recent was the scent?" she asked.

"Quite recent. But I didn't see any cats there." *Except Tigerclaw*, he added silently. But Fireheart decided not to tell Bluestar that part of the story. The leader was in no mood to listen to any more accusations against her deputy, and he had no evidence anyway that Tigerclaw had had anything to do with the unknown cats.

"Rogues from the Twolegplace, perhaps?" Bluestar guessed. "Thank you, Fireheart. I'll tell the patrols to keep a lookout when they go that way. I don't suppose they're any threat to ThunderClan, but we can't be too careful."

Fireheart padded toward the camp with a vole clamped firmly in his jaws. The sun shone from a brilliantly blue sky, and already, two days after his meeting with Princess, most of the snow was gone. Buds were swelling and a mist of tiny green leaves was beginning to cover the trees. More important, prey was reappearing in the forest. Already it was easier to replenish the pile of fresh-kill, and for the first time in moons the Clan was full-fed.

Fireheart arrived in the clearing to find the queens raking old bedding out of the nursery. When he had dropped his prey on the pile of fresh-kill, he went across to give them a hand, pleased to see that Cloudkit was helping too.

"I'm going to show the other kits the good moss place!"

the kit mewed proudly as he staggered past with a load of bedding.

"Good idea," Fireheart agreed. He'd noticed that even after Tigerclaw relieved him of his duties with the elders, Cloudkit had gone on helping. Maybe at last the kit was feeling some spark of loyalty toward his adopted Clan. "Watch out for badgers, though!"

Just then he saw Goldenflower emerge from the nursery, pushing a ball of soiled moss in front of her. Her belly was round with the weight of the kits she was carrying.

"Hello, Fireheart," she meowed. "Isn't it great to see the sun again?"

Fireheart gave the queen's shoulder a friendly lick. "Soon it'll be newleaf," he mewed. "Just in time for your kits. If you—" He broke off and spun around as he heard Tigerclaw's voice behind him, speaking his name.

"Fireheart, if you've nothing better to do than stand gossiping with the queens, I have a job for you."

Fireheart bit back an angry response. He'd been hunting all morning, and paused for only a few moments to talk to Goldenflower.

"I want you to take a patrol along the border of RiverClan," the deputy went on. "No cat has been that way for a few days, and now the snow has gone we need to renew the scent markings. And make sure no RiverClan cats are hunting in our territory. If they are, you know what to do!"

"Yes, Tigerclaw," Fireheart mewed. Hedgehogs must be growing wings, he thought, if Tigerclaw had chosen him to lead a patrol! Then he realized that Tigerclaw was too clever to behave hostilely toward him in public. The deputy would be careful to treat him just the same as any other Clan warrior, in case Bluestar noticed.

But I still don't trust you! Fireheart thought. Aloud he meowed, "Whom shall I take with me?"

"Any cat you like. Or do you need me to hold your paw?" Tigerclaw added with a sneer.

"No, Tigerclaw." By now Fireheart could barely keep his tongue curbed; he would have loved to swipe a claw over the deputy's scarred muzzle. He mewed a hasty good-bye to Goldenflower, and headed for the warriors' den. Sandstorm was there, lying on her side and energetically washing, while Graystripe and Runningwind shared tongues nearby.

"Who's up for a patrol?" Fireheart called. "Tigerclaw wants us to check the RiverClan border."

Graystripe scrambled to his paws right away at the mention of RiverClan, while Runningwind got up more slowly. Sandstorm paused in her washing and looked up at Fireheart. "Just when I was hoping for a bit of peace," she complained. "I've been hunting since dawn." But her tone was good-humored, not remotely as unfriendly as she was when he had first arrived in the Clan, Fireheart thought, and almost at once she got up and shook herself. "All right," she mewed. "Lead on."

"What about Brackenpaw?" Fireheart asked Graystripe. "Do you want to bring him along?"

"Whitestorm and Mousefur took the apprentices out,"

Runningwind explained. "*All* of the apprentices—more fool them! They're hunting fresh-kill for the elders."

Fireheart led the way out of the camp, feeling a tingle in his paws as he leaped up the side of the ravine. It felt like moons since he'd had a good run without snow to freeze his paws off, and he wanted to stretch his muscles. "We'll head for the Sunningrocks," he meowed, "and then follow the border up to Fourtrees."

He set a brisk pace through the trees, but not so fast that he failed to notice the brilliant green fronds of new bracken beginning to unfurl, or the first pale buds of primroses pushing out of their green coverings. Birdsong filled the air, and the fresh scent of growing things.

He slowed down to a walk as the patrol approached the edge of the forest. Ahead of him he could hear the sound of the river, free at last from its bonds of ice. "We're almost at the border," he meowed quietly. "From here on we have to keep alert. There may be RiverClan cats about."

Graystripe stopped and opened his jaws to drink in scent from the breeze. "I can't smell any," he reported. Fireheart wondered if he was disappointed that Silverstream wasn't nearby. "Besides, they'll have plenty of prey now that the river's unfrozen," Graystripe added. "Why should they come and steal ours?"

"I wouldn't put anything past RiverClan," growled Runningwind. "They'd steal the fur off your back if you didn't keep an eye on them."

Fireheart saw Graystripe beginning to bristle. "Come on,

then," he meowed hastily, trying to distract his friend before he said something that gave away his divided loyalties. "Let's go." He raced away through the last of the trees and burst out onto open ground. What he saw there brought him skidding to a halt, and the memory of his dream crashed into his mind like a thunderclap.

In front of the cats, the land sloped gently down to the river—or what had been the river. Swelled by the melting snow, the fast-flowing water had burst the banks and risen until it lapped the grass barely a rabbit-length from Fireheart's paws. The tips of reeds just showed above it; farther upstream, the Sunningrocks were gray islands in the midst of a shimmering silver lake.

The thaw had certainly come, but now the river was in full flood.

CHAPTER 11

"Great StarClan!" breathed Sandstorm.

The other two cats grunted in agreement, but Fireheart was speechless with horror. He had instantly recognized the shining expanse of water, and now he recalled Spottedleaf's ominous words: "Water can quench fire."

Fear chilled him as he struggled to understand how this flood could threaten his Clan, so that he was hardly aware of Graystripe trying to attract his attention until the big gray cat pressed up close to his side. Panic flared in Graystripe's amber eyes, and Fireheart didn't need to ask why. His friend was afraid for Silverstream.

The land was lower on the RiverClan bank, so the flood-waters could spread much farther. As for the camp on the island . . . Fireheart wondered how much of that was under-water. He had grown to like Silverstream in spite of his concerns, and he felt a grudging respect for Mistyfoot and Graypool, too. He didn't want to imagine them driven out of their camp, or worse, drowned.

Runningwind had padded right to the water's edge and was gazing out across the river. "RiverClan isn't going to like this," he remarked. "And a good thing, too. It'll keep them off our territory."

Fireheart felt Graystripe tense at the note of satisfaction in Runningwind's voice. He shot his friend a warning glance. "Well, we can't patrol the border now," he pointed out. "We'd better get back to camp and report this. Come on, Graystripe," he added firmly, seeing the warrior look once more with anguish across the swollen river.

As soon as Bluestar heard the news she leaped to the top of the Highrock and gave the familiar call: "Let all cats old enough to catch their own prey join here beneath the Highrock for a Clan meeting."

At once cats began to pour out of their dens and into the clearing. Fireheart took his place at the front of the crowd, noticing with a prickle of annoyance that Cloudkit had come bouncing along after Brindleface, although he was too young to attend the meeting. He saw Yellowfang and Cinderpaw listening from the mouth of the fern tunnel. Even Brokentail emerged from his den, nudged along by Mousefur.

The bright morning was coming to an end. Clouds were massing to cover the face of the sun, and the gentle breeze had strengthened until a stiff wind blew across the clearing, flattening the fur of the cats who crouched around the Highrock. Fireheart shivered, and didn't know whether it was from cold or apprehension.

"Cats of ThunderClan," meowed Bluestar. "Our camp may be in danger. The snow has gone, but the river has burst its banks. Part of our territory is already flooded."

A chorus of dismay rose from the Clan, but Bluestar raised her voice above the yowls. "Fireheart, tell the Clan what you have seen."

Fireheart stood up and described how the river had overflowed near the Sunningrocks.

"It doesn't sound that dangerous to us," meowed Darkstripe when he had finished. "We have plenty of territory left for prey. Let RiverClan worry about the floods."

A murmur of approval broke out, although Fireheart noticed that Tigerclaw stayed silent. He sat at the base of the Highrock, motionless except for the twitching tip of his tail.

"Silence!" spat Bluestar. "The water could spread here before we know it. Something like this is bigger than Clan rivalry. I don't want to hear that any RiverClan cats have died from these floods."

Fireheart noticed a hot glow in her eyes as she spoke, as if her words meant more than she had said. Puzzled, he remembered how angry Bluestar had been with him for speaking to RiverClan warriors; yet now her strength of feeling suggested a current of sympathy running deep within her.

Patchpelt spoke up from among the elders. "I remember the last time the river overflowed, many moons ago. Cats from all Clans drowned. Prey drowned, too, and we went hungry even though our paws stayed dry. This is not just RiverClan's problem."

"Well said, Patchpelt," meowed Bluestar. "I remember those days, too, and I hoped I would never have to see such times again. But since it has happened, these are my orders: No cat is to go out alone. Kits and apprentices must not leave the camp without at least one warrior. Patrols will go out to discover how far the floods reach—Tigerclaw, see to it."

"Yes, Bluestar," meowed the deputy. "I'll send out hunting patrols, too. We must build up a stock of prey before the water rises any farther."

"Good idea," agreed Bluestar. She raised her voice again to address the whole Clan. "The meeting is over. Go to your duties." She leaped down lightly from the Highrock and padded across to talk with Patchpelt and the other elders.

Fireheart was waiting to see if Tigerclaw would choose him for a patrol when he noticed Graystripe edging away from the circle of cats. Fireheart headed after him, and caught up just as he broke for the gorse tunnel. "Where do you think you're going?" he hissed in the gray warrior's ear. "Bluestar just said that no cat should go out alone."

Graystripe turned a panicky look on him. "Fireheart, I *have* to see Silverstream," he protested. "I have to be sure she's okay."

Fireheart let out a long sigh of exasperation. He understood how his friend was feeling, but he could hardly have chosen a worse time to go visiting his mate. "How will you get across the river?" he asked.

"I'll manage," Graystripe promised grimly. "It's only water."

"Don't be such a mouse-brain!" Fireheart spat, remembering the time Graystripe had fallen through the ice, when

Silverstream had rescued him. "You nearly drowned once before. Wasn't that enough for you?"

Graystripe didn't answer; he just swung around and made for the tunnel again.

Fireheart glanced over his shoulder. The other cats in the clearing were breaking up into small groups under Tigerclaw's direction, ready to go out on patrol. "Stop, Graystripe!" he hissed, halting his friend at the entrance to the tunnel. "Wait there."

Once he was sure Graystripe had done as he asked, he bounded across the clearing toward the deputy. "Hey, Tigerclaw," he meowed. "Graystripe and I are ready to go. We'll check the RiverClan boundary downstream of the Sunningrocks, all right?"

Tigerclaw narrowed his eyes, clearly displeased that Fireheart had taken it upon himself to choose which area he was going to patrol. But he had no reason to refuse, especially with Bluestar in earshot. "All right," he growled. "Try to bring some prey back, as well."

"Yes, Tigerclaw," Fireheart replied, dipping his head before turning to race back to Graystripe. "Okay," he panted. "We're on patrol, so at least no cat will wonder where we've gone."

"But you—" Graystripe began to protest.

"I know you have to go," Fireheart meowed. "But I'm coming with you."

He felt a prickle of guilt as he spoke. Even on patrol, he and Graystripe wouldn't be expected to cross Clan boundaries. Bluestar would be furious if she knew that two of her warriors were risking their lives to go into enemy territory when their own Clan needed them so badly. But Fireheart couldn't just stand there and let Graystripe go alone. His friend could be swept away in the floods and never return.

"Thanks, Fireheart," murmured Graystripe as they left the tunnel. "I won't forget this."

Side by side, the two warriors scrambled up the steep, rocky slope. As they headed into the forest, retracing the steps of their earlier patrol, Fireheart noticed how muddy the ground was underpaw. The melted snow had soaked the earth like the heaviest rainfall, even without the deadly spread of floodwater from the river.

When they reached the edge of the trees Fireheart realized that the water had risen even farther. The Sunningrocks were almost submerged now, and the current swirled around them in tight circles. "We'll never make it across there," he meowed.

"Let's head downstream," Graystripe suggested. "We might be able to use the stepping stones."

"We can try," Fireheart mewed uncertainly. He was about to follow his friend when he thought he heard something—a thin, wailing sound, above the wind and the rushing of the torrent. "Wait," he called. "Did you hear that?"

Graystripe looked back, and both cats stood, ears pricked, straining to catch the sound. Then Fireheart heard it again— the panic-stricken mewing of kits in distress.

"Where are they?" he meowed, looking all around and up into the trees. "I can't see them!"

"There." Graystripe flicked his tail in the direction of the Sunningrocks. "Fireheart, they'll drown!"

Fireheart saw that the current had driven a mat of twigs and debris up against the Sunningrocks. Two kits balanced precariously on it, their tiny mouths stretched wide as they wailed for help. Even as Fireheart watched, the current tugged at the mat, threatening to sweep it away. "Come on," he yowled to Graystripe. "We've got to reach them somehow."

Taking a deep breath, he waded into the flood. The water soaked into his fur at once, and a paralyzing, icy chill crept up his legs. The tug of the current made it harder to stay on his paws with every step he took.

Graystripe splashed in behind him, but when the water reached his belly fur he stopped. "Fireheart . . ." he choked out.

Fireheart twisted around to give him a comforting nod. He could understand how the river might terrify Graystripe, after his near-drowning a few moons ago. "Stay there," he meowed. "I'll try to push the mat over to you."

Graystripe nodded, trembling too violently to speak. Fireheart waded forward a few more paces, then launched himself into the current and began to swim, thrashing his legs instinctively to push himself through the black water. They were upstream of the Sunningrocks; if StarClan was kind, he should be carried down toward the kits.

For a moment he lost sight of them in the wind-ruffled waves, though he could still hear their terrified cries. Then the smooth gray bulk of a Sunningrock loomed up beside him. He kicked out strongly, fearing for one panic-stricken heartbeat that he would be swept right past.

The current swirled; Fireheart's paws worked furiously, and the river tossed him against the rock, driving the breath out of his body. He scrabbled at the rough surface, bracing himself against the rushing water, and found himself face-to-face with the two kits.

They were both very small—still suckling from their mother, Fireheart guessed. One was black and one gray, their fur plastered against their tiny bodies, and their brilliant blue eyes wide with terror. They were crouched on a tangled mat of twigs, leaves, and Twoleg rubbish, but when they saw Fireheart they started to scramble toward him. The mat lurched and their wails grew louder as river water sloshed over them.

"Keep still!" Fireheart gasped, paddling madly against the current. Briefly he wondered if he could climb onto the rock and haul the kits up with him, but he was not sure how long it would be before the Sunningrocks were completely submerged. His best plan was still to push the mat over to Graystripe. Looking back, he saw that his friend had already moved downstream, into a good position to catch the mat as it was swept toward him.

"Here we go," Fireheart muttered. "StarClan help us!" He pushed himself off from the rock, thrusting at the mat with his muzzle to guide it into the current. The two kits whimpered and flattened themselves against the twigs.

Fireheart put every last scrap of energy into pushing the

mat ahead of him with his nose and paws. He could feel exhaustion draining the strength from his limbs. His fur was soaked, and he was so cold he could hardly breathe. Raising his head and blinking water out of his eyes, he realized with horror that he had lost sight of Graystripe and the bank. It seemed as if there was nothing in the world but the churning water, the fragile mat of twigs, and the two terrified kits.

Then he heard Graystripe's voice, sounding close by. "Fireheart! Fireheart, here!"

Fireheart thrust again at the mat, trying to propel it toward the voice. It spun away from him, and his head went under. Coughing and choking, he clawed his way back to the surface, to see Graystripe pacing on dry land just a few tail-lengths away.

For a heartbeat Fireheart felt relief that he was nearly there. Then he focused his blurred eyes on the kits again, and fear pulsed through him. The mat was beginning to break up.

Fireheart watched helplessly as the twigs underneath the gray kit gave way and the tiny creature was plunged into the torrent.

CHAPTER 12

♣

"No!" Graystripe yowled, launching himself after the drowning kit.

Fireheart lost sight of them. The kit left on the mat squealed desperately, trying to cling to the twigs as they were split apart by the current. With the last of his strength Fireheart drove himself forward, sank his teeth into the little creature's scruff, and kicked out for dry ground.

Within moments he felt stones under his paws and managed to stand. Stone-limbed with weariness, he staggered out and dropped the black kit on the grass at the edge of the flood. Its eyes were closed; he was not sure if it was still alive.

Glancing downstream, he saw Graystripe splashing out of the shallows, with the gray kit gripped firmly in his teeth. He padded up to Fireheart and set it gently on the ground.

Fireheart nosed both kits. They were lying very still, but when Fireheart looked closer he could see the faint rise and fall of their flanks as they breathed. "Thank StarClan," he muttered. He began to lick the black kit as he had seen the queens in the nursery do to their little ones, rasping his tongue against the lie of the fur to rouse the kit and warm it. Graystripe crouched beside him and did the same for the gray kit.

Soon the black kit twitched and coughed up a mouthful of river water. It took longer for the gray kit to respond, but at last it too coughed up water and opened its eyes.

"They're alive!" exclaimed Graystripe, his voice filled with relief.

"Yes, but they won't live long without their mother," Fireheart pointed out. He sniffed the black kit carefully. The river water had washed off much of the Clan scent, but he could still detect a faint trace. "RiverClan," he mewed, unsurprised. "We'll have to take them home."

Fireheart's courage almost deserted him for good at the thought of crossing the swollen river. He had almost drowned rescuing the kits, and he felt exhausted. His limbs were cold and stiff, and his fur was soaked. He wanted nothing more than to creep into his own den and sleep for a moon.

Graystripe, still crouched over the gray kit, looked as if he felt the same. His thick gray fur was flattened against his body, and his amber eyes were wide with anxiety. "Do you think we can get across?" he meowed.

"We've got to, or the kits will die." Forcing himself to his paws, Fireheart picked up the black kit again by its scruff and headed downstream. "Let's see if we can cross by the stepping-stones, like you said." Graystripe padded after him, carrying the gray kit through the wet grass at the edge of the floodwater.

When the river was at its usual level, the stepping-stones

were an easy route across for RiverClan cats. The longest leap from rock to rock was no more than a tail-length, and RiverClan controlled the territory here on both sides of the river.

Now floodwater completely covered the stones. But where they had once broken the surface, a dead tree, its bark stripped away, lay across the river. Fireheart guessed that some of its branches had been caught on the submerged stepping-stones. "Thank StarClan!" he exclaimed. "We can use the tree to cross." He adjusted his grip on the kit and waded out into the flood toward the splintered end of the tree trunk. The kit, seeing the churning water barely a mouse-length below its nose, began to mewl and struggle feebly.

"Keep still, both of you," growled Graystripe gently, as he set down the gray kit for a moment to adjust his grip. "We're going to find your mother."

Fireheart wasn't sure if his terrified kit was even old enough to understand, but at least it went limp again so it was easier to carry. He had to lift his head high to keep the tiny creature clear of the water as he floundered toward the tree. He reached it without needing to swim and sprang upward, clawing for a grip on the soft, rotting wood. Once he had pulled himself up, his main concern was keeping a pawhold on the smooth, slippery trunk. Gingerly placing each of his paws in a straight line, Fireheart padded toward the opposite bank with the river churning beneath him, sucking at the tree as if it wanted to sweep it, and its burden of cats, away downstream. Fireheart glanced back to see Graystripe following with the gray kit, his face creased with determination.

At the far end the trunk divided into a tangle of broken branches. Fireheart ducked down to squeeze through them, being careful not to let the kit's fur catch on the splinters. It was harder to find a pawhold as the branches tapered, and he ran out of anything that might bear his weight when there was still a gap of a couple of fox-lengths separating him from the far side of the river. Fireheart took a deep breath, flexed his hindlegs, and leaped. His front paws hit the bank while his hind paws kicked madly in the rushing current. As water splashed up, the kit started to struggle again. Fireheart kept his teeth clenched in its neck fur as he sank his front claws into the soft earth and scrabbled upward until he stood safely on the bank. He lurched forward a few paces and set the kit down gently.

Glancing around, he saw Graystripe pulling himself out of the water a little way downstream. He lowered the gray kit to the ground and shook himself. "The river water tastes foul," he spat.

"Look on the bright side," Fireheart suggested. "At least it should disguise your scent. The RiverClan cats won't know that you're the warrior who's been trespassing on their territory. If they ever found out—"

He broke off as three cats crashed out of the bushes just beyond Graystripe. Fireheart braced himself as he recognized Leopardfur, the RiverClan deputy, and the warriors Blackclaw and Stonefur. Forcing his tired legs to move, he picked up the black kit and padded along the bank to stand beside Graystripe. The gray warrior hauled himself to his paws, and the two cats set down their burdens and faced their enemies together.

Fireheart wondered if the RiverClan cats had overheard what he was saying to Graystripe. He knew that he and Graystripe were too exhausted to stand up to a patrol of strong, fresh warriors, and his head spun as he tried to summon enough energy for a fight into his frozen paws. But to his relief, the RiverClan cats halted a few tail-lengths away.

"What's this?" growled Leopardfur. Her golden-spotted fur bristled, and her ears were flattened against her head.

Beside her, Blackclaw stood with his lips drawn back in a snarl. "Why are you trespassing on our territory?" he demanded.

"We're not trespassing," Fireheart meowed quietly. "We pulled two of your kits out of the river and wanted to bring them home."

"Do you think we nearly drowned ourselves just for fun?" Graystripe blurted out.

Stonefur paced forward until he was close enough to sniff the two kits. "It's true!" His blue eyes widened. "They're Mistyfoot's missing kits!"

Fireheart stiffened in amazement. He knew that Mistyfoot had recently had kits, but hadn't realized that the kits they had rescued were hers. He was even more thankful now that they had been able to save the kits' lives, but he knew they mustn't let any of these cats know that Mistyfoot had friends in ThunderClan.

Leopardfur did not relax the fur on her shoulders. "How

do we know you saved the kits?" she snarled. "You might have been trying to steal them."

Fireheart stared at her. After risking their lives in the floodwater, he couldn't believe that they were actually being accused of stealing the kits. "Don't be such a mouse-brain!" he spat. "No cat from ThunderClan tried to steal your kits when we could walk across the river on the ice. Why do you think we'd try it now? We nearly drowned!"

Leopardfur looked thoughtful, but Blackclaw stalked up and thrust his head aggressively into Fireheart's face. Fireheart snarled, ready to counter a blow.

"Blackclaw!" Leopardfur meowed sharply. "Back off! We'll let these cats explain themselves to Crookedstar, and see if he believes them."

Fireheart opened his mouth to protest, but left the words unspoken. They would have to go with the RiverClan cats; in their exhausted state he and Graystripe had no hope of winning a fight. At least Graystripe would be able to check on Silverstream. "All right," Fireheart meowed. "I just hope your Clan leader can see the truth when it's in front of his nose."

Leopardfur led the way along the bank, while Blackclaw picked up one kit and stalked threateningly alongside Fireheart and Graystripe. Stonefur brought up the rear, carrying the other kit.

When they reached the island where the RiverClan cats had their camp, Fireheart saw that a wide channel of racing water separated it from the ridge of dry ground, wrenching at the overhanging boughs of the willow trees. No cats were visible through the reeds, and Fireheart could see silver water lapping among the bushes that concealed the camp.

Leopardfur paused, her eyes widening with alarm. "The water has risen since we left camp," she meowed.

As she spoke, a yowl came from behind them at the top of the slope, where Fireheart and Graystripe had hidden to talk to Silverstream. "Leopardfur! Up here!"

Fireheart turned to see the RiverClan leader, Crookedstar, emerging from the shelter of the bushes. His pale tabby coat was soaked, fur sticking out in all directions, and his twisted jaw made him look as if he were mocking the patrol and their prisoners.

"What happened?" Leopardfur demanded as she reached her leader.

"The camp is flooded," Crookedstar replied. His voice was flat with defeat. "We've had to move up here."

As he spoke, two or three other cats emerged cautiously from the bushes. Fireheart noticed Graystripe brighten when he saw one of them was Silverstream.

"And what have you brought us?" Crookedstar went on. He narrowed his eyes at Fireheart and Graystripe. "ThunderClan spies? As if we didn't have enough trouble!"

"They found Mistyfoot's kits," Leopardfur told him, nodding to Stonefur and Blackclaw to bring forward the kits. "They claim they pulled them out of the river."

"I don't believe a word of it!" spat Blackclaw, setting down the kit he carried. "You can't trust a ThunderClan cat."

At the mention of the kit, Silverstream had turned and

disappeared rapidly under the bushes again. Crookedstar padded forward and sniffed the pathetic bundles. By now they had begun to recover from their ordeal and were trying to sit up, though they still looked completely waterlogged.

"Mistyfoot's kits went missing when the camp flooded," Crookedstar remarked, turning his cold green gaze on Fireheart and Graystripe. "How do you come to have them?"

Fireheart exchanged an exasperated glance with Graystripe, exhaustion making him short-tempered. "We flew across the river," he mewed sarcastically.

A loud yowling interrupted him. Mistyfoot broke out of the bushes and came racing over to them. "My kits! Where are my kits?" She crouched over the tiny scraps of fur, staring wildly around as if she thought the other cats would try to take them away from her. Then she began licking them furiously, trying to comfort both of them at once. Stonefur pressed up close against her and mewed comfortingly into her ear.

Silverstream followed more slowly and stood beside her father, Crookedstar, eyeing the ThunderClan cats. Fireheart was relieved to see her gaze pass with apparent indifference over Graystripe. She would not give them away, he was sure.

More cats emerged after her and gathered curiously around. Fireheart recognized Graypool, who gave no sign that she had ever seen him before, and Mudfur, the RiverClan medicine cat, who crouched beside Mistyfoot to examine the kits.

All of the RiverClan cats were wet through, and the fur clinging to their bodies showed they were skinnier than ever.

Fireheart had always thought of RiverClan cats as plump and sleek, wellfed on fish from the river. That was until Silverstream told him that Twolegs had stayed by the river during greenleaf and stolen or scared away most of their prey. The Twolegs had left the forest now, during leaf-bare, but RiverClan had been unable to hunt when the river froze. And instead of bringing much-needed food, the thaw had driven them out of their camp completely.

In spite of his pang of pity, Fireheart could also see the unfriendliness in their eyes, the hostility in their flattened ears and twitching tail tips. Fireheart knew he and Graystripe would have to work hard to convince Crookedstar that they had really saved the kits.

The Clan leader was at least prepared to give them a chance to explain. "Tell us what happened," Crookedstar ordered.

Fireheart began at the point when he had heard the kits wailing and seen them stranded on the mat of debris in the river.

"Since when have ThunderClan cats risked their lives for us?" Blackclaw broke in contemptuously as Fireheart described how he had pushed the kits through the torrent to the riverbank.

Fireheart bit back an angry retort, and Crookedstar hissed at the warrior, "Quiet, Blackclaw! Let him speak. If he's lying, we'll find out soon enough."

"He's not lying." Mistyfoot looked up from where she was still nuzzling her kits. "Why should ThunderClan steal kits when all the Clans are finding it hard to feed themselves?"

"Fireheart's story makes sense," Silverstream observed calmly. "We had to abandon the camp and shelter in these bushes when the water started to rise again," she explained to Fireheart. "When we came to move Mistyfoot's kits, we could find only two of them. The other two were missing. The whole nursery floor had been washed away. They must have been swept along the river to where you found them."

Crookedstar nodded slowly, and Fireheart realized that the hostility of the RiverClan cats was fading—all except for Blackclaw, who turned his back on the ThunderClan warriors with a snort of disgust.

"In that case, we're grateful to you," meowed Crookedstar, though he sounded grudging, as if he could hardly bear to be in debt to a pair of ThunderClan cats.

"Yes," mewed Mistyfoot. She looked up again, her eyes glowing softly with gratitude. "Without you, my kits would have died."

Fireheart dipped his head in acknowledgment. Impulsively, he asked, "Is there anything we can do for you? If you can't go back to your camp, and if prey's scarce because of the flood—"

"We need no help from ThunderClan," growled Crookedstar. "RiverClan cats can look after themselves."

"Don't be such a fool." It was Graypool who spoke, with a glare at her leader. Fireheart felt a new surge of respect for her; he guessed that not many cats would dare to take that tone with Crookedstar. "You're too proud for your own good," the elder rasped. "How can we feed ourselves, even with the thaw? There are no fish to eat. The river's practically poisoned; you know it is."

"What?" Graystripe exclaimed; Fireheart was too shocked to say anything.

"It's all the fault of the Twolegs," Graypool explained to them. "Last newleaf, the river was clean and full of fish. Now it's filthy with Twoleg rubbish from their camp."

"And the fish are poisoned," Mudfur added. "Cats who eat them fall ill. I've treated more cats for bellyache this leaf-bare than in all the time since I've been the medicine cat."

Fireheart stared at Graystripe, and then back at the hungry RiverClan cats. Most of them couldn't meet his eyes, as if they were ashamed that a cat of another Clan should know about their troubles. "Then let us help," he urged them all. "We'll catch prey for you in our territory and bring it to you, until the floods have gone and the river is clean."

Even as he made the offer, he knew that he was breaking the warrior code that demanded loyalty to his own Clan alone. Bluestar would be furious with him if she found out he was prepared to share ThunderClan's precious prey like this. But Fireheart couldn't bring himself to abandon another Clan in their need. *Bluestar herself said our welfare depends on having four Clans in the forest*, he reminded himself. *Surely it's the will of StarClan.*

"Would you really do this for us?" asked Crookedstar slowly, his eyes narrowing with suspicion.

"Yes," Fireheart meowed.

"And I'll help too," promised Graystripe, with a glance at Silverstream.

"Then the Clan thanks you," grunted Crookedstar. "None of my cats will challenge you in our territory until the floods go down and we can return to our camp. But after that, we will fend for ourselves again." He turned and led the way back to the bushes. His subdued cats followed him, casting glances back at Fireheart and Graystripe as they went. Not all of them, Fireheart could see, trusted them or believed in their offer of help.

Last to go was Mistyfoot, nudging her kits to their paws and guiding them up the slope. "Thank you both," she murmured. "I won't forget this."

Fireheart and Graystripe were left alone as the RiverClan cats disappeared into the bushes. As they picked their way down the slope again toward the river, Graystripe shook his head in disbelief. "Hunting for another Clan? We must be mad."

"What else could we do?" Fireheart retorted. "Let them starve?"

"No! But we'll have to be careful. We'll be crowfood if Bluestar finds out."

Or Tigerclaw, Fireheart added silently. *He already suspects Graystripe and I have friends in RiverClan. And we could be about to prove him right.*

CHAPTER 13

It was a cold, gray morning. Fireheart dragged himself reluctantly out of his warm nest, and padded over to nudge Graystripe.

"Wha . . . ?" Graystripe twitched and settled down again with his tail wrapped over his nose. "Go away, Fireheart."

Fireheart lowered his head and butted the broad gray shoulder. "Come on, Graystripe," he whispered into his friend's ear. "We've got to hunt for RiverClan."

At that, Graystripe levered himself upright and parted his jaws in an enormous yawn. Fireheart felt just as tired as his friend; supplying RiverClan with fresh-kill as well as keeping up with their duties in ThunderClan was taking up all their time and energy. They had crossed the river with prey several times, and so far their luck had held. No ThunderClan cat had found out what they were doing.

Stretching, Fireheart glanced cautiously around the den. Most of the warriors were curled among the moss, too sound asleep to ask awkward questions. Tigerclaw was just a mound of dark tabby fur in his nest.

Fireheart slipped out between the branches of the den. At first he thought that all the other cats were asleep; then he saw Brindleface appear at the entrance to the nursery and lift her face to sniff the air. As if she didn't like the raw, damp wind that greeted her, she retreated almost at once.

Fireheart looked back at Graystripe, who was shaking scraps of moss off his coat. "Okay," he meowed. "We can go now."

The two cats bounded across the clearing toward the gorse tunnel. Just as they reached it, a familiar voice behind them called out, "Fireheart! Fireheart!"

Fireheart froze and turned around. Cloudkit was scampering toward him, yowling, "Fireheart! Wait for me!"

"Fireheart," growled Graystripe, "why does your kin always turn up at the most awkward moment?"

"StarClan knows." Fireheart sighed.

"Where are you going?" Cloudkit panted excitedly as he skidded to a stop in front of the warriors. "Can I come with you?"

"No," Graystripe told him. "Only apprentices can go out with warriors."

Cloudkit shot Graystripe a look of dislike. "But I'll be an apprentice soon. Won't I, Fireheart?"

"'Soon' isn't 'now,'" Fireheart reminded him, struggling to keep calm. If they hung around much longer, the whole Clan would be awake and wanting to know where they were going. "You can't come this time, Cloudkit. We're going out on a special warrior mission."

Cloudkit's blue eyes grew round with wonder. "Is it a secret?"

"Yes," hissed Graystripe. "Especially from nosey kits."

"I wouldn't tell any cat," Cloudkit promised eagerly. "Fireheart, *please* let me come."

"No." Fireheart exchanged an exasperated glance with Graystripe. "Look, Cloudkit, go back to the nursery now, and maybe I'll take you out later for some hunting practice. Okay?"

"Okay . . . I suppose." Cloudkit looked sulky, but he turned around and trailed off in the direction of the nursery.

Fireheart watched him until he reached the entrance, and then slipped into the mouth of the tunnel. Moments later he was racing up the ravine with Graystripe at his side.

"I just hope Cloudkit doesn't tell the whole Clan we went out early on a special mission," puffed Graystripe.

"We'll worry about that later," Fireheart panted.

The two warriors headed for the stepping-stones. The fallen tree was still there to help them cross the river, and hunting close by meant they had less distance to carry the fresh-kill, and were less likely to be spotted.

By the time they reached the edge of the forest, the day-light had grown stronger, but the sunrise was hidden behind a mass of gray cloud. There was a spatter of rain in the wind. Fireheart couldn't help feeling that all sensible prey would be curled up in their holes. He raised his head and sniffed. The breeze carried the scent of squirrel, fresh and not far away. Cautiously he began to stalk through the trees. Soon he caught sight of his prey searching among the debris at the foot of an oak tree. As he watched, it sat up and began to nibble on an acorn held between its front paws.

"If it knows we're here," Graystripe breathed in his ear, "it'll be up that tree in a flash."

Fireheart nodded. "Circle around," he murmured. "Come at it from that side."

Graystripe slid away from him, a silent gray shape in the shadows of the trees. Fireheart flattened himself into the hunter's crouch with the ease of long practice, and began to creep up on the squirrel. He saw its ears prick, and its head swiveled around as if something had alarmed it; perhaps it had seen a flicker of movement from Graystripe, or caught his scent.

While it was distracted, Fireheart hurled himself across the open ground. His claws pinned the squirrel to the forest floor, and Graystripe ran forward to finish the struggle.

"Well done," Fireheart grunted.

Graystripe spat out a mouthful of fur. "It's a bit old and stringy, but it'll do."

The two warriors continued their hunt until they had killed a rabbit and a couple of mice. By then, although he could not see the sun, Fireheart knew it must be near sunhigh. "We'd better take this to RiverClan," he meowed. "They're bound to miss us back at the camp soon."

Stumbling slightly under the weight of the squirrel and one of the mice, he led the way to the fallen tree. To his relief, the water was no higher, and the crossing seemed easier now that he had done it several times. All the same, Fireheart felt uneasy as he scrambled through the branches, knowing that he was in full view of any ThunderClan cat who happened to be patrolling the forest's edge.

He and Graystripe swam the last couple of fox-lengths and pulled themselves out of the river on the RiverClan side. When they had shaken the water out of their fur they slunk quickly toward the bushes where RiverClan had made their temporary camp.

A cat must have been on watch, because as they approached, Leopardfur emerged from the bushes. "Welcome," she meowed, sounding a lot friendlier than she had when she first came upon them with the two kits they had rescued.

Fireheart followed her into the shelter of the hawthorn branches, remembering how he and Graystripe had hidden there to wait for Silverstream. The RiverClan cats had worked hard since the floods forced them out of their camp, bringing moss for bedding and scraping out a place beside the roots of a large bush where fresh-kill could be stored. Today this was little more than a pitiful collection of a few mice and a couple of blackbirds, which made the ThunderClan warriors' contribution all the more necessary. Fireheart dropped his prey onto the pile, and Graystripe did the same.

"Is that more fresh-kill?" Stonefur appeared with Silverstream just behind him. "Great!"

"We have to feed the elders and the nursing queens first," Leopardfur reminded him.

"I'll take something for the elders," Silverstream offered. She turned a long look on Graystripe and meowed, "You can help me. Fetch that rabbit, will you?"

Fireheart felt a sudden jolt of alarm. Surely Silverstream

wouldn't risk spending time alone with Graystripe in the middle of her own camp? On their earlier visits, she had kept her distance.

Graystripe didn't need another invitation. "Sure," he mewed, grabbing the rabbit and following Silverstream out of the bushes.

"They've got the right idea," meowed Stonefur. "Fireheart, do you want to bring the squirrel to the nursing queens? Then they can thank you themselves."

Feeling somewhat dazed, Fireheart agreed. Following Stonefur, he reflected again on how strange it was to look at the RiverClan warrior and know that he was half ThunderClan, especially since Stonefur himself didn't share that knowledge.

In the makeshift nursery, Fireheart was pleased to see Mistyfoot again, stretched out on her side while her kits suckled contentedly. But he couldn't help worrying about Graystripe. Once he had greeted the queens, and helped them divide up the squirrel, he murmured to Stonefur, "Can you show me where Graystripe went? We ought to be getting back, before any cat notices we're missing."

"Sure, this way," meowed Stonefur. He led Fireheart to a spot farther along the ridge where three or four elders were crouched on a bed of heather and bracken, tucking into the fresh-kill. Already not much was left of the rabbit except a few scraps of fur.

Graystripe and Silverstream were watching in silence, sitting side by side but not quite touching, with their tails wrapped around their paws. As soon as they saw Fireheart they sprang up and padded over to him.

Graystripe's yellow eyes blazed with a mixture of excitement and fear. "Fireheart!" he blurted out. "You won't believe what Silverstream's just told me!"

Fireheart glanced behind him, but Stonefur was already disappearing off into the bushes. The elders, having just eaten, looked sleepy, and none of them was paying any attention to Graystripe.

"Okay, what?" Fireheart mewed, his fur starting to prickle with unease. "But keep your voice down."

Graystripe looked ready to burst out of his skin. "Fireheart," he whispered, "Silverstream is going to have my kits!"

CHAPTER 14

❧

His heart thudding, Fireheart looked from Graystripe to Silverstream. She quivered with happiness, her green eyes glowing with pride. "Your kits?" he echoed in alarm. "Are you both out of your minds? This is disastrous!"

Graystripe blinked and would not meet his friend's eyes. "Not . . . not necessarily. I mean, these kits will join us together forever."

"But you come from different Clans!" Fireheart protested. From the uneasiness in Graystripe's expression, he guessed that his friend knew very well what difficulties the kits would cause. "You can't ever claim these kits as your own, Graystripe. And Silverstream," he added, turning toward the RiverClan cat, "you won't be able to tell anyone in your Clan who the father is."

"I don't care," Silverstream insisted, giving her chest fur a quick lick. "*I'll* know. That's all that matters."

Graystripe looked as if he wasn't too sure of that. "It's stupid that they can't know," he muttered. "We haven't done anything to be ashamed of." He pressed himself against Silverstream's flank and shot Fireheart a helpless glance.

"I know that's what you feel," Fireheart agreed heavily. "But it's no good, Graystripe; you know it isn't. These will be RiverClan kits." His heart sank at the thought of the trouble this could cause in the future. When these kits grew to be warriors, Graystripe might have to fight against them! He would be torn between loyalty to his blood kin, and loyalty to his Clan and the warrior code. Fireheart could not see any way for him to keep faith with both.

Had it been the same with Mistyfoot and Stonefur? he wondered. Had their ThunderClan parents ever had to fight against them? He remembered Oakheart, trying to defend them from ThunderClan attack; how had the RiverClan warrior explained that to them? It was an impossible situation, and now it would all begin again with a new set of kits.

But Fireheart knew it was pointless to say this now. Glancing up and down the line of bushes in case any cat was approaching, he meowed, "It's time we were going. It must be sunhigh. They'll miss us back at camp."

Graystripe touched his nose gently to Silverstream's. "Fireheart's right," he murmured. "We must go. And don't worry," he added. "They'll be the most beautiful kits in the forest."

Silverstream's eyes narrowed with affection, and her voice came in a deep purr. "I know. We'll find a way to get through this." She stood watching as Fireheart and Graystripe left the bushes and padded down the slope toward the flooded river. Graystripe kept looking back, as if he could hardly bear to leave her.

Fireheart felt as if he were carrying a cold, heavy stone in his chest. *How long can this go on*, he wondered, *before some cat finds out?*

He was still feeling weighed down with anxiety as they crossed the tree trunk and went back into ThunderClan territory, though he tried hard to push the problem out of his mind. Right now it was more important to decide what to say if any cat had noticed their absence.

"I think we should hunt for a bit," he told Graystripe. "Then at least—"

An excited meow from the edge of the forest interrupted him. "Fireheart! Fireheart!"

Fireheart stared in disbelief as a small white body crashed out of the bracken at the edge of the trees. Cloudkit!

"Oh, mousedung!" muttered Graystripe.

Fireheart padded across the grass, his heart sinking. "Cloudkit, what are you doing here?" he demanded. "I told you to stay in the nursery."

"I tracked you," Cloudkit announced proudly. "All the way from camp."

As he looked at the kit's shining blue eyes, Fireheart felt sick with apprehension. Their chances of slipping back into camp with a story of early hunting had just vanished. Cloudkit must have seen them crossing the river.

"I followed your scent trail right up to the stepping-stones," Cloudkit went on. "Fireheart, what were you and Graystripe doing in RiverClan territory?"

Before Fireheart could think of a reply, another voice broke in—a low, menacing growl. "Yes, that's what I would like to know, too."

Fireheart felt the strength drain out of his paws as he looked up to see Tigerclaw shouldering his way through the crisp brown bracken.

"Fireheart's really brave!" mewed Cloudkit, while Fireheart stood with his mouth half-open, panic turning his brain to feathers. "He went out on a special warrior mission—he told me so."

"Did he now?" hissed Tigerclaw, an interested gleam in his eyes. "And did he tell you what this special warrior mission was?"

"No, but I can guess." Cloudkit trembled with excitement. "He's been with Graystripe to spy on RiverClan. Fireheart, did you—"

"Quiet, kit," snapped Tigerclaw. "Well?" he challenged Fireheart. "Is that true?"

Fireheart glanced at Graystripe. His friend was frozen, his yellow eyes staring in horror at the deputy; obviously there would be no helpful suggestions from him.

"We wanted to see how far the floods went," Fireheart meowed. That was not exactly a lie.

"Oh?" Tigerclaw paused while he looked deliberately in all directions and then asked, "What happened to the rest of your patrol? And some cat must have sent you," he added, before Fireheart could reply. "It wasn't me, even though I sent out all the other patrols."

"We just thought . . ." Graystripe began feebly.

Tigerclaw ignored him. He thrust his huge head so close to Fireheart that he could smell the deputy's hot, rancid breath. "If you ask me, *kittypet*, you're far too friendly with RiverClan. You might have been over there to spy—or you might be spying *for* them. Which side are you on?"

"You've no right to accuse me!" Anger made Fireheart's fur bristle. "I'm loyal to ThunderClan."

A deep growl came from Tigerclaw's throat. "Then you won't mind if we tell Bluestar about this expedition of yours. And we'll see if *she* thinks you're so loyal. As for you . . ." He glared down at Cloudkit, who tried to meet his amber gaze boldly, but couldn't help retreating a pace or two. "Bluestar ordered that no kits were to leave camp alone. Or do you think Clan orders don't apply to you, like your kittypet kin?"

For once, Cloudkit didn't reply; his blue eyes looked scared.

Tigerclaw swung around and stalked back toward the trees. "Come on; we're wasting time. Follow me, all of you," he snarled.

When they reached the camp, Fireheart saw Bluestar standing at the foot of the Highrock. A patrol made up of Whitestorm, Longtail, and Mousefur was reporting to her.

"The stream is flooded as far as the Thunderpath," Fireheart heard Whitestorm say. "If the water doesn't go down, we won't be able to make it to the next Gathering."

"There's still time before—" Bluestar broke off when she

saw Tigerclaw approach her. "Yes, what is it?"

"I've brought these cats to you," the deputy growled. "One disobedient kit, and two traitors."

"Traitors!" echoed Longtail. His eyes met Fireheart's with an unpleasant gleam. "Just what I'd expect of a kittypet," he sneered.

"That's enough," Bluestar ordered, with the faintest hint of a snarl in her voice. She dipped her head toward the cats in the patrol. "You may go, all of you." She turned back to Tigerclaw as they moved away. "Tell me what happened."

"I saw this kit leaving camp," Tigerclaw began, flicking his tail toward Cloudkit, "after you ordered that no kits or apprentices should go out without a warrior. I went to fetch him back, but when I got into the ravine, I realized he was following a scent trail." He paused, and glared challengingly at Fireheart and Graystripe. "The trail led to the stepping-stones downstream from the Sunningrocks. And what should I see there but these two brave warriors"—he spat the words out—"crossing back from RiverClan territory. When I asked them what they were doing, they gave me some fish-and-mouse story about checking to see how far the floods stretched."

Fireheart braced himself for Bluestar's anger, but the Clan leader remained calm. "Is this true?" she asked.

During the journey back from the stepping-stones, Fireheart had had time to think. He couldn't imagine the trouble he would be in if he tried to lie to Bluestar again. Now, seeing the wisdom in her face and the penetrating look in her blue eyes, he knew he had to tell her the truth. "Yes," he admitted. "We can explain, but . . ." He shot a glance at Tigerclaw.

Bluestar closed her eyes for a long moment. When she opened them again, her expression was as unreadable as ever. "Tigerclaw, I'll deal with this. You may go."

The deputy looked as if he was going to object, but under Bluestar's clear gaze he kept silent. He gave her a curt nod and marched off toward the pile of fresh-kill.

"Now, Cloudkit," meowed Bluestar, turning to the white kit. "Do you know why I ordered kits and apprentices not to go out alone?"

"Because the floods are dangerous," replied Cloudkit sullenly. "But I—"

"You disobeyed me and you must be punished. That is the Clan law."

For a moment Fireheart thought that Cloudkit was about to protest, but to his relief the kit just dipped his head and mewed, "Yes, Bluestar."

"Tigerclaw got you to help the elders for a few days recently, didn't he? Very well, you can continue with those duties. It is an honor to serve the other cats in the Clan, and you must learn that it is an honor to obey Clan orders, too. Go now, and see if they have any jobs for you."

Cloudkit bowed his head again and scampered off across

the clearing, his tail held high. Fireheart suspected he quite enjoyed looking after the elders, and that his punishment wasn't as bad as it might have been. He couldn't help worrying that Cloudkit still hadn't learned his lesson about respecting the ways of the Clan.

Bluestar settled down on the ground with her paws tucked under her. "Tell me what happened," she invited the warriors.

Taking a deep breath, Fireheart explained how he and Graystripe had rescued the RiverClan kits, and been taken to the camp by RiverClan warriors.

"Except we couldn't go into their camp," he meowed. "It's underwater. They're staying in the bushes on higher ground for now."

"I see . . ." murmured Bluestar.

"They haven't much shelter," Fireheart went on. "And they're finding it hard to catch prey. They told us that the Twolegs have poisoned the river. Cats get ill if they eat the fish."

As he spoke he caught a worried look from Graystripe, as if his friend thought it was dangerous to reveal so many of RiverClan's weaknesses. Some cats, Fireheart knew, would see this as a good chance to attack RiverClan. But he believed Bluestar was not like that. She would never try to take advantage of another cat's troubles, especially not in leaf-bare.

"So we felt we had to do something," he finished. "We . . . we offered to catch prey for RiverClan in our territory, and we've been taking fresh-kill across the river to them. Today

Tigerclaw saw us coming back."

"We're not traitors," Graystripe put in. "We only wanted to help."

Bluestar turned to him, then back to Fireheart again. She looked stern, but there was a glimmer of understanding in her eyes. "I understand," she murmured. "I even respect your good intentions. All cats have the right to survive, whatever their Clan. But you know perfectly well that you can't take matters into your own paws like that. You acted deceitfully in slipping away on your own. You lied to Tigerclaw—or at least you didn't tell him all the truth," she added, before Fireheart could protest. "And you hunted for another Clan before your own. This is not how warriors behave."

Fireheart swallowed uncomfortably and looked sideways at Graystripe. His friend's head was bowed and he was staring at his paws in shame.

"We know all that," Fireheart admitted. "We're sorry."

"Feeling sorry isn't always enough," Bluestar meowed, with an edge to her voice. "You will have to be punished. And since you haven't acted like warriors, we'll see if you can remember what it's like to be apprentices. From now on, you can hunt for the elders and see to their needs. And when you hunt, you'll have another warrior to supervise you."

"What?" Fireheart couldn't help the word escaping in a mew of outrage.

"You have broken the warrior code," Bluestar reminded him. "Since you can't be trusted, you'll go with someone who can. There must be no more visits to RiverClan."

"But . . . we won't *be* apprentices again, will we?" Graystripe meowed anxiously.

"No." Bluestar allowed a gleam of amusement to soften her eyes. "You are still warriors. A leaf cannot return to the bud. But you will live as apprentices until I think you have learned your lesson."

Fireheart forced himself to breathe evenly. He was so proud to be a warrior of ThunderClan, and shame overwhelmed him at the thought of losing his warrior's privileges. But he knew there was no use arguing with Bluestar, and deep inside he admitted the punishment was fair. He bowed his head respectfully. "Very well, Bluestar."

"And we really are sorry," Graystripe added.

"I know." Bluestar nodded to him. "You may go, Graystripe. Fireheart, stay a moment."

Surprised, Fireheart waited a little nervously to find out what Bluestar wanted.

The Clan leader waited until Graystripe was out of earshot. Then she asked, "Tell me, Fireheart, have any RiverClan cats died in the floods?" She sounded distracted, and for once she didn't meet Fireheart's eyes. "Any warriors?"

"Not that I know of," Fireheart admitted. "Crookedstar didn't say that any cat had drowned."

Bluestar frowned, but she didn't ask any more. She gave a tiny nod, as if to herself. Then, after a brief hesitation, she dismissed Fireheart. "Find Graystripe and tell him you may both eat," she ordered, her voice expressionless and firm again. "And send Tigerclaw to me."

Fireheart bowed his head and stood up to leave. On his way across the clearing, he glanced back at Bluestar. The gray she-cat was still crouched at the foot of the rock, her eyes staring into the far distance. He couldn't help feeling puzzled by his leader's urgent questions.

Why should she be so worried about RiverClan warriors? he wondered.

CHAPTER 15
❧

"Well, *if it isn't our newest* apprentice, Firepaw!"

Fireheart looked up from his vole to see Longtail swaggering toward him, his tail waving in the air. "Ready for a training session?" the warrior sneered. "Tigerclaw sent me to be your mentor."

Taking his time, Fireheart swallowed the last of the vole and rose to his paws. He could guess what had happened. Bluestar had told Tigerclaw about the punishment, and Tigerclaw had wasted no time in organizing the first patrol. Naturally he would choose the cat who disliked Fireheart the most to supervise his hunting.

Beside him, Graystripe jumped up and took a pace toward Longtail. "Watch what you say," he snarled. "We're not apprentices!"

"That's not the way I heard it," replied Longtail, swiping his tongue appreciatively over his jaws as if he had just swallowed a tasty morsel.

"Then we'd better put you right," Fireheart hissed, beginning to lash his tail. "Do you want me to tear your other ear?"

Longtail took a step back. He was clearly remembering

Fireheart's arrival in the camp. He had fought Longtail fiercely, showing no fear in spite of the warrior's "kittypet" taunts. Fireheart knew that even if the other cats let Longtail forget his defeat, his torn ear would remind him forever.

"You'd better watch it," the warrior blustered. "Tigerclaw'll have your tails off if you touch me."

"It would be worth it," Fireheart retorted. "Call me Firepaw once more, and you'll find out."

Longtail said nothing, only turning his head aside to lick his pale fur. Fireheart relaxed his threatening stance. "Come on, then," he grunted. "If we're going to hunt, let's get on with it."

He and Graystripe led the way out of the gorse tunnel and up the side of the ravine. Longtail followed, loudly suggesting where to hunt as if he were in charge, but once they were in the forest Fireheart and Graystripe did their best to ignore him.

The day was cold and gray, and a thin rain had begun to fall. Prey was hard to find. Graystripe caught sight of movement in some bracken fronds and went to investigate, but Fireheart was almost ready to give up by the time he saw a chaffinch pecking around the roots of a hazel bush. He dropped into a crouch, creeping forward paw by paw while the bird pecked on unawares.

He was preparing to pounce, his haunches rocking from side to side, when Longtail jeered, "Call that a crouch? I've seen better on a three-legged rabbit!" As soon as he spoke the chaffinch fluttered away in a panic, letting out a loud alarm call.

Fireheart whirled around furiously. "That was your fault!" he snarled. "As soon as it heard you—"

"Rubbish," meowed Longtail. "Don't make excuses. You couldn't catch a mouse if it sat between your paws."

Fireheart flattened his ears and bared his teeth, but as he braced himself for a fight, he suddenly wondered if Longtail was deliberately provoking him. Longtail would have a fine story to tell Tigerclaw if Fireheart attacked him.

"Fine," Fireheart growled through his teeth. "If you're so good, show us how it's done."

"As if there'll be any prey left, after the racket that bird made when you scared it," Longtail sneered.

"Now who's making excuses?" Fireheart spat back.

Before Longtail could reply, Graystripe emerged from the bracken with a vole in his jaws. He dropped it beside Fireheart and began to kick earth over it to bury it until they were ready to return to camp.

Longtail used the interruption to turn away and stalk toward the tunnel Graystripe had made in the bracken.

Graystripe watched him go. "What's the matter with him? He looks as if he's swallowed mouse bile."

Fireheart shrugged. "Nothing. Come on, let's keep going."

After that, Longtail left them alone, and by sunset the two young warriors had collected a respectable pile of fresh-kill to carry back to the camp.

"You take some to the elders," Fireheart suggested to Graystripe as they dragged the last pieces in. "I'll see to

Yellowfang and Cinderpaw." He chose a squirrel and headed toward the medicine cat's den. Yellowfang was standing outside the cleft in the rock, with Cinderpaw sitting in front of her. Fireheart's former apprentice looked happy and alert. She was sitting very straight, with her tail wrapped around her paws, and her blue eyes were fixed on Yellowfang as she listened to the old cat.

"We can chew up ragwort leaves and mix them with crushed juniper berries," rasped Yellowfang. "It makes a good poultice for aching joints. Do you want to try doing it?"

"Okay!" Cinderpaw mewed enthusiastically. She sprang up and sniffed the heap of herbs Yellowfang had laid on the ground. "Does it taste bad?"

"No," answered Yellowfang, "but try not to swallow it. A bit won't hurt you, but too much will give you a bellyache. Yes, Fireheart, what do you want?"

Fireheart crossed the clearing, dragging the squirrel between his front paws. Cinderpaw was already crouching in front of the ragwort, chewing vigorously, but she flicked her tail at Fireheart in greeting.

"This is for you," Fireheart mewed as he dropped the squirrel beside Yellowfang.

"Oh, yes, Runningwind told me you were back on apprentice duties," Yellowfang growled. "Mouse-brain! You might have known some cat would find out you were helping RiverClan."

"Well, it's done now." Fireheart didn't want to talk about his punishment.

To his relief, Yellowfang seemed happy to change the subject. "I'm glad you've come," she meowed, "because I want a word with you. You see that poultice?" She lifted her muzzle toward the green mash of chewed leaves Cinderpaw was making.

"Yes."

"It's for Smallear. He's in my den now, with the worst case of stiff joints I've seen in moons. He can hardly move. And if you ask me, it's all because his nest was recently lined with damp moss." Her tone was mild, but her yellow eyes burned into Fireheart's.

Fireheart felt his heart sink. "This is about Cloudkit, isn't it?"

"I think so," mewed Yellowfang. "He's been careless about the bedding he's brought in. If you ask me, he hasn't bothered to shake the water off."

"But I showed him how—" Fireheart broke off. He had troubles enough of his own, he thought; it wasn't fair that he had to keep sorting out Cloudkit as well. He took a deep breath. "I'll have a word with him," he promised.

"Do that," grunted Yellowfang.

Cinderpaw sat up, spitting out scraps of ragwort. "Is that chewed enough?"

Yellowfang inspected her work. "Excellent," she meowed.

Cinderpaw's blue eyes glowed with the praise, while Fireheart glanced appreciatively at the old medicine cat. It gave him a warm glow to see how Yellowfang made Cinderpaw feel useful and needed.

"Now you can fetch the juniper berries," Yellowfang went on. "Let's see . . . three should be enough. You know where I keep them?"

"Yes, Yellowfang." Cinderpaw headed for the split in the rock, bouncing in spite of her limp, her tail lifted high. At the mouth of the den she looked back. "Thanks for the squirrel, Fireheart," she meowed, before she disappeared.

Yellowfang looked after her approvingly and let out a rusty purr. "Now there's a cat who knows what she's doing," she murmured.

Fireheart agreed. He wished he could say the same about his own kin. "I'll go and find Cloudkit right now." He sighed, touching his nose to Yellowfang's flank before padding out of her den.

The white kit was not in the nursery, so Fireheart tried the elders' den. As he entered, he heard Halftail's voice. "So the leader of TigerClan stalked the fox for a night and a day, and on the second night— Hello, there, Fireheart. Come to listen to the story?"

Fireheart glanced around. Halftail was curled up in the moss with Patchpelt and Dappletail nearby. Cloudkit was crouched in the shelter of the big tabby's body, his blue eyes wide with wonder as he pictured the mighty black-striped cats of TigerClan. A few scraps of fresh-kill lay on the floor of the den, and from the smell of mouse that clung to Cloudkit's fur, Fireheart guessed that the elders had let him share.

"No, thanks, Halftail," he meowed. "I can't stay. I just

wanted to talk to Cloudkit. Yellowfang says he's been bringing in damp bedding."

Dappletail let out a snort. "What nonsense!"

"She's been listening to Smallear," meowed Patchpelt. "He'd complain if StarClan descended from Silverpelt themselves to bring his bedding."

Fireheart's fur prickled with embarrassment. He hadn't expected to find the elders making excuses for Cloudkit. "Well, have you or haven't you?" he demanded, glaring at the kit.

Cloudkit blinked up at him. "I *tried* to get it right, Fireheart."

"He's only a kit," Dappletail pointed out fondly.

"Yes, well . . ." Fireheart scraped his paws on the floor of the den. "Smallear has got aching joints."

"Smallear has had aching joints for seasons," meowed Halftail. "Since well before this kit was littered. You mind your own business, Fireheart, and let us mind ours."

"Sorry," Fireheart muttered. "I'll go, then. Cloudkit, just make sure you're extra careful about damp moss in the future, okay?"

He started backing out of the den. As he left, he heard Cloudkit meow, "Go on, Halftail. What did TigerClan's leader do then?"

Fireheart was glad to escape into the clearing. He couldn't help thinking that Cloudkit probably had been careless over the moss, but it looked like the rest of the elders wouldn't have a word said against him. Free to take fresh-kill for himself now that he had hunted for the elders, Fireheart was trotting over to the heap when he noticed

Brokentail lying outside his den. Tigerclaw was beside him, and the two cats were sharing tongues like old friends.

Unexpectedly moved by the sight, Fireheart paused. Was this Tigerclaw's merciful side making a rare appearance? He could just hear the rumble of Tigerclaw's voice, though he was too far away to make out the words. Brokentail replied briefly, looking much more relaxed, as if he was responding to the deputy's friendliness.

Suddenly all of Fireheart's old doubts about bringing Tigerclaw to justice welled up inside him. Every cat knew that Tigerclaw was a fierce and courageous fighter, and that he handled the responsibilities of a deputy with effortless confidence. Fireheart had never seen anything to show that he had the compassion of a true leader, until now, with Brokentail. . . .

Fireheart's mind whirled. Perhaps Bluestar had been right, that Tigerclaw was innocent of Redtail's death. Perhaps Cinderpaw's accident had been just that, instead of a trap. *What if you've been wrong all along?* Fireheart thought. *Suppose Tigerclaw is just what he seems to be: a loyal and efficient deputy?*

But he couldn't make himself believe it. And as Fireheart padded more slowly over to the pile of fresh-kill, he wished to the tips of his claws that he could be freed from the burden of what he knew.

CHAPTER 16

Fireheart stepped out of the ferns that enclosed the apprentices' den and stretched out his front paws. It was just after sunrise, and the sky was already a pale eggshell blue, promising fine weather after days of cloud and rain.

In Fireheart's opinion, sleeping in the apprentice den was the worst part of his punishment. Every time he went in there, Thornpaw and Brightpaw stared at him with huge eyes, as if they couldn't believe what they were seeing. Brackenpaw just looked acutely embarrassed, while Swiftpaw—encouraged by his mentor, Longtail, Fireheart guessed—openly sneered. Fireheart found it hard to relax, and his sleep was broken by dreams in which Spottedleaf bounded toward him, meowing a warning that he could never remember when he woke.

Now Fireheart stretched his jaws in a massive yawn and settled down to give himself a thorough wash. Graystripe was still sleeping; soon Fireheart would have to wake him and find a warrior to supervise them on yet another hunting patrol.

As Fireheart washed, he saw Bluestar and Tigerclaw sitting at the foot of the Highrock, deep in conversation. Idly he wondered what they were talking about. Then Bluestar gave a flick of her tail to summon him. Fireheart sprang up at once and bounded across the camp.

"Fireheart," Bluestar meowed as he approached, "Tigerclaw and I think you've been punished enough. You and Graystripe can be full warriors again."

Fireheart felt almost giddy with relief. "Thank you, Bluestar!" he meowed.

"Let's hope it's taught you a lesson," growled Tigerclaw.

"Tigerclaw is going to lead a patrol up to Fourtrees," Bluestar went on before Fireheart could respond. "In two nights the moon will be full, and we need to know if we can make it to the Gathering. Tigerclaw, will you take Fireheart with you?"

Fireheart couldn't interpret the gleam in the deputy's amber eyes. He didn't look pleased—Tigerclaw never did— but there was a certain dark satisfaction, as if he would enjoy putting Fireheart through his paces. Fireheart didn't care. He was thrilled that Bluestar was trusting him with a real warriors' mission again.

"He can come," Tigerclaw meowed. "But if he puts a paw wrong, I'll want to know the reason why." His dark coat rippled as he heaved himself to his paws. "I'll find another cat to go with us."

Fireheart watched him as he strode across the clearing and disappeared into the warriors' den.

"This will be an important Gathering," murmured Bluestar beside him. "We need to find out how the other

Clans are coping with the floods. It's important for our Clan to be there."

"We'll find a way, Bluestar," Fireheart assured her.

But his confidence drained rapidly away a moment later when he saw Tigerclaw reappear from the den. The cat who followed him out was Longtail. It looked as if Tigerclaw had chosen the third member of the patrol deliberately to disadvantage Fireheart.

Fireheart felt a hard lump of apprehension in his stomach. He wasn't sure that he wanted to go out alone with Tigerclaw and Longtail. The memory of the battle with RiverClan was still too fresh, when Tigerclaw had watched him struggling with a fierce warrior and made no move to help him. And Longtail had been his enemy ever since he had set paw in the camp.

For a moment, fearful pictures of the two cats turning on him in the depths of the forest and murdering him whirled through Fireheart's mind. Then he shook himself. He was scaring himself like a kit listening to some elder's tale. No doubt Tigerclaw would make unreasonable demands of him, and Longtail would enjoy every moment, but Fireheart wasn't afraid of being challenged. He'd show them that he was a warrior equal to them in every way that mattered!

Saying a respectful good-bye to Bluestar, he raced across the clearing and followed Tigerclaw and Longtail out of the camp.

The sun rose higher, and the sky turned to a deep blue as the cats journeyed through the forest toward Fourtrees. The ferns were weighted with glittering drops of dew that clung to Fireheart's fur as he brushed past. Birds sang, and branches rustled with freshly opened leaves. Newleaf had really come at last.

As he padded after Tigerclaw, Fireheart was distracted by tempting movements in the undergrowth as prey scurried to and fro. After a while the deputy let them stop and hunt for themselves. He was in an unusually good mood, Fireheart thought, relaxing enough to praise the flame-pelted warrior as he pounced on a particularly speedy vole. Even Longtail kept his unfriendly comments to himself.

When they went on, Fireheart's stomach was warm and full from the vole he had eaten. His uneasy feelings vanished. On a day like this he couldn't help feeling optimistic, sure that they would soon have good news to take back to Bluestar.

Then they reached the top of a slope and looked down toward the stream that crossed ThunderClan territory, separating them from Fourtrees. Tigerclaw let out a long, soft hiss, and Longtail yowled in dismay.

Fireheart shared their exasperation. Usually the stream was shallow enough for cats to cross easily, keeping their paws dry by leaping from rock to rock. Now the water had spread into a glistening sheet on either side, while the current churned swiftly along the original course of the stream.

"Fancy crossing that?" spat Longtail. "I don't."

Without a word, Tigerclaw began padding upstream, following the edge of the floodwater toward the Thunderpath.

The land sloped gently upward, and before long, Fireheart could see that the shining surface was broken by tussocks of grass and clumps of bracken poking above the water.

"This isn't as deep as when Whitestorm last reported," Tigerclaw meowed. "We'll try to cross here."

Fireheart had his doubts that the water would be shallow enough, but he kept them to himself. He knew if he objected, he would just get the usual sneers about his soft kittypet background. Instead he quietly followed Tigerclaw, who was already wading into the flood. He couldn't help noticing that Longtail's ears twitched nervously as he splashed in beside him.

The water felt cold as it lapped at Fireheart's legs. He picked his way carefully, tracing a zigzag course toward the nearest bank of the stream by springing from one clump of grass to the next. Drops of water glittered in the sunlight as he splashed forward. Once a frog wriggled out from under his paws, almost making him lose his balance, but he righted himself by sinking his claws heavily into a waterlogged tussock.

In front of him, the current was brown where it had stirred up mud from the streambed. It was much too wide for a cat to leap, and the stepping-stones were completely submerged. *I hope Tigerclaw doesn't expect us to swim*, Fireheart thought with a wince.

Even as the words went through his mind, he heard Tigerclaw's yowl from farther upstream. "Come here! Look at this!"

Fireheart splashed toward him. The deputy, with Longtail beside him, was standing at the edge of the stream. A branch was lodged in front of them, swept into place by the current so that it stretched from one bank to the other.

"Just what we need," Tigerclaw grunted in satisfaction. "Fireheart, check that it's safe, will you?"

Fireheart gazed doubtfully at the branch. It was much thinner than the fallen tree that he had used to cross to RiverClan's territory. Twigs poked out in all directions, still with dead leaves dangling from them. Every few moments the whole branch gave a slight jerk, as if the current wanted to sweep it away again.

With any other senior warrior, or even Bluestar, Fireheart would have discussed how safe the branch was before he set paw on it. But no cat questioned an order from Tigerclaw.

"Scared, kittypet?" Longtail taunted him.

Determination burned in Fireheart's belly. He would *not* show fear in front of these cats and let them have the pleasure of reporting it to the rest of the Clan. Gritting his teeth, he stepped onto the end of the branch.

Immediately it sagged under his paws, and he dug his claws in hard, fighting for balance. He could see brown water racing a mouse-length below, and for a few heartbeats he thought he would plunge straight into it.

Then he steadied himself. He began to move forward cautiously, placing his paws in a straight line one after the other. The slender branch bounced under his weight with every step. Twigs caught in his fur, threatening his balance. *We'll never get to the Gathering like this*, Fireheart thought.

Gradually he drew closer to the middle of the stream,

where the current was strongest. The branch tapered until it was barely as thick as his tail, making it harder to find a pawhold. Pausing, Fireheart measured the distance left; was he close enough to leap safely yet?

Then the branch lurched under him. Instinctively he gripped tighter with his claws. He heard Tigerclaw yowl, "Fireheart! Get back!"

For a heartbeat Fireheart swayed precariously. Then the branch lurched again and suddenly it was free, racing along with the surging water. Fireheart slipped sideways, and thought he heard Tigerclaw yowl once more as the waves closed over his head.

CHAPTER 17

❧

As he plunged into the stream Fireheart managed to keep one clawhold on the branch. He felt as if he were fighting a spiky wooden enemy, twigs that lashed at him and raked through his fur while his breath bubbled into the dark water. His head broke the surface briefly, but before he could gasp in air the branch twisted and rolled him under again.

Terror made him strangely calm, as if time had slowed down. Part of Fireheart's mind told him to let go of the branch and fight his way to the surface, but he knew that if he did that he would risk his life; the current was far too strong for him to swim. The force of the water meant there was nothing he could do but dig his claws in and endure. *StarClan help me!* he thought frantically.

His senses were just beginning to ebb into a tempting darkness when the branch rolled over again and brought him back to the surface. Choking and spitting he clung to it, with water churning along on either side of him. He could not see the bank. He tried to haul himself farther out of the water, but his sodden fur was too heavy and his limbs were growing stiff with cold. He did not know how long he could hold on.

Just as he felt that he was about to let go, something brought the branch to a jarring stop. It shuddered along its whole length, almost throwing Fireheart off. As he clung on desperately, he heard a cat screech his name. Twisting his head, he saw that the other end of the branch was jammed against a rock that jutted out into the stream.

Longtail was crouched on the rock, leaning down toward him. "Move, kittypet!" he growled.

With his last drop of energy, Fireheart scrambled along the length of the branch. Twigs whipped across his face. He felt the branch lurch again and flung himself at the rock, his front paws scraping at it while his hind legs thrust through the water. His paws had barely touched stone when the branch was swept away from underneath him.

For a heartbeat Fireheart thought he would follow it. The rock was smooth; there was no purchase for his paws. Then Longtail reached down and Fireheart felt his teeth meet in the scruff of his neck. With the other cat's help he managed to claw his way upward until he was crouching on the top of the rock. Shivering, he coughed up several mouthfuls of stream water before he looked up. "Thanks, Longtail," he gasped.

The warrior's face was expressionless. "It was nothing."

Tigerclaw padded up from behind the rock. "Are you hurt?" he demanded. "Can you walk?"

Shakily, Fireheart pushed himself to his paws. Water streamed off his coat as he shook himself. "I-I'm fine, Tigerclaw," he stammered.

Tigerclaw stepped backward to avoid the spinning droplets from Fireheart's fur. "Watch it; we're all wet enough already." Approaching Fireheart again he gave a rapid sniff down the length of his body. "Back to camp for you," he ordered. "In fact, we'll all go back. No cat can get across that water; you've proved that, if nothing else."

Fireheart nodded and wordlessly followed the deputy back into the forest. Colder and more tired than he could ever remember being before, he wanted nothing more than to curl up and sleep in a patch of sunlight.

But while his limbs felt like waterlogged stone, his mind was a whirlpool of fear and suspicion. Tigerclaw had sent him out onto the branch, when any cat could see it was dangerous. Fireheart couldn't help wondering if Tigerclaw had deliberately dislodged it, to make sure that he was flung into the swollen stream.

Not if Longtail was watching, he decided. After all, Longtail had rescued him; much as Fireheart disliked Longtail, he had to admit that the pale tabby would stick rigidly to the Clan code when another warrior needed his help.

Even so, Tigerclaw could have shifted the branch without letting Longtail see, or perhaps Longtail hadn't understood what was happening. Fireheart would have liked to ask him, but he knew that if he did the question would be reported to Tigerclaw.

Then he glanced at Tigerclaw, and saw the deputy glaring at him with unmasked hatred. As Fireheart met the amber stare, he saw Tigerclaw's eyes narrow as if with an unspoken threat. And in that moment Fireheart *knew* that somehow Tigerclaw had tried to murder him. This time he had failed. *But what about next time?* Fireheart's tired brain shied away from what was all too obvious. Next time, Tigerclaw would make sure he did not fail.

By the time he reached the camp, the warm newleaf sun had dried Fireheart's fur, but he was so exhausted he could scarcely put one paw in front of another.

Sandstorm, who was sunning herself outside the warriors' den, sprang up as soon as she saw him and bounded over to his side. "Fireheart!" she exclaimed. "You look awful! What happened?"

"Nothing much," Fireheart mumbled. "I was—"

"Fireheart went for a swim, that's all," Tigerclaw interrupted. He looked down at the young warrior. "Come on. We need to report to Bluestar." He strode across to the Highrock with Longtail at his heels. As Fireheart staggered after them, Sandstorm padded close beside him, pressing her warm body against his for support.

"Well?" Bluestar asked when the cats stood in front of her. "Did you find somewhere to cross?"

Tigerclaw shook his massive head. "It's impossible. The water's too high."

"But every Clan should attend the Gathering," Bluestar pointed out. "StarClan will be angry if we don't try to find a dry route. Tigerclaw, tell me exactly where you went."

Tigerclaw began to describe the events of the morning in

more detail, including Fireheart's attempt to cross by the branch. "It was brave but foolish," he growled. "I thought he'd paid with his life."

Sandstorm looked around, impressed, but Fireheart knew as well as Tigerclaw that he had had no choice about getting onto the branch.

"Be more careful in the future, Fireheart," Bluestar warned. "You'd better see Yellowfang in case you've caught a chill."

"I'm fine," Fireheart told her. "I just need to sleep, that's all."

Bluestar's eyes narrowed. "That was an order, Fireheart."

Stifling a yawn, Fireheart bowed his head respectfully. "Yes, Bluestar."

"Come to the den when you've finished," meowed Sandstorm, giving him a lick. "I'll fetch you some fresh-kill."

Fireheart mewed his thanks and stumbled unsteadily to Yellowfang's den. The clearing was empty, but when he called Yellowfang's name the old medicine cat poked her head out of the gap in the rock.

"Fireheart? Great StarClan, you look like a squirrel that's fallen out of its tree! What happened to you?"

She padded toward him as he explained. Cinderpaw limped out behind her and sat beside Fireheart, her blue eyes wide as she heard how he had nearly drowned.

Seeing her, Fireheart could not help remembering how she had been injured beside the Thunderpath—another accident arranged by Tigerclaw? Not to mention the cold-blooded murder of Redtail. His head spinning with fatigue, Fireheart wondered how he could possibly stop Tigerclaw before another cat died for the deputy's ruthless ambition.

"Right," rasped Yellowfang, interrupting his troubled thoughts. "You're a strong cat, and you probably haven't taken a chill, but we'll check you to make sure. Cinderpaw, what should we look for when a cat gets a soaking?"

Cinderpaw sat up straight with her tail wrapped around her paws. Eyes fixed on Yellowfang, she recited, "Poor breathing, sickness, leeches in his fur."

"Good," grunted Yellowfang. "Off you go, then."

Very carefully, Cinderpaw sniffed along the length of Fireheart's body, parting his fur with one paw to make sure that no leeches had fastened themselves onto his skin. "Breathing okay, Fireheart?" she asked gently. "Do you feel sick?"

"No, everything's fine," Fireheart mewed. "I just want to sleep for a moon."

"I think he's all right, Yellowfang," Cinderpaw reported. She pressed her cheek against Fireheart's and gave him a couple of quick licks. "Just don't go jumping in any more rivers, eh?"

Yellowfang let out a throaty purr. "All right, Fireheart, you can go and sleep now."

Cinderpaw flicked up her ears in surprise. "Aren't you going to check him as well? What if I've missed something?"

"No need," meowed Yellowfang. "I trust you, Cinderpaw." The old cat stretched, arching her skinny back, and then relaxed. "I've been meaning to say something to you for a while," she went on. "I see so many mouse-brained cats around here that it's a real joy to find one with some sense. You've learned quickly, and you're good with sick cats."

"Thank you, Yellowfang!" Cinderpaw burst out, her eyes round with surprise at Yellowfang's praise.

"Be quiet, I haven't finished. I'm getting old now, and it's time I started to think about finding an apprentice. Cinderpaw, how would you feel about becoming ThunderClan's next medicine cat?"

Cinderpaw leaped to her paws. Her eyes were sparkling and she quivered with excitement. "Do you really mean it?" she whispered.

"Of course I mean it," Yellowfang growled. "I don't talk for the pleasure of hearing my own voice, unlike some cats."

"In that case, yes," Cinderpaw murmured, lifting her head with dignity. "I'd like that better than anything in the whole world!"

Fireheart felt his heart begin to beat faster with happiness. He had worried so much for Cinderpaw, at first when he thought she might die, then when it became clear that her injured leg would stop her from becoming a warrior. He remembered how she had wondered desperately what she could make of her life. And now it looked as if Yellowfang had found the perfect solution. Seeing the young she-cat so happy and excited about the future was more than Fireheart had ever hoped for.

Fireheart went back to the warriors' den on lighter paws to

share fresh-kill with Sandstorm and then to sleep. When he awoke, the light in the den was red from the rays of the setting sun.

Graystripe was nudging him. "Wake up," his friend meowed. "Bluestar has just called a meeting."

Fireheart left the den to find Bluestar already standing on the top of the Highrock. Yellowfang was beside her, and when all the cats were assembled it was the old medicine cat who spoke first.

"Cats of ThunderClan," she rasped, "I have an announcement to make. As you know, I am not a young cat. It's time I took an apprentice. So I've chosen the only cat I can put up with." Yellowfang let out an amused purr. "And the only cat who can put up with me. Your next medicine cat will be Cinderpaw."

A chorus of pleased meows broke out. Cinderpaw sat at the foot of the rock, her eyes shining and her fur sleekly groomed. She lowered her head shyly as the Clan congratulated her.

"Cinderpaw." Bluestar made herself heard above the noise. "Do you accept the post of apprentice to Yellowfang?"

Cinderpaw lifted her head to look up at her leader. "Yes, Bluestar."

"Then at the half moon you must travel to Mothermouth, to be accepted by StarClan before the other medicine cats. The good wishes of all ThunderClan will go with you."

Yellowfang half jumped, half slithered down from the rock, and padded up to Cinderpaw to touch noses with her.

Then the rest of the Clan gathered around the new apprentice. Fireheart caught sight of Brackenpaw pressing close to his sister, his eyes glowing with pride, and even Tigerclaw went up to her and meowed a few words. It was clear that Cinderpaw was a popular choice for this important position.

As he waited to give Cinderpaw his congratulations, Fireheart could not help wishing that all his own problems could be solved as smoothly.

CHAPTER 18

The sun began to set for the third time since Fireheart had almost drowned. The young warrior was washing himself outside his den, scraping his tongue across his fur. He kept imagining that he could still taste the muddy water. As he twisted his head to wash his back, he heard the pad of approaching paws, and looked up to see Tigerclaw looming over him.

"Bluestar wants you to go to the Gathering," the deputy growled. "Meet her outside her den—and bring Sandstorm and Graystripe." He stalked away before Fireheart could reply.

Fireheart got up and stretched. Glancing around, he spotted Graystripe and Sandstorm eating beside the patch of nettles, and hurried over to join them. "Bluestar has chosen us to go to the Gathering," he announced.

Sandstorm finished off her blackbird and swiped a pink tongue around her jaws. "But can we get to the Gathering?" she meowed, sounding puzzled. "I thought the stream was impossible to cross."

"Bluestar said StarClan would be angry if we didn't try," Fireheart mewed. "She wants to talk to us now—maybe she has a plan."

Graystripe spoke through a mouthful of vole. "I just hope she doesn't expect us to swim." In spite of his words, his eyes shone with excitement as he gulped the rest of the fresh-kill and sprang to his paws. Fireheart knew he must be looking forward to a chance to see Silverstream, and he wondered if they had managed to meet in the time since he and Graystripe had been caught crossing the river after their ill-fated hunting mission for RiverClan.

Fireheart thought of Silverstream's kits, and he wondered how Graystripe would be able to bear seeing them grow up in another Clan. Would Silverstream ever be able to tell them that Graystripe, the ThunderClan warrior, was their father? Fireheart tried to put the questions out of his mind as he and his friends crossed the clearing to the Highrock. Bluestar was sitting outside her den, with Whitestorm, Mousefur, and Willowpelt already by her side. A moment later Tigerclaw and Darkstripe joined them.

"As you know, the moon is full tonight," Bluestar began when all the cats were gathered around her. "It will be hard to get to Fourtrees, but StarClan would expect us to do all we can to find a dry route. So I've chosen warriors only—this will be no journey for elders or apprentices, or queens expecting kits. Darkstripe, you led a patrol to examine the stream this morning. Report what you found."

"The water's going down," meowed Darkstripe. "But not fast enough. We patrolled as far as the Thunderpath, and there's nowhere a cat could cross without swimming."

"The stream's narrower up there," mewed Willowpelt.

"Could we jump across?"

"Maybe, if you grew wings," Darkstripe replied. "If all you've got is your own paws . . . "

"But that has to be the best place to try," insisted Whitestorm.

Bluestar nodded. "We'll start there," she decided. "Maybe StarClan will lead us to a safe place." She rose to her paws and led her cats quietly out of the camp.

The sun had gone down, and twilight blurred the shapes of the forest. In the distance an owl hooted, and Fireheart could hear the rustle of prey in the undergrowth, but the warriors were too intent on their journey to hunt. Bluestar took them straight through the trees to the place where the stream emerged from a hard stone tunnel underneath the Thunderpath. Their usual route to Fourtrees did not pass this close to the Thunderpath, and Fireheart wondered what his leader was planning to do. When they reached the tunnel, he saw that floodwater spread out on either side, reflecting the pale light of the rising moon. Water covered the Thunderpath as well, and as the cats watched they saw a monster pass by, moving slowly, throwing up a filthy wave from its round black paws.

Once the monster had disappeared into the distance, Bluestar led her cats to the water's edge on the hard surface of the Thunderpath. She sniffed the water, wrinkling her nose at the stench, and cautiously put one paw into the flood. "It's shallow enough here," she meowed. "We can walk up the Thunderpath until we're on the other side of the stream, and get to Fourtrees along the border with ShadowClan."

Walk up the Thunderpath! Fireheart felt his coat begin to prickle with fear at the thought of deliberately following the tracks of the monsters. Cinderpaw's accident had shown him what they could do to a cat, and she had only been at the edge.

"What if another monster comes?" asked Graystripe, voicing Fireheart's fear.

"We will keep to the side," Bluestar replied calmly. "You saw how slowly that monster was moving. Maybe they don't like getting their paws wet."

Fireheart saw that Graystripe still looked doubtful. He shared his friend's worries, but there was no point in protesting any more. Tigerclaw would just berate them for being cowards.

"Bluestar, wait," called Whitestorm as the Clan leader waded into the water. "Remember how low our territory is on the other side of this stream? I can't help thinking it will be flooded there, too. I don't think we'll get to Fourtrees without going onto ShadowClan territory, which is higher."

A cat close to Fireheart let out a faint hiss, and Fireheart felt another pang of fear. A band of warriors setting paw across the border of a Clan with which they had recently battled? If a patrol caught them, they would think it was an invasion.

Bluestar paused with water lapping over her paws, and looked back at Whitestorm. "Maybe," she acknowledged, "but we'll have to risk it, if it's the only way."

She set off again without giving her cats any time to protest. There was nothing to do but follow. Fireheart splashed along the edge of the Thunderpath just behind Whitestorm. Tigerclaw brought up the rear to keep a lookout for monsters coming up from behind.

At first everything was quiet, except for a single monster traveling in the other direction on the opposite side of the Thunderpath. Then Fireheart heard the familiar growling and the splash of an approaching monster.

"Look out!" Tigerclaw yowled from the end of the line.

Fireheart froze, pressing himself against the low wall that edged the Thunderpath as it crossed the stream. Darkstripe scrambled on top of it and crouched there, baring his teeth at the monster as it passed. For a moment its strange, glittering colors were reflected in the stinking water, and a wave washed out from it, soaking Fireheart as far as his belly fur.

Then it was gone, and Fireheart could breathe again.

As they reached the other side of the stream Fireheart could see that Whitestorm was right. The low-lying land on the ThunderClan side was covered with water. There was nothing to do but continue along the edge of the Thunderpath until the land rose and was dry enough to walk on.

Stepping thankfully off the paw-achingly hard Thunderpath, Fireheart raised his head and opened his jaws. A strong, rank stench filled his scent glands—the scent of ShadowClan! They had followed the Thunderpath out of ThunderClan territory, and now a swath of ShadowClan land lay between them and the Gathering at Fourtrees.

"We shouldn't be here," Willowpelt murmured uneasily.

If Bluestar heard the comment, she ignored it, quickening

the pace until they were racing across the sodden turf. There were few trees here, and the close-cropped grass offered no cover for trespassing cats. Fireheart's heart was beating fast, and not only from the speed of their journey. If ShadowClan cats caught them, they would be in trouble, but Fourtrees was not far away, and their luck might hold.

Then he caught sight of a dark shadow streaking over the ground ahead of them, on a course to intercept Bluestar at the head of her patrol. More shadows followed, and a furious yowling split the quiet of the night.

For a heartbeat Bluestar quickened her pace, as if she thought she could outrun the challengers. Then she slowed to a stop. Her warriors did the same. Fireheart stood panting; the shadows drew closer, and he saw that they were ShadowClan cats, headed by their leader, Nightstar.

"Bluestar!" he spat as he halted in front of the ThunderClan leader. "Why have you brought your cats onto ShadowClan land?"

"In these floods, it was the only way to reach Fourtrees," Bluestar replied, her voice low and steady. "We mean no harm, Nightstar. You know there's a truce for the Gathering."

Nightstar hissed, his ears flattened against his head and his fur bristling. "The truce holds at Fourtrees," he snarled. "There is no truce here."

Instinctively, Fireheart dropped into a defensive crouch. The ShadowClan cats—apprentices and elders as well as warriors—slipped silently into a semicircle around the smaller band from ThunderClan. Like Nightstar, their coats were bristling and their tails lashed in anger. Their hostile eyes reflected the cold light of the moon. Fireheart knew that if it came to a fight, ThunderClan was hopelessly outnumbered.

"Nightstar, I'm sorry," meowed Bluestar. "We would never trespass on your territory without good reason. Please let us pass."

Her words did nothing to appease the ShadowClan cats. Cinderfur, the ShadowClan deputy, moved up beside his leader, a dim shape in the moonlight. "I think they're here to spy," he growled softly.

"Spy?" Tigerclaw shouldered his way forward to stand next to Bluestar, his head thrust out toward Cinderfur until their noses were less than a mouse-length apart. "What can we spy on here? We're nowhere near your camp."

Cinderfur curled back his lip to reveal thorn-sharp teeth. "Give us the word, Nightstar, and we'll tear them apart."

"You can try," growled Tigerclaw.

For a few heartbeats Nightstar was silent. Fireheart's muscles tensed. Beside him, Graystripe growled low in his throat. Mousefur bared her teeth at the nearest ShadowClan warrior, and Sandstorm's pale golden eyes shone with readiness to fight.

"Keep back," Nightstar grunted at last to his warriors. "We'll let them pass. I want ThunderClan cats at the Gathering." Though his words were friendly, he hissed them through bared teeth. Suddenly suspicious, Fireheart whispered to Graystripe, "What does he mean by that?"

Graystripe shrugged. "Dunno. We've seen nothing of

ShadowClan since the floods started. Who knows what they're up to?"

"We'll even give you an escort," Nightstar went on, narrowing his eyes. "Just to make sure you get to Fourtrees safely. We wouldn't want ThunderClan to be scared off by an angry mouse, would we?"

A murmur of agreement rose from the ShadowClan warriors. They shifted so that they surrounded the ThunderClan cats on all sides. With a faint nod, Nightstar set off beside Bluestar. The other cats followed, the ShadowClan patrol matching ThunderClan step for step.

ThunderClan headed for the Gathering completely encircled by their enemies.

The moon was at its height as Fireheart and the other ThunderClan cats were herded into the hollow beneath the four oak trees. A fierce, cold light poured down over the members of RiverClan and WindClan who were already assembled. All of them turned to stare curiously at the group descending the slope. Fireheart knew that he and the rest of his Clan must look like prisoners. He stalked along proudly, head and tail held high, defying any cat to say that they had been beaten.

To his relief, the ShadowClan cats slipped away into the shadows as soon as they reached the hollow. Bluestar headed straight for the Great Rock with Tigerclaw at her side. Fireheart looked around for Graystripe, and found that his friend had already disappeared; a moment later he caught sight of him approaching Silverstream, but the silver tabby was surrounded by other RiverClan cats, and Graystripe could only hover nearby, looking frustrated.

Fireheart suppressed a sigh. He knew how much Graystripe must be longing to see Silverstream again, especially now she was expecting kits, but there was a huge risk in meeting at a Gathering, where any cat could catch them together.

"What's up with you?" Mousefur made him jump. "You look as if you've got something on your mind."

Fireheart stared at the brown warrior. "I . . . I was thinking about what Nightstar said," he improvised rapidly. "Why did he say he wants ThunderClan cats here?"

"Well, I'm sure of one thing. He's not being kind and helpful," Sandstorm mewed, coming up with Willowpelt beside her. She licked one paw and drew it over her ear. "We'll find out soon enough."

"Trouble's coming," Willowpelt meowed over one shoulder as she went to join a group of WindClan queens. "I can feel it in my paws."

Uneasier than ever, Fireheart padded back and forth under the trees, listening with one ear to the cats around him. Most of them were sharing harmless gossip, catching up on news from other Clans, and he heard nothing about what ShadowClan were planning. He noticed, though, that all the ShadowClan cats he passed glared at him, still fiercely hostile. And he caught one or two of them glancing up at the Great Rock as if they were impatient for the meeting to start.

At last a yowling sounded from the top of the rock, and the murmuring from the cats below died away. Fireheart found a place at the edge of the hollow where he had a good view of the four Clan leaders, their silhouettes black against the sky.

Sandstorm settled herself beside him, crouching with her paws tucked under her chest. "Now for it," she whispered expectantly.

Nightstar stepped forward, stiff-legged with barely suppressed fury. "Cats of all Clans, listen to me!" he demanded. "Listen, and remember. Until last greenleaf, Brokenstar was leader of ShadowClan. He was—"

Tallstar, the leader of WindClan, stepped forward to stand beside Nightstar. "Why do you speak that hated name?" he growled. His eyes flashed, and Fireheart knew he was remembering how Brokenstar and his warriors had driven WindClan out of their territory.

"Hated, yes," Nightstar agreed. "And with good reason, which you know as well as any cat, Tallstar. He stole kits from ThunderClan. He forced kits from his own Clan into battle too early, and they died. In the end he was so bloodthirsty that we—his own Clan—drove him out. And where is he now?" Nightstar's voice rose to a shriek. "Was he left to die in the forest, or scavenge a living among the Twolegs? No! Because there are cats here tonight who have taken him in. They are traitors to the warrior code, and to every other cat in the forest!"

Fireheart exchanged an uneasy glance with Sandstorm. He

could see what was coming, and by the troubled look she gave him in return, so could she.

"ThunderClan!" Nightstar yowled. "ThunderClan are sheltering Brokenstar!"

CHAPTER 19

❧

Shocked and angry caterwauls rose up from the cats surrounding the Great Rock. Every muscle in Fireheart's body urged him to creep backward into the bushes and hide from their fury. It took all his strength to stay where he was. Sandstorm pressed against his side, as shaken as he was, and he found her warmth comforting.

On top of the Great Rock, Tallstar whipped around to face Bluestar. "Is this true?" he snarled.

Bluestar did not reply to him at once. With great dignity, she stepped forward and faced Nightstar. The moonlight glowed on her fur, turning it to silver, so that Fireheart could almost believe that a warrior of StarClan had leaped down from Silverpelt to join them. She waited until the noise from below had died down. "How do you know this?" she coolly asked Nightstar when she could make herself heard. "Have you been spying on our camp?"

"Spying!" Nightstar spat the word out. "There's no need to spy when your apprentices gossip so freely. My warriors heard this at the last Gathering. Do you dare to stand here now and tell me they are wrong?"

As he spoke, Fireheart remembered seeing Swiftpaw with the ShadowClan apprentices at the end of the last Gathering. No wonder the young cat had looked guilty, if he had been telling his friends all about ThunderClan's prisoner, so soon after Bluestar had ordered all her Clan to keep quiet!

Bluestar hesitated. Fireheart felt a pang of sympathy for her. Many of her own Clan had been unhappy with her decision to shelter blind Brokentail. How was she going to defend herself in front of the other Clans?

Tallstar crouched in front of her, his ears flattened. "Is it true?" he repeated.

For a moment Bluestar did not speak. Then she lifted her head defiantly. "Yes, it's true," she meowed.

"Traitor!" spat Tallstar. "You know what Brokenstar did to us."

Bluestar's tail tip twitched; even from his place below the rock Fireheart could see the strain in every muscle of her body, and knew she was struggling to keep calm. "No cat *dares* to call me traitor!" she hissed.

"*I* dare," retorted Tallstar. "You are nothing but a traitor to the warrior code, if you are willing to give shelter to that . . . that heap of *foxdung*!"

All around the clearing WindClan cats leaped to their paws, yowling in support of their leader. "Traitor! Traitor!"

At the foot of the Great Rock, Tigerclaw and Deadfoot, the WindClan deputy, faced each other with their hackles raised, lips drawn back to show their sharp teeth, their noses no more than a mouse-length apart.

Fireheart sprang up too, his fighting instinct sending energy to his paws. He caught a glimpse of Willowpelt snarling at the WindClan queens with whom she had been sharing tongues a few moments before. A couple of ShadowClan warriors paced threateningly toward Darkstripe, and Mousefur leaped to his side, ready to attack.

"Stop!" Bluestar yowled from her place on the Great Rock. "How can you break the truce like this? Would you risk the wrath of StarClan?"

As she spoke, the moonlight began to fade. Every cat in the clearing froze. Looking up, Fireheart saw a wisp of cloud passing over the face of the moon. He shivered. Was that a warning from StarClan, because the Clans seemed about to break the sacred truce? Clouds had covered the moon once before, a sign of StarClan's anger that had brought the Gathering to an end.

As the cloud passed away the moonlight strengthened again. The moment of crisis had passed. Most of the cats sat down, though they continued to glare at one another. Whitestorm pushed himself between Deadfoot and Tigerclaw, and started to mew urgently into the ThunderClan deputy's ear.

On the top of the Great Rock, Crookedstar stepped forward to stand beside Bluestar. He looked calm; Fireheart realized that of all the Clans, RiverClan had least reason to hate Brokentail. He had not crossed the river into their territory, or stolen their kits.

"Bluestar," he meowed, "tell us why you have done this."

"Brokentail is blind," Bluestar replied, her voice ringing out so that every cat in the clearing could hear her. "He is an old, defeated cat. He is no danger, not anymore. Would you have him starve to death in the forest?"

"Yes!" Nightstar's voice rose, shrill and insistent. "No death is too cruel for him!" Flecks of foam spun from the ShadowClan leader's lips. He thrust his head aggressively toward Tallstar and snarled, "Will you forgive the cat who drove you out?"

For a moment Fireheart wondered why Nightstar should be so frantic, so intent on whipping up Tallstar's hatred like this. He was Clan leader now. What harm could a blind prisoner do him?

Tallstar flinched away from the ShadowClan leader, clearly taken aback by his fury. "You know how much this means to my Clan," he meowed. "We will never forgive Brokenstar."

"Then I tell you, you're wrong," meowed Bluestar. "The warrior code tells us to show compassion. Tallstar, don't you remember what ThunderClan did for you when you were defeated and driven out? We found you and brought you home, and later we fought beside you against RiverClan. Have you forgotten what you owe us?"

Far from soothing Tallstar, Bluestar's words angered the WindClan leader more than ever. He stalked up to her, his fur bristling. "Does ThunderClan claim to own us?" he spat out. "Is *that* why you brought us back, to bow to your wishes and accept your decisions without question? Do you think

WindClan has no honor?"

Bluestar bowed her head in the face of the WindClan leader's fury. "Tallstar," she meowed. "You're right that no Clan can own another. That's not what I meant. But remember how you felt when you were weak, and try to show compassion now. If we drive Brokentail out to die, we're no better than he is."

"Compassion?" spat Nightstar. "Don't give us tales fit for kits, Bluestar! What compassion did Brokenstar ever show?" Yowls of agreement filled the air as he spoke. Nightstar added, "You must drive him out now, Bluestar, or I'll want to know the reason why."

Bluestar's eyes narrowed to glittering blue slits. "Don't tell me how to run my Clan!"

"I'll tell you this," Nightstar growled. "If ThunderClan keeps on sheltering Brokenstar, you can expect trouble. ShadowClan will see to that."

"And WindClan," snarled Tallstar.

For a moment Bluestar was silent. Fireheart knew she knew how dangerous it was to make enemies of two Clans at once, especially when some of her own cats were unhappy with her decision to take care of Brokentail. "ThunderClan does not take orders from other Clans," she meowed at last. "We do what we think is right."

"Right?" Nightstar jeered. "To shelter that bloodthirsty—"

"Enough!" Bluestar interrupted. "No more argument. There's other business to discuss at this Gathering, or had you forgotten?"

Nightstar and Tallstar exchanged a glance, and while they hesitated Crookedstar stepped forward to report on the floods and the damage done to the RiverClan camp. They let him speak, though Fireheart didn't think that many cats were listening. The hollow was buzzing with shocked speculation about Brokentail.

Sandstorm pressed closer to Fireheart and mewed in his ear, "I knew there'd be trouble over Brokentail, as soon as Nightstar started to speak."

"I know," Fireheart replied. "But Bluestar can't send him away now. It would look as if she were giving in. No cat would respect her after that, not from ThunderClan or any Clan."

Sandstorm gave a low purr of agreement. Fireheart tried to concentrate on the rest of the Gathering, but it was difficult. He couldn't help being aware of the hostile glares on all sides from the cats of WindClan and ShadowClan, and he wished the Gathering were over.

It seemed a long time before the moon began to sink and cats began to divide into their patrols for the journey home. In silent accord, the ThunderClan warriors bounded up to Bluestar as soon as she left the Great Rock and made a protective circle around her. Fireheart guessed they were all as uncertain as he was that the truce would hold.

As the warriors formed up around Bluestar, Fireheart caught sight of Onewhisker, slipping past on his way to join a group of WindClan cats. Their eyes met, and Onewhisker paused. "I'm sorry about this, Fireheart," he meowed softly. "*I haven't forgotten how you brought us home.*"

"Thanks, Onewhisker," Fireheart replied. "I wish—"

He broke off as Tigerclaw pushed his way into the circle of cats, glaring at them and baring his teeth at Onewhisker, who backed away toward the WindClan cats. Fireheart braced himself for a rebuke, but the deputy stalked straight past him.

"I hope you're satisfied," Tigerclaw snarled at Bluestar as he took his place beside her. "Now two Clans are yowling for our blood. We should have thrown out that piece of vermin long ago."

Fireheart couldn't help feeling surprised by Tigerclaw's hostility toward the ThunderClan prisoner. Not long before, he had seen Tigerclaw sharing tongues with Brokentail, as if the deputy were reconciled to the cat staying in the Clan. But maybe it wasn't so surprising that he had been ruffled—as they all had—by the clash with WindClan and ShadowClan.

"Tigerclaw, this is no place to argue among ourselves," Bluestar told him quietly. "When we get back to camp—"

"And how do you intend to get back?" It was Nightstar who interrupted, pushing his way past the ThunderClan warriors. "Not the way you came, I hope. If you set one paw on ShadowClan territory, we'll rip you to pieces." He turned and slipped away into the shadows without waiting for a reply.

For a moment Bluestar looked confused. There was no other way back to the ThunderClan camp, Fireheart knew, unless they tried to swim the stream. He shivered at the thought of the fierce current that had almost cost him his life. Would they have to stay at Fourtrees until the floodwater went down? Then he caught the scent of RiverClan, and turned to see Crookedstar approaching with some of his warriors.

"I heard that," the pale tabby tom addressed Bluestar. "Nightstar is wrong. At a time like this, all cats should help one another." He glanced at Fireheart as he spoke, and Fireheart guessed he was remembering how Fireheart and Graystripe had helped RiverClan by sharing prey. But none of the ThunderClan cats here, except for Bluestar, knew anything about that, and Fireheart heard some uneasy murmurings from the warriors around him.

"I can offer you a way home," Crookedstar continued. "To get here, we crossed the river by the Twoleg bridge. If you go that way, you can travel through our territory and cross back lower down—there's a dead tree caught up by the stepping-stones."

Before Bluestar could speak, Tigerclaw hissed, "And why should we trust RiverClan?"

Crookedstar ignored him, his amber eyes on Bluestar as he waited for her response. She dipped her head respectfully. "Thank you, Crookedstar. We accept your offer."

The RiverClan leader nodded briefly and turned to escort her out of the clearing. There was still some muttering among the ThunderClan cats as Bluestar led her warriors through the bushes and up the slope out of the hollow. Cats from ShadowClan and WindClan hissed at them, even though RiverClan warriors flanked them protectively on both sides. Fireheart realized with a jolt that the divisions within the forest had shifted in the space of a single Gathering.

He was relieved when they reached the top of the slope and left the hostile Gathering behind them. He noticed Graystripe trying to edge his way closer to Silverstream, but another of the RiverClan queens was in his way, giving Silverstream a lick from time to time.

"You're sure you're not tired?" the queen fussed. "It's a long journey when you're expecting kits."

"No, Greenflower, I'm fine," Silverstream replied patiently, casting a frustrated glance at Graystripe over her friend's head.

Tigerclaw brought up the rear of the ThunderClan patrol, swinging his huge head aggressively from side to side as if he expected the RiverClan cats to attack at any moment.

Bluestar, on the other hand, seemed to be quite at ease traveling with the other Clan. Once they were away from Fourtrees she let Crookedstar take the lead, while she dropped back to join Mistyfoot. "I hear you have kits," she meowed, her voice level. "Are they well?"

Mistyfoot looked slightly surprised to be addressed by the ThunderClan leader. "Two . . . two of them were swept away in the river," she stammered. "Fireheart and Graystripe saved them."

"I'm sorry. You must have been frightened for them," Bluestar murmured, her blue eyes soft with sympathy. "I'm glad ThunderClan warriors were able to help. Did your kits recover?"

"Yes, they're fine now, Bluestar." Mistyfoot still seemed bewildered at being questioned so closely by the ThunderClan leader. "They're all fine. They'll be apprentices soon."

"And I'm sure they'll make fine warriors," Bluestar mewed warmly.

Watching his leader and the RiverClan queen walking step for step, Fireheart couldn't help thinking how their blue-gray fur shone almost identically in the moonlight. They had the same neat, compact bodies, and when they had to leap over a log that lay in their path they both flexed their limbs with the same economical ripple of muscles. Stonefur, coming up behind, was a copy of his sister, with a silver sheen to his coat and an enviable deftness of movement.

If cats from different Clans could look so alike, Fireheart wondered, why couldn't they think alike too? Why did there have to be so much quarreling between them? Uncomfortably he remembered the antagonism shown toward his Clan by ShadowClan and WindClan, and their bitterness over Bluestar's defense of Brokentail. As he padded toward the bridge, alert for the scent of Twolegs, Fireheart felt the cold winds of war beginning to sweep over the forest.

On the second dawn after the Gathering, Fireheart woke in the warriors' den to find that Graystripe had already left. The hollow in the moss where his friend had been sleeping was quite cold.

Gone to meet Silverstream, Fireheart thought with a sigh of resignation. It was hardly surprising, now that Graystripe knew she was going to have his kits, but it meant that Fireheart would have to cover for his absence again.

Yawning widely, Fireheart pushed his way through the

outer branches of the bush, and shook moss from his coat while he looked around the clearing. The sun was beginning to edge its way above the bracken wall, casting long shadows over the bare ground. The sky was pure, cloudless, and blue. Birdsong all around held the promise of easy prey.

"Hey, Brackenpaw!" Fireheart called to the apprentice, who sat blinking at the entrance to his den. "Do you want to go hunting?"

Brackenpaw leaped to his paws and raced across the clearing to Fireheart. "Now?" he asked, delight shining in his eyes.

"Yes, now," meowed Fireheart, suddenly sharing the young cat's eagerness. "I could do with a nice fresh mouse, couldn't you?"

Brackenpaw fell in behind him as they headed for the gorse tunnel. He hadn't even asked where Graystripe was, Fireheart realized. Graystripe had never taken his duties as mentor seriously, he thought with a pang of worry. He had been more interested in Silverstream right from the start. Meanwhile, Fireheart himself had more or less taken over Brackenpaw's training. He enjoyed it, and he liked the serious-minded ginger tom, but he was troubled that loyalty to the Clan didn't mean more to Graystripe.

He put these thoughts aside as he led Brackenpaw up the ravine, avoiding the muddy streambed where the floodwater was drying up. It was hard to be sad or anxious on a bright, warm day like this. With the floods receding more and more every day, there was no longer any danger that ThunderClan would be driven out of their camp by rising water.

At the top of the ravine, Fireheart paused. "Okay, Brackenpaw," he meowed. "Have a good sniff. What can you smell?"

Brackenpaw stood with his head erect, his eyes closed, and his jaws parted to drink in the breeze. "Mouse," he mewed at last. "Rabbit, and blackbird, and . . . some other bird I don't know."

"That's woodpecker," Fireheart told him. "Anything else?"

Brackenpaw concentrated, and his eyes snapped open in alarm. "Fox!"

"Fresh?"

The apprentice sniffed again and then relaxed, looking a bit ashamed of himself. "No, stale. Two or three days old, I think."

"Good, Brackenpaw. Now, you head that way, as far as the two old oaks, and I'll go this way." He watched Brackenpaw for a few moments as the apprentice moved slowly into the shadow of the trees, stopping every few paces to taste the air. A flutter of wings under a bush distracted Fireheart; turning his head he saw a thrush, flapping to keep its balance as it tugged a worm out of the soil.

Fireheart crouched down and crept toward it paw by paw. The thrush pulled the worm free and started to tuck in; Fireheart bunched his muscles for the pounce.

"Fireheart! Fireheart!"

Brackenpaw's frantic meow split the silence. His paws crunched on dead leaves as he tore through the trees toward Fireheart. Though Fireheart hurled himself at the thrush it had been given too much warning. It flew up to a low branch, squawking in panic, while Fireheart's paws thudded onto the empty ground.

"What do you think you're doing?" Fireheart swung around angrily to face the apprentice. "I'd have caught that thrush, and now listen to it! Every bit of prey in the forest will—"

"Fireheart!" Brackenpaw gasped out, skidding to a halt in front of him. "They're coming! I could smell them; then I saw them!"

"Smell who? Who's coming?"

Brackenpaw's eyes were round with fear. "ShadowClan and WindClan!" he meowed. "They're coming to invade our camp!"

CHAPTER 20

❧

"Where? How many warriors?" Fireheart demanded.

"Over there." Brackenpaw flicked his tail toward the deeper forest. "I don't know how many. They're creeping through the undergrowth."

"Okay." Fireheart thought quickly, trying to ignore the sudden thumping of his heart. "Go back to camp. Warn Bluestar and Tigerclaw. We need some warriors out here right now."

"Yes, Fireheart." Brackenpaw spun around and raced off down the ravine.

As soon as he had gone, Fireheart headed into the forest, prowling with new caution beneath the arching ferns. At first all seemed quiet, though it wasn't long before he picked up the rank scent of many intruding cats—the scents of WindClan and ShadowClan.

Somewhere ahead, a bird sounded a stuttering alarm call. Fireheart took cover behind a tree. He could still see nothing. His fur prickled with anticipation.

He bunched his hindquarters and sprang, clawing his way up the trunk of the tree until he could scramble onto a low branch. Crouching there, he peered down through the leaves.

The forest floor seemed empty, with not even a beetle stirring. Then Fireheart caught sight of a fern quivering. Something flashed white and was gone. Moments later a dark head poked out of the undergrowth below the tree. Fireheart recognized Nightstar.

A soft mew came from him. "Follow me!"

The ShadowClan leader emerged from the bracken and raced across a stretch of open ground. A band of cats streamed after him; Fireheart grew even more tense when he saw how many. Warriors from WindClan and ShadowClan bore down on his camp together; Fireheart saw Tallstar and Cinderfur, Deadfoot and Stumpytail, Wetfoot and Onewhisker, running side by side as if they were littermates.

Not long ago, these cats had been fighting each other in the snowbound WindClan camp. Now they were united in their hatred of Brokentail and of ThunderClan for sheltering him.

Fireheart knew he would have to fight them. Even though he thought of the WindClan warriors as his friends, he would have to stand by his leader and his own Clan.

As Fireheart braced himself to spring down, he heard a single furious caterwaul from the direction of the camp, and recognized Tigerclaw's voice summoning the warriors to battle. For all his distrust of the deputy, Fireheart couldn't help feeling relieved. Right now, ThunderClan needed all of Tigerclaw's fierce courage and fighting skills.

Fireheart scrambled down the tree, hit the ground with all

four paws, and streaked toward the battle, no longer trying to hide from the invaders. When he broke out of the trees, he saw that the open ground at the top of the ravine was covered with a mass of writhing, spitting cats. Tigerclaw and Nightstar wrestled together, clawing furiously. Darkstripe had pinned down a WindClan warrior. Mousefur flung herself, screeching in fury, on top of Cinderfur. Morningflower, a WindClan queen, raked her claws down Longtail's flank and sent him howling back down the slope.

Fireheart sprang at Morningflower, anger pounding through his veins. He couldn't help remembering how he had helped this same queen carry her kit on the way back to WindClan's camp after Brokenstar had driven out her Clan. She leaped around as Fireheart landed beside her, and pulled back just as she was about to swipe him with her claws. For a few heartbeats both cats stared at each other. Morningflower's eyes were filled with sorrow, and Fireheart could see that she too remembered what they had endured together. He could not bring himself to strike her, and after a moment she backed away from him and disappeared into the heaving mass of cats.

Before he could draw breath, a cat slammed into Fireheart from behind, knocking him onto the damp ground. He scrabbled vainly to get up. Twisting his neck, he gazed up into the fierce eyes of the ShadowClan warrior Stumpytail; a heartbeat later the ShadowClan warrior's teeth sank into his shoulder. Letting out a yowl of pain, Fireheart battered at Stumpytail's belly with his back legs, clawing out great clumps of his brown tabby fur. Stumpytail's blood spattered him as the ShadowClan warrior reared back in agony and was gone.

Fireheart scrambled up and looked around, panting. The fiercest fighting had shifted to the bottom of the ravine. The enemy cats were pushing forward, clearly determined to invade the camp. The outnumbered ThunderClan warriors were unable to keep them back. And where was Bluestar?

Then Fireheart saw her. With Whitestorm and Dustpelt, she crouched at the entrance to the gorse tunnel, ready to bar the way with her life. Already Onewhisker and Wetfoot had broken through Tigerclaw's defense, and as Fireheart stared, horrified, Wetfoot flung himself at Bluestar.

Fireheart raced along the top of the ravine. Out of the whole of ThunderClan, only he and Yellowfang knew that Bluestar was on the last of her nine lives. If she died in this battle, ThunderClan would be without a leader—or worse, would be left to the control of Tigerclaw.

When he was above the tunnel entrance, Fireheart plunged straight down the slope, his paws barely touching the treacherously steep rocks, to land, skidding, in the thick of the fight. His teeth tore into Wetfoot's neck, dragging the warrior off Bluestar. The ThunderClan leader slashed her claws at the gray tabby tom until he scrabbled backward and fled.

A wave of fighting cats bore down on Fireheart and the other cats by the gorse tunnel. Fireheart bit and scratched instinctively without knowing which cat he was fighting. Sharp claws slashed his forehead and blood began trickling into his eyes. He took a gasping breath, feeling as if he were about to suffocate in the rank scent of his enemies.

Then he heard Bluestar meowing close to his ear. "They're pushing through the wall! Fall back—defend the camp!"

Fireheart scrabbled to keep on his paws as the invaders carried the battle into the tunnel itself. The gorse tore at his fur like hostile claws. It was impossible to fight here, so he turned along his own length and struggled through the gorse into the camp.

In the clearing, Willowpelt, Runningwind, and Sandstorm had rushed to guard the nursery, ready to protect the nursing queens and their kits. Longtail, hastily licking his wounds, stood outside Brokentail's den with Brackenpaw beside him. Among the branches of the fallen tree, Fireheart could just make out the dark tabby fur and sightless eyes of the former ShadowClan leader. He couldn't help feeling a pang of frustration that they were being attacked for the sake of this cruel and murderous cat.

Nightstar and Onewhisker were the first to break out of the tunnel, streaking across the open ground toward Brokentail's den. Tallstar pushed his way through the thorny hedge and joined them. More of the invaders followed.

"Stop them!" Fireheart yowled, rallying the Clan warriors as he raced across the clearing. "They want Brokentail!" He threw himself on Nightstar, rolling the black tom over on the dusty ground. He couldn't help wondering how many ThunderClan cats really wanted to defend the former ShadowClan leader. Many of them would no doubt be happy to hand him over to the other Clans. But Fireheart also felt sure that they would stay loyal; whatever they felt in their hearts, they would fight for ThunderClan.

He pinned Nightstar down, his teeth buried in the leader's bony shoulder. Nightstar writhed under him and then heaved upward. Fireheart lost his balance and suddenly found that he was trapped—the warrior, though old, was still ferociously strong.

Nightstar bared his fangs, his eyes gleaming. All of a sudden he reared back, letting Fireheart go. Shaking blood from his eyes, Fireheart saw that Brackenpaw had leaped at the ShadowClan leader and was clinging to his back with all four paws. Nightstar tried vainly to shake him off and then rolled over, crushing Brackenpaw against the ground. The apprentice let out a furious howl.

Fireheart slashed at Nightstar with claws outstretched, but Tallstar thrust between them, trying to reach Brokentail's den. To his dismay, Fireheart felt himself being forced backward.

Then Tigerclaw was there. The huge deputy was bleeding from many wounds and his fur was plastered with mud, but his amber eyes still burned with the fire of battle. He swiped a massive paw at Tallstar, bowling him over and sending him scrambling away.

More ThunderClan cats appeared: Whitestorm, Mousefur, Runningwind, and Bluestar herself. The tide of battle turned. The invaders started to retreat, breaking for the tunnel and the gaps in the bracken around the clearing. Fireheart watched, panting, as Onewhisker vanished at the tail end of the fleeing invaders. The battle was over.

Brokentail stayed crouching in his den, his head low as he stared unseeing at the ground. He had made not one sound during the battle. Fireheart wondered if he even knew what his adopted Clan had risked for him.

Close by, Brackenpaw struggled to his paws. Fur hung raggedly from one shoulder, and his coat was smeared with dust and blood, but his eyes glowed.

"Well done," Fireheart meowed. "You fought like a warrior."

The apprentice's eyes shone even brighter.

Meanwhile the battered ThunderClan cats were gathered around Bluestar. All were muddy and bleeding, and they looked as exhausted as Fireheart felt. At first they were silent, their heads lowered. Fireheart could sense no triumph in their victory.

"You brought this on us!" It was Darkstripe who spoke, angrily confronting Bluestar. "You made us keep Brokentail here, and now we've been torn to pieces defending him. How long before one of us is killed for his sake?"

Bluestar looked troubled. "I never thought it would be easy, Darkstripe. But we must do what we believe is right."

Darkstripe spat at her with contempt. "For Brokentail? For a couple of mousetails I'd kill him myself!"

Several of the other warriors mewed their agreement.

"Darkstripe." Tigerclaw shouldered his way through the assembled cats to stand beside Bluestar, who looked suddenly old and fragile beside the huge dark tabby. "This is your leader you're talking to. Show some respect."

For a heartbeat Darkstripe glared at them both, then bowed his head. Tigerclaw swung his massive head, sweeping his amber gaze over all the cats.

"Fireheart, go and fetch Yellowfang," meowed Bluestar.

Fireheart turned toward the medicine cat's den, to see that she was already running stiffly across the clearing, followed closely by Cinderpaw. Quickly the two cats began to check the warriors' wounds, searching out the ones who needed the most urgent treatment. As Fireheart waited for his turn, he saw another cat appear from the camp entrance. It was Graystripe. His fur was sleek and unmarked; a couple of pieces of fresh-kill dangled from his jaws.

Before Fireheart could move, Tigerclaw broke away from Cinderpaw and strode across to meet Graystripe in the middle of the clearing. "Where have you been?" he demanded.

Graystripe looked bewildered. He dropped the fresh-kill and meowed, "Hunting. What on earth happened here?"

"What does it look like?" snarled the deputy. "WindClan and ShadowClan invaded, trying to get at Brokentail. We needed every warrior, but it seems that you weren't here. Where were you?"

With Silverstream, Fireheart answered silently. He thanked StarClan that at least Graystripe had brought back some prey, so he had a genuine reason for being away from camp.

"Well, how was I to know what was happening?" Graystripe protested to the deputy, beginning to look annoyed. "Or do I have to ask your permission before I set paw out of camp?"

Fireheart winced—Graystripe should have known better than to provoke Tigerclaw like that, but perhaps guilt was making him reckless.

Tigerclaw growled low in his throat. "You're away too often for my liking—you and Fireheart."

"Hang on!" Fireheart was stung into replying. "I was here today when the cats attacked. And it's not Graystripe's fault that he wasn't."

Tigerclaw let his cold gaze rest on Graystripe, and then Fireheart. "Just be careful," he spat. "I've got my eye on you—both of you." He swung around and stalked back to Cinderpaw.

"Like I care," Graystripe muttered, but he didn't meet Fireheart's eyes.

While Graystripe went to take his prey to the pile of fresh-kill, Fireheart limped back to the medicine cats to have his wounds seen to.

"Hmph!" growled Yellowfang as she ran an expert eye over him. "If they'd pulled out much more of your fur, you'd look like an eel. But none of the wounds is deep. You'll live."

Cinderpaw came up with a wad of cobweb, which she pressed to the scratch over Fireheart's eye. Gently she touched her nose to his. "You were brave, Fireheart," she whispered.

"Not really." Fireheart felt embarrassed. "We all did what we had to do."

"But it's not easy," Yellowfang rasped unexpectedly. "I've fought battles in my time, and I know. Bluestar," she went on, turning to the leader and facing her squarely, "thank you. It means a lot to me that you'd risk your Clan to protect Brokentail."

Bluestar shook her head. "There's no need for thanks, Yellowfang. It's a matter of honor. Despite what Brokentail has done, he deserves our compassion now."

The old medicine cat bowed her head. Softly, so that only Bluestar and Fireheart could hear, she mewed, "He has brought great danger to my adopted Clan, and for that I am sorry."

Bluestar moved closer to her and gave her gray coat a comforting lick. For a moment the expression in her eyes was that of a mother soothing a fretful kit. A picture came into Fireheart's mind of the Clan leader padding through the forest on the night of the Gathering, and the moonlight that shone on three silver coats—on Bluestar, Mistyfoot, and Stonefur.

Fireheart gasped. Was that really what he had seen? Three cats so identical that they could be nothing else but *kin*? Mistyfoot and Stonefur were sister and brother, he knew . . . and Graypool had told him that they had once borne the scent of ThunderClan.

Was it possible that Bluestar's kits hadn't died all those moons ago? Could it be that Mistyfoot and Stonefur were the ThunderClan leader's lost kits?

CHAPTER 21

When Cinderpaw had finished tending to Fireheart's wounds, he went to find Graystripe. His friend was hunched up inside the warriors' den, his golden eyes troubled.

He looked up as Fireheart slipped between the branches. "I'm sorry," he blurted out. "I know I should have been here. But I *had* to see Silverstream. I couldn't get near her on the night of the Gathering."

Fireheart sighed. For a moment, he had considered sharing his suspicions about Mistyfoot and Stonefur with his friend, but now he realized that Graystripe had more than enough worries of his own. "It's okay, Graystripe. Any of us could have been away, patrolling or hunting. But if I were you, I'd stick around camp for the next few days, and make sure Tigerclaw sees you."

Graystripe scraped absently at a piece of moss. Fireheart guessed he had already arranged to meet Silverstream again. "There's something else I wanted to tell you," he meowed, deciding not to try to argue about this now. "About Brackenpaw." Quickly he described how he and the apprentice had gone out early, and how Brackenpaw had scented the invading band of cats. "He fought well, too," Fireheart remarked. "I think it's time he became a warrior."

Graystripe let out a purr of agreement. "Does Bluestar know this?"

"Not yet. You're Brackenpaw's mentor. You ought to recommend him."

"But I wasn't there."

"That doesn't matter." Fireheart gave his friend a nudge. "Come on, let's go and talk to Bluestar now."

The ThunderClan leader and most of the warriors were still in the clearing, while Yellowfang and Cinderpaw distributed cobwebs to stop bleeding and poppy seeds for pain. Brindleface had brought out her kits to see what was going on, and Cloudkit was frisking around, pestering one warrior after another with questions about the battle. Brackenpaw was there, too, giving himself a thorough wash; Fireheart was relieved that he didn't seem too badly hurt.

The two warriors went up to Bluestar, and Fireheart once more told the story of Brackenpaw's skill at scenting their enemies, and his bravery in the battle. "It's thanks to Brackenpaw that we had any warning at all," he meowed.

"We think he should be made a warrior," Graystripe added.

Bluestar nodded thoughtfully. "I agree. Brackenpaw showed himself worthy today." She got up, paced into the middle of her cats, and raised her voice. "Let all cats old enough to catch their own prey join here beneath the Highrock for a Clan meeting."

Goldenflower appeared at once from the nursery, followed by Speckletail, and Smallear limped slowly from the elders' den. When they had gathered around Bluestar, she meowed, "Brackenpaw, come here."

Brackenpaw looked up, surprised, and padded nervously over to Bluestar. Fireheart could see he had not the least idea what was coming.

"Brackenpaw, it was you who warned the Clan today, and you fought bravely in the battle," Bluestar meowed. "It is time for you to become a warrior."

The apprentice's mouth fell open. His eyes blazed with excitement as Bluestar pronounced the ritual words.

"I, Bluestar, leader of ThunderClan, call upon my warrior ancestors to look down on this apprentice. He has trained hard to understand the ways of your noble code, and I commend him to you as a warrior in his turn." She fixed her blue gaze on Brackenpaw. "Brackenpaw, do you promise to uphold the warrior code and to protect and defend this Clan, even at the cost of your life?"

Brackenpaw trembled slightly, but his voice was steady as he meowed, "I do."

"Then by the powers of StarClan, I give you your warrior name. Brackenpaw, from this moment you will be known as Brackenfur. StarClan honors your forethought and your determination, and we welcome you as a full warrior of ThunderClan."

When she finished speaking Bluestar stepped up to Brackenfur and rested her muzzle on his bowed head.

Brackenfur licked her shoulder respectfully, then walked over to stand between Fireheart and Graystripe.

The watching cats raised their voices to chant the new warrior's name. "Brackenfur! Brackenfur!" They began to press around him, congratulating him and wishing him well. His mother, Frostfur, pressed her muzzle against his flank, while her dark blue eyes glowed with delight.

"Tonight you have to keep vigil alone," mewed Sandstorm, giving Brackenfur a friendly nudge. "Thank StarClan! The rest of us can have a night off!"

Brackenfur was too overwhelmed to answer properly, but he broke into a deep, contented purr. "Th-Thank you, Graystripe," he stammered. "And you, Fireheart."

Fireheart felt a rush of pride to see the cat made a warrior at last, almost as though Brackenfur had been his own apprentice. It made up, a little, for knowing that he would never go through this with Cinderpaw. StarClan had a different fate for her. Now that the ceremony was done, weariness swept over Fireheart. He was about to go back to the warriors' den when he caught sight of Cinderpaw limping rapidly over to her brother.

"Congratulations, Brackenfur!" she mewed, her blue eyes sparkling as she covered his ears with licks.

Brackenfur's purring faltered and his eyes looked troubled. "You should have been with me," he murmured, gently nosing her injured leg.

"No, I'm fine as I am," Cinderpaw insisted. "You'll have to be a warrior for both of us. And I'll have to settle for being the greatest medicine cat this forest has ever seen!"

Fireheart gazed at the dark gray she-cat with admiration. He knew that Cinderpaw really was happy to be Yellowfang's apprentice. She would be a fine medicine cat. But she would have been a fine warrior too. It took a special spirit, he thought, not to begrudge her brother's triumph. As always, the sight of Cinderpaw's injury reminded Fireheart of Tigerclaw. Fireheart was so sure the deputy had caused her accident, and had also tried to drown him just recently. Yet today Tigerclaw had fought with the strength of StarClan. Without him, they could have lost the battle. *If you prove his treachery*, Fireheart asked himself, *who will defend ThunderClan then?*

After the raid, Fireheart was relieved to see Graystripe keeping his promise to stay around the camp, patrolling or hunting or helping Yellowfang and Cinderpaw to replenish their supplies. Tigerclaw said nothing, but Fireheart hoped he had noticed.

However, on the third morning Fireheart was woken by movement in the nest beside him, and opened his eyes in time to see Graystripe sliding out of the den. "Graystripe?" he muttered, but his friend vanished without replying.

Careful not to disturb Sandstorm, who was sleeping on his other side, Fireheart got up and slipped out between the branches. He emerged blinking into the clearing and saw Graystripe disappearing into the gorse tunnel. He also saw Darkstripe, crouched beside the pile of fresh-kill, looking up with a vole dangling from his jaws. His eyes were fixed on the tunnel entrance.

Fireheart felt a heavy weight like a cold stone in his belly. If Darkstripe had seen Graystripe leave, that meant Tigerclaw would know about it before very long. And then the deputy would want to know exactly where Graystripe had been. He might even follow him, and catch him with Silverstream.

Almost unconsciously, Fireheart started forward. He forced himself to walk briskly, but without any special urgency. As he passed the heap of fresh-kill, he called out, "Morning, Darkstripe! We're just off to hunt. It's the early cat that catches the prey, you know!" Without waiting for Darkstripe's response, he entered the tunnel. Once he had left the clearing, he put on speed, racing to the top of the ravine. Graystripe was out of sight already but his scent was strong, leading unwaveringly to the Sunningrocks.

But they agreed only to meet at Fourtrees, he thought.

Fireheart pelted along, ignoring the tempting sounds and smells of prey in the undergrowth. He had hoped to catch Graystripe and divert him before his friend reached Silverstream, just in case Tigerclaw was already out in the forest, but by the time he came within sight of the Sunning-rocks he had seen no sign of him. Fireheart paused on the edge of the trees and drank in the scented air. Graystripe was close by, he was sure, and he could scent Silverstream as well, but the scents of both cats were overlaid with something that set Fireheart's fur bristling—the smell of blood!

At that moment, he heard a thin, eerie wailing from the rocks ahead, the unmistakable sound of a cat in deep distress. "Graystripe!" he yowled. He shot forward and hurled himself up the sloping surface of the nearest rock. What he saw from the top brought him to a skidding stop.

Below, in a deep gully between this rock and the next, Silverstream lay on her side. As Fireheart stared, appalled, a strong spasm traveled down the length of her body, and her legs twitched. She let out another chilling wail.

"Graystripe!" Fireheart gasped.

Graystripe was crouched beside Silverstream, frantically licking her heaving flank. He looked up at the sound of Fireheart's voice. "Fireheart! It's the kits—the kits are coming, and it's all going wrong. Fetch Yellowfang!"

"But—" Fireheart bit off his protest. His paws were already moving, carrying him down from the rock and back across the stretch of open ground toward the trees.

Fireheart ran as he had never run before, but even so, a small, cold part of his mind was telling him this was the end. Every cat in the Clans would find out about Graystripe and Silverstream now. What would Bluestar and Crookedstar do to them when it was all over?

Almost before he knew it he was back at the camp. He hurled himself down the ravine, almost bowling Cinderpaw over at the entrance to the tunnel. She reared back with a meow of protest, scattering the herbs she had gathered. "Fireheart, what—"

"Where's Yellowfang?" Fireheart panted.

"Yellowfang?" Cinderpaw suddenly grew more serious as she sensed Fireheart's desperation. "She went over to Snakerocks. It's the best place to find yarrow."

Fireheart gathered himself to go on running, then paused, frustrated. It would take too much time to fetch Yellowfang from Snakerocks. Silverstream needed help now!

"What's the matter?" mewed Cinderpaw.

"There's a cat—Silverstream—by the Sunningrocks. She's having her kits, but something's gone wrong."

"Oh, StarClan help her!" exclaimed Cinderpaw. "I'll come. Wait there—I need to fetch supplies." She vanished into the mouth of the gorse tunnel. Fireheart waited, scrabbling his paws with impatience, until at last he saw movement in the tunnel again. But it wasn't Cinderpaw; it was Brackenfur.

"Cinderpaw sent me for Yellowfang," he called as he bounded past Fireheart, heading up the ravine.

At last Cinderpaw reappeared. Her jaws were clamped on a leaf-wrapped bundle of herbs. She flicked her tail at Fireheart as she approached, signaling that he should lead the way.

Every step of that journey was torment for Fireheart. Cinderpaw did her best, but her damaged leg slowed her down. Time seemed to stretch out. With a pang of horror, Fireheart remembered his dream, of a faceless silver queen who faded away, leaving her kits crying helplessly in the dark. Had that been Silverstream?

As soon as the Sunningrocks came in sight, Fireheart bounded ahead of Cinderpaw. When he reached the foot of the rock, he saw another cat crouched on the top, looking down into the gully where Graystripe and Silverstream were. Cold paws clutched Fireheart's heart. There was no mistaking Tigerclaw's massive body and dark coat. Darkstripe must have notified him, and the deputy had followed Graystripe's scent. Fireheart had passed him on his dash back to camp without realizing it.

"Fireheart," growled Tigerclaw, turning his head as Fireheart scrambled up the rock. "What do you know about this?"

Fireheart looked down into the gully. Silverstream still lay on her side, but the powerful rippling down her body had ebbed away into weak spasms. She had stopped wailing now; Fireheart guessed she was too exhausted. Graystripe huddled close to her. He made a low, crooning noise deep in his chest, and his yellow eyes were fixed on the she-cat's face. Fireheart didn't think that either of them had realized Tigerclaw was there.

Before Fireheart could answer the deputy's question, Cinderpaw came skidding around the bottom of the rock and squeezed along the gully to Silverstream's side. She dropped the bundle of herbs and stooped to sniff the silver-gray queen.

"Fireheart!" she called a moment later. "Get down here! I need you!"

Ignoring a furious hiss from Tigerclaw, Fireheart leaped down into the gully, scraping his claws painfully on the sheer rock. As his paws touched the ground, Cinderpaw came to meet him. She was carrying a very small kit with its eyes closed and ears flat to its head, and dark gray fur plastered to its body.

"Is it dead?" Fireheart whispered.

"No!" Cinderpaw set down the kit and patted it toward him. "Lick, Fireheart! Make it warm, get its blood flowing."

As soon as she had finished speaking she turned in the narrow space and went back to Silverstream. Her body blocked Fireheart's view of what was happening, but he heard the apprentice medicine cat begin to meow reassuringly, and an anxious question from Graystripe.

Fireheart bent over the kit and rasped his tongue over its tiny body. For a long time it didn't respond, and he began to think Cinderpaw had been wrong, and the kit was dead after all. Then he felt a tiny shiver run through it and it opened its jaws in a soundless mew. "It's alive!" he gasped.

"Told you," Cinderpaw called to him. "Keep licking. There's another one coming, any moment now. That's right, Silverstream . . . you're doing fine."

Tigerclaw had come down from the rock and was standing in the mouth of the gully with a look of thunder on his face. "That's a RiverClan cat," he hissed. "Will one of you tell me what's going on?"

Before any cat had time to reply, Cinderpaw let out a shout of triumph. "You've done it, Silverstream!" Moments later she turned with a second tiny kit in her jaws, and set it down in front of Tigerclaw. "Here. Lick."

Tigerclaw glared at her. "I'm not a medicine cat."

Cinderpaw's blue eyes blazed as she rounded on the deputy. "You've got a tongue, haven't you? Lick, you useless lump of fur. Do you want the kit to die?"

Fireheart flinched, half expecting Tigerclaw to hurl himself at her and slash her open with his powerful claws. Instead, the dark tabby bowed his huge head and began to lick the second kit.

At once Cinderpaw turned back to Silverstream. Fireheart heard her meow, "You need to swallow this herb. Here, Graystripe, make her eat as much as she can. We've got to stop the bleeding."

Fireheart paused for a moment in his own vigorous licking. His kit was breathing evenly now, and it seemed to be out of danger. He wished he knew what was happening in the gully ahead of him; he heard Cinderpaw growl, "Hold on, Silverstream," and a louder, panicky meow from Graystripe: "Silverstream!"

At the sound of his friend's distress, Fireheart could not stay back any longer. Leaving the kit, he pushed forward until he could crouch beside Cinderpaw. He was in time to see Silverstream raise her head and feebly lick Graystripe's face. "Good-bye, Graystripe," she whispered. "I love you. Take care of our kits."

Then the silver tabby's body gave a massive shudder. Her head fell back, her paws jerked, and she was still.

"Silverstream!" whispered Cinderpaw.

"No, Silverstream, no." Graystripe's mew was very soft. "Don't go. Don't leave me." He bent over the limp body, nuzzling her gently. She did not move.

"Silverstream!" Graystripe reared up and flung back his head. His wails of grief split the quiet air. "Silverstream!"

Cinderpaw crouched over the body for a few moments more, nudging at Silverstream's fur, but at last she admitted defeat. She sat up and stared ahead, her blue eyes bleak and cold.

Fireheart got up and padded over to her. "Cinderpaw, the kits are safe," he murmured.

The look she gave him made his heart freeze. "But their mother is dead. I lost her, Fireheart."

The rocks were still echoing to Graystripe's dreadful wailing. Tigerclaw appeared, scrambling past the other cats, and reached out a massive paw to cuff the gray warrior behind the ear. "Stop that moaning."

Graystripe fell silent, more out of shock and exhaustion, Fireheart thought, than obedience to the deputy's order.

Tigerclaw glared around at all of them. "*Now* will some cat tell me what's going on? Graystripe, do you know this RiverClan cat?"

Graystripe looked up. His eyes had gone dull and cold, like pebbles. "I loved her," he whispered.

"What—these are *your* kits?" Tigerclaw seemed stunned.

"Mine and Silverstream's." A faint spark of defiance kindled in Graystripe. "I know what you'll say, Tigerclaw. Don't bother. I don't care." He turned back to Silverstream, pressing his nose against her fur and murmuring softly to her.

Meanwhile, Cinderpaw had roused herself enough to

examine the two kits. "I think they'll live," she mewed, though to Fireheart she sounded less certain than before. "We need to get them back to camp, to find a queen to suckle them."

Tigerclaw spun around to face her. "Are you *mad*? Why should ThunderClan raise them? They're half-breeds. No Clan will want them."

Cinderpaw ignored him. "Fireheart, you take that one," she ordered. "I'll carry the other."

Fireheart twitched his whiskers in agreement, but before he picked up the kit he walked over to Graystripe and pressed his body against his friend's broad gray shoulder. "Do you want to come with us?"

Graystripe shook his head. "I have to stay here and bury her," he whispered. "Here, between RiverClan and ThunderClan. After this, not even her own Clan will want to mourn her."

Fireheart felt his heart break for his friend, but there was nothing more he could do to help. "I'll come back soon," he promised. More softly, though he was past caring if Tigerclaw heard him or not, he added, "I will mourn her with you, Graystripe. She was brave, and I know she loved you."

His friend did not respond. Fireheart picked up the kit with his teeth, and left Graystripe beside the cat he had loved more than his Clan, more than honor, more than life itself.

CHAPTER 22

❧

Tigerclaw went on ahead, and by the time Fireheart and Cinderpaw reached the camp with Silverstream's kits, the whole Clan knew what had happened. Warriors and apprentices had gathered outside their dens, watching in silence. Fireheart could almost smell their shock and disbelief.

Bluestar stood at the entrance to the nursery as if she was waiting for them. Fireheart half expected her to turn them away, refusing to take care of a different Clan's kits, but she only meowed quietly, "Come inside."

In the heart of the bramble thicket, all was dim and quiet. Brindleface was curled around her kits, asleep in a heap of gray and tawny fur with Cloudkit's white coat shining among them like a patch of snow. Close by her, in a nest of moss lined with downy feathers, Goldenflower lay on her side, suckling her new kits. One was a pale ginger color like Goldenflower herself, and the other a dark tabby.

"Goldenflower," murmured Bluestar, "I have something to ask you. Can you manage two more? Their mother has just died."

Goldenflower raised her head, her startled look softening

when she saw the two helpless scraps of fur dangling from Fireheart's and Cinderpaw's mouths. They had begun to wriggle feebly, giving out thin, high-pitched mews of fear and hunger.

"I suppose—" Goldenflower began.

"Wait," Speckletail interrupted; she had padded into the nursery just behind Fireheart. "Before you agree to anything, Goldenflower, ask Bluestar to tell you whose kits these are."

Fireheart felt a pang of anxiety. Though Speckletail was a good mother, she had a ferocious temper, and he guessed she would not look kindly on kits that were neither one Clan nor the other.

"I would not hide such a thing from her," Bluestar meowed calmly. "Goldenflower, these are Graystripe's kits. Their mother was Silverstream—a RiverClan cat."

Goldenflower's eyes widened in astonishment, and Brindleface, roused from her doze, pricked up her ears.

"Graystripe must have been slinking off for moons to see her," Speckletail hissed. "What loyal cat would do that? They both betrayed their Clans. There's bad blood in those kits."

"Nonsense," Bluestar spat back, her hackles suddenly raised. Fireheart winced—he had rarely seen his leader so angry. "Whatever we think about Graystripe and Silverstream, the kits are innocent. Will you take them, Goldenflower? They'll die without a mother."

Goldenflower hesitated, and then let out a long breath. "How can I say no? I have plenty of milk."

Speckletail let out a snort of disapproval and pointedly

turned her back as Fireheart and Cinderpaw gently laid the kits in Goldenflower's nest. The pale ginger queen bent over to guide them toward her belly, and their miserable squeaking died away as they burrowed into the warmth of her body and found a place to suckle.

"Thank you, Goldenflower," purred Bluestar.

Fireheart realized that she was looking down at the young kits with an expression of longing. He wondered if she was thinking about her own lost kits, and his doubts about what had really happened to them came flooding back. Could they possibly be Mistyfoot and Stonefur, alive and well in RiverClan? Did she have any idea?

His thoughts were interrupted when Cinderpaw turned abruptly and made her way out of the den. Fireheart followed her, to find her crouching outside with her head bowed onto her front paws. "What's the matter?" he asked.

"Silverstream died." Fireheart could hardly hear her muffled reply. "I let her die."

"That's not true!"

Cinderpaw looked up, blinking. Her eyes were blue pools of misery. "I'm supposed to be a medicine cat. I'm supposed to save lives."

"You saved the two kits," Fireheart reminded her, moving closer and pressing the side of his face against her cheek.

"But I didn't save Silverstream."

A wave of sympathy washed over Fireheart. He understood how Cinderpaw felt, and he wanted to tell her she was wrong to blame herself, but he didn't have the words. Feeling useless and saddened, he began to lick her gently.

"What's going on?" Fireheart looked up to see Yellowfang standing in front of them, a puzzled frown on her broad gray face. "What's this I hear about Graystripe and a RiverClan queen?"

Cinderpaw didn't even seem to notice that her mentor was there. It was left to Fireheart to explain.

"Cinderpaw was brilliant," he told the elderly medicine cat. "Those kits would have died without her."

Yellowfang nodded. "I've seen Tigerclaw," she rasped. "Brackenfur was taking me to the Sunningrocks when we ran into him. He's furious about the kits. But he's not furious with you, Cinderpaw," she added. "He knows you did your duty, just as any medicine cat would."

Cinderpaw glanced up at that. "I'll never be a medicine cat," she spat bitterly. "I'm useless. I let Silverstream die."

"What?" snarled Yellowfang angrily, arching her skinny gray body. "That's the most mouse-brained thing I've ever heard."

"Yellowfang—" Fireheart began to protest at her harsh tone, but the medicine cat ignored him.

"You did your best, Cinderpaw," she growled. "No cat can do more."

"But it wasn't good enough," Cinderpaw pointed out dully. "If you'd been there, you would have saved her."

"Oh? StarClan told you that, did they? Cinderpaw, sometimes cats die, and no cat can do anything about it." She let out a rusty mew, half laughter, half scolding. "Not even me."

"But I *lost* her, Yellowfang."

"I know. And that's a hard lesson." Now there was rough sympathy in the old cat's meow. "But I've lost cats before now—more cats than I care to count. Every medicine cat in the world has. You live with it. You go on." She nudged Cinderpaw with her battle-scarred muzzle, and went on nudging until the younger cat rose unsteadily to her paws. "Come on. There's work to be done. Smallear's complaining about his aching joints again."

She herded Cinderpaw in the direction of her den and paused to glance over her shoulder at Fireheart. "Don't worry," she told him. "She'll be fine."

Fireheart watched the two cats cross the clearing and vanish into Yellowfang's den.

"You can trust Yellowfang." At the sound of the quiet meow, Fireheart turned to see Bluestar. "She'll see Cinderpaw through this."

The Clan leader was sitting just outside the nursery, her tail wrapped neatly over her paws. In spite of all the turmoil of Silverstream's death and the discovery of Graystripe's illicit relationship, she looked as calm as ever.

"Bluestar," Fireheart meowed hesitantly, "what will happen to Graystripe now? Will he be punished?"

Bluestar looked thoughtful. "I can't answer that yet, Fireheart," she admitted. "I need to discuss it with Tigerclaw and the other warriors."

"Graystripe couldn't help himself," Fireheart blurted out loyally.

"Not help himself—when he betrayed his Clan and the warrior code to be with Silverstream?" Bluestar's eyes glinted, but her tone was not as angry as Fireheart would have expected. "I promise you one thing," she added. "I'll do nothing until the shock has died down. We need to consider the whole matter carefully."

"You're not really shocked, though, are you?" Fireheart dared to ask. "Had you guessed it was happening?" He half expected Bluestar not to answer. She held him motionless for several heartbeats with her penetrating blue gaze. There was wisdom in her eyes, he saw, and even pain.

"Yes, I suspected," she mewed at last. "It's a leader's place to know things. And I'm not exactly blind at the Gatherings."

"Then . . . then why didn't you stop it?"

"I hoped Graystripe would remember his loyalty to the Clan on his own," Bluestar replied. "I knew that even if he didn't, something would happen to end it, sooner or later. I only wish it had not ended so tragically, for both of them. Though I don't know how Graystripe would have coped with watching his own kits grow up in another Clan."

"You understand about that, don't you?" The words were out before Fireheart had a chance to think about what he was saying. "It happened to you."

Bluestar stiffened and Fireheart flinched at the sudden blaze of anger in her eyes. Then she relaxed, and the anger was replaced by a distant look of memory and loss.

"You guessed," she murmured. "I thought you might. Yes, Fireheart, Mistyfoot and Stonefur were once my kits."

CHAPTER 23

✤

"Come," Bluestar ordered. She began to walk slowly across the camp toward her den, leaving Fireheart with no choice but to follow. Once inside, she told him to sit down, and settled herself on her bedding.

"How much do you know?" she asked Fireheart, her blue eyes searching his.

"Only that Oakheart once brought two ThunderClan kits to RiverClan," Fireheart admitted. "He told Graypool—that's the queen who suckled them—that he didn't know where they had come from."

Bluestar nodded, her gaze softening. "I knew Oakheart would stay loyal to me," she murmured. She raised her head. "He was the kits' father," she added. "Did you guess that much?"

Fireheart shook his head. But it made sense, then, that Oakheart had been so desperate for Graypool to care for the helpless kits. "What exactly happened to your kits?" he demanded, curiosity making him unguarded. "Oakheart didn't *steal* them, did he?"

The Clan leader's ears flicked impatiently. "Of course

not." Her eyes met Fireheart's, suddenly clouded with a pain he could not begin to imagine. "No, he didn't steal them. I gave them away."

Fireheart stared in disbelief. There was nothing he could do but wait for the she-cat to explain.

"My warrior name was Bluefur," she began. "Like you, I wanted nothing more than to serve my Clan. Oakheart and I met at a Gathering early one leaf-bare, when we were still young and foolish. We were not mates for long. When I discovered I was to have kits, I intended to bear them for ThunderClan. No cat asked me who the father was—if a queen does not wish to tell, that is her choice."

"But then . . . ?" Fireheart prompted.

Bluestar's eyes were fixed on a point far away, as if she were staring into the distant past. "Then our Clan deputy, Tawnyspots, decided to retire. I knew I had a good chance of being chosen to take his place. Our medicine cat had already told me that StarClan held a great destiny for me. But I also knew the Clan would never take a queen nursing kits as deputy."

"So you gave them away?" Fireheart could not keep the note of disbelief out of his voice. "Couldn't you have waited until they had left their nursery? Surely you could have been made deputy once the kits were old enough to care for themselves."

"It wasn't an easy decision," Bluestar told him, her voice rough with pain. "That was a bitter leaf-bare. The Clan was half-starved and I had barely enough milk to feed my kits. I knew that in RiverClan they would be well cared for. In those days the river was full of fish, and RiverClan cats never went hungry."

"But to lose them . . ." Fireheart blinked at the sharpness of pain he felt in sympathy.

"Fireheart, I don't need you to tell me how difficult my choice was. I lay awake for many nights, deciding what to do. What was best for the kits . . . what was best for me . . . and what was best for the Clan."

"There must have been other warriors ready to be deputy?" Fireheart was still struggling to accept that Bluestar had been so ambitious that she would have given away her own kits.

Bluestar jerked her chin up defiantly. "Oh, yes. There was Thistleclaw. He was a fine warrior, strong and brave. But his answer to every problem was to fight. Should I have watched him be made deputy, and then leader, and let him force the Clan into unnecessary wars?" She shook her head sadly. "He died as he lived, Fireheart, a few seasons before you came to join us, attacking a RiverClan patrol on the border. Wild and arrogant to the last. I couldn't stand by and let him destroy my Clan."

"Did you give the kits to Oakheart yourself?"

"Yes. I spoke to him at a Gathering, and he agreed to take them. So one night I crept out of the camp and took them to the Sunningrocks. Oakheart was waiting, and he took two of them across the river."

"Two of them?" Fireheart was startled. "You mean there

were more than two?"

"There were three." Bluestar bowed her head; her mew was scarcely audible. "The third kit was too weak to cope with the journey. He died with me, by the river."

"What did you tell the rest of the Clan?" Fireheart thought back to the Gathering, when Patchpelt had said only that Bluestar had "lost" her kits.

"I . . . I made it look as if they had been taken from the nursery by a fox or a badger. I tore a hole in the nursery wall just before I left, and when I came back, I said that I had been hunting and had left my kits sleeping safely." Her whole body trembled, and Fireheart could tell that confessing to this lie was causing Bluestar more pain than losing a life.

"Every cat searched," she went on. "And I searched too, even though I knew there was no hope of finding them. The Clan was devastated for me." She dropped her head onto her paws. Forgetting for a moment that she was his leader, Fireheart crossed the floor of the den and gave Bluestar's ears a gentle lick.

Once again he remembered his dream, and the faceless queen who had faded away, leaving her kits to cry for her. He had thought the queen was Silverstream, but now he realized she was Bluestar as well. The dream had been both prophecy and Clan memory. "Why are you sharing this with me?" he asked.

When Bluestar looked up, Fireheart could hardly bear to see the sorrow in her eyes.

"For many seasons I put the kits out of my mind," she

answered. "I became deputy, and then leader, and my Clan needed me. But lately, with the floods, and the danger to RiverClan—and your discoveries, Fireheart, making me hear again what I knew very well already . . . And now another pair of kits who are half RiverClan, half ThunderClan. Perhaps this time I can make better decisions."

"But why tell *me*?" Fireheart repeated.

"Perhaps after so long I want a cat to know the truth," meowed Bluestar with a slight frown. "I think you of all cats might understand, Fireheart. Sometimes there are no right choices."

But Fireheart was not sure that he understood at all. His mind was whirling. On one paw he could picture the young warrior, Bluefur, fiercely ambitious, determined to do the best for her Clan, even if it meant unimaginable sacrifices. On the other, he saw a mother grieving for the kits she had abandoned so long ago. And what was probably more real to him than either, the gifted leader who had done what she felt was best and borne the pain of it alone.

"I won't tell another cat," he promised, realizing how much she must trust him to have revealed her secrets to him like this.

"Thank you, Fireheart," she replied. "There are difficult times ahead of us. The Clan doesn't need more trouble." She rose to her paws and stretched as if she had been curled up in a long sleep. "Now I must speak with Tigerclaw. And you, Fireheart, had better go and find your friend."

❈   ❈   ❈

The sun was beginning to sink, turning the river into a ribbon of reflected fire, as Fireheart returned to the Sunningrocks. Graystripe crouched beside a patch of freshly turned earth at the top of the riverbank, his gaze fixed on the blazing water.

"I buried her on the shore," he whispered as Fireheart padded up and sat down beside him. "She loved the river." He raised his head to where the first stars of Silverpelt were beginning to appear. "She hunts with StarClan now," he mewed softly. "Someday I'll find her again, and we'll be together."

Fireheart was unable to speak. He pressed himself more closely to Graystripe's side, and the two cats crouched there in silence as the bloodred light faded.

"Where did you take the kits?" Graystripe meowed at last. "They should have been buried with her."

"Buried?" Fireheart echoed. "Graystripe, didn't you know? The kits are alive."

Graystripe stared at him, jaws gaping, his golden eyes beginning to glow. "They're alive—Silverstream's kits—my kits? Fireheart, where are they?"

"In the ThunderClan nursery." Fireheart gave him a quick lick. "Goldenflower is suckling them."

"But she won't keep them—will she? Does she know they're Silverstream's?"

"The whole Clan knows," Fireheart told him reluctantly. "Tigerclaw saw to that. But Goldenflower doesn't blame the kits, and neither does Bluestar. They'll be cared for,

Graystripe; they really will."

Graystripe scrambled to his paws, moving stiffly after his long vigil. He looked doubtfully at Fireheart, as if he couldn't believe that ThunderClan would really accept the kits. "I want to see them."

"Come on, then," mewed Fireheart, feeling a surge of relief that his friend felt ready to face the Clan again. "Bluestar sent me to bring you home."

He led the way through the darkening forest. Graystripe padded after him, but he kept casting glances back, as if he couldn't bear to leave Silverstream behind. He did not speak, and Fireheart let him be silent with his memories.

When they reached the camp, the curious murmuring groups of warriors and apprentices had broken up, and everything looked normal for a warm newleaf evening. Brackenfur and Dustpelt crouched by the nettle patch, sharing a piece of fresh-kill, and outside the apprentices' den Thornpaw and Brightpaw were rolling around in a play fight while Swiftpaw looked on. Tigerclaw and Bluestar were nowhere to be seen.

Fireheart breathed a sigh of relief. He wanted Graystripe left alone, at least until he had visited the kits, without being troubled by blame or hostility from his fellow warriors.

Then, on their way to the nursery, they passed Sandstorm. She halted abruptly, glancing from Fireheart to Graystripe and back again.

"Hi," Fireheart mewed, trying to sound as friendly as he always did. "We're going to visit the kits. See you in the den later?"

"*You* can," Sandstorm growled, with a glare at Graystripe. "Just keep *him* away from me, that's all." She stalked off, her head and tail held high.

Fireheart's heart sank. He remembered how hostile Sandstorm had been to him when he first joined the Clan. It had taken her a long time to thaw toward him. How long would it be before she would treat Graystripe as a friend again?

Graystripe flattened his ears against his head. "She doesn't want me here. No cat does."

"*I* do," Fireheart meowed, hoping he sounded sufficiently encouraging. "Come on; let's go and see your kits."

CHAPTER 24

Fireheart leaped from one stepping-stone to the next across the swiftly flowing river. The floodwater had retreated and the stones were clearly visible again. It was the day after Silverstream had died; the sky was gray with a thin drizzle of rain, as if StarClan were mourning her too.

Fireheart was on his way to take the news of Silverstream's death into RiverClan, although he had not sought Bluestar's permission first. He had slipped away without telling any cat because he thought Silverstream's Clan had the right to know what had happened to her. And he suspected that not every cat in ThunderClan would agree with him.

Reaching the opposite bank, Fireheart stood with his head raised, tasting the air for fresh scents. He caught one almost at once, and a heartbeat later a small tabby tom appeared from the ferns above the path.

He hesitated, looking startled, before sidling down the bank to confront Fireheart. "You're Fireheart, aren't you?" he meowed. "I recognize you from the last Gathering. What are you doing on our side of the river?"

He was trying to sound confident, but Fireheart could

detect nervousness in his voice. He was a very young cat—an apprentice, Fireheart guessed, anxious at being away from the camp without his mentor.

"I'm not here to fight, or to spy," Fireheart promised. "I need to talk to Mistyfoot. Will you fetch her for me?"

The apprentice hesitated again, as if he would have liked to protest. Then the habit of obeying warriors' orders won over, and he padded along the riverside in the direction of the RiverClan camp. Fireheart watched him go and scrambled up the bank to a spot where he could lie concealed in the bracken until Mistyfoot appeared.

It was a long time before she came, but at last Fireheart caught sight of her familiar blue-gray shape trotting rapidly toward him. Familiar because of Bluestar, he realized with a jolt. His leader's daughter was practically her double. To his relief she was alone. As she paused to sniff the air, he called out softly to her, "Mistyfoot! Up here!"

Mistyfoot's ears twitched; moments later she was pushing her way into the ferns beside him. "What is it?" she meowed, looking worried. "Is it about Silverstream? I haven't seen her since yesterday."

Fireheart felt as if a bone were lodged in his throat. He swallowed uncomfortably. "Mistyfoot," he mewed, "it's bad news. I'm so sorry . . . Silverstream is dead."

Mistyfoot fixed him with wide blue eyes full of disbelief. "Dead?" she echoed. "She can't be!" Before Fireheart could respond, she added more harshly, "Did some of your ThunderClan warriors catch her over there?"

"No, no," Fireheart replied quickly. "She was at the Sunningrocks with Graystripe, and the kits started to come. Something was wrong . . . there was a lot of blood. We did everything we could, but . . . oh, Mistyfoot, I'm so sorry."

Pain flooded into Mistyfoot's eyes as he explained. She let out a long, low wailing sound, her head flung back and her claws digging into the ground. Fireheart moved closer to try to comfort her, and felt every muscle in her body rigid with tension. There were no words he could say that would do any good.

At last the terrible wailing died away and Mistyfoot relaxed a little. "I knew no good could come of it," she murmured. There was no anger or accusation in her voice, only a weary sadness. "I told her not to meet Graystripe, but would she listen? And now . . . I can't believe I'll never see her again."

"Graystripe buried her by the Sunningrocks," Fireheart told her. "If you'll meet me there one day, I'll show you the place."

Mistyfoot nodded. "I'd like that, Fireheart."

"Her kits are alive," Fireheart added, in an attempt to ease some of the queen's grief.

"Her kits?" Mistyfoot sat up, alert again.

"Two kits," mewed Fireheart. "They're going to be fine."

Mistyfoot blinked, suddenly deep in thought. "Will ThunderClan want them, when they're half RiverClan?"

"One of our queens is suckling them," Fireheart assured her. "The Clan's angry with Graystripe, but no cat would take it out on the kits."

"I see." Mistyfoot was silent for a while, still thoughtful, and then rose to her paws. "I must get back to camp and tell the Clan. They don't even know about Graystripe. I can't imagine what I'm going to say to Silverstream's father."

Fireheart knew how she felt. Many warrior fathers did not stay close to their kits, but Crookedstar had maintained a close bond with Silverstream. His grief at her death would be mixed with anger that she had betrayed her Clan by taking Graystripe as a mate.

Mistyfoot gave Fireheart a quick lick on the forehead. "Thank you," she mewed. "Thank you for coming to tell me."

Then she was gone, sliding rapidly through the ferns. Fireheart waited until she was out of sight before he padded down the pebbly shore and crossed the stepping stones back to his own territory.

Hunger roused Fireheart from sleep. Peering through the dim light in the warriors' den, he saw that Graystripe had left his nest already. *Oh, no!* Fireheart thought irritably. *He's gone off to meet Silverstream again!* Then he remembered.

Two dawns had passed since Silverstream's death. The shock the Clan felt about her affair with Graystripe was beginning to die down, though none of the warriors except Fireheart and Brackenfur would talk to Graystripe or go on patrols with him. Bluestar had still not announced what his punishment would be.

Fireheart stretched and yawned. All night his sleep had

been disturbed by Graystripe twitching and whimpering, but the weariness inside him went deeper than that. He couldn't see how the Clan could possibly recover from the blow that had been struck by the discovery of Graystripe's disloyalty. There was an atmosphere of uncertainty and distrust that dulled conversation and cut short the familiar rituals of sharing tongues.

With a determined shake, Fireheart slipped out through the branches and padded over to the pile of fresh-kill. The sun was rising, dappling the camp with golden light. As he bent to pick out a plump vole, he heard a voice calling, "Fireheart! Fireheart!"

Fireheart turned. Cloudkit was racing across the clearing toward him from the nursery. Brindleface and the rest of her kits followed more slowly, and to Fireheart's surprise Bluestar was with them.

"Fireheart!" Cloudkit panted, skidding to a stop in front of him. "I'm going to be an apprentice! I'm going to be an apprentice *now!*"

Fireheart dropped the vole. He couldn't help feeling cheered up when he saw the kit's excitement, along with a twinge of guilt that he had completely forgotten Cloudkit was approaching his sixth moon.

"You'll mentor him, of course, Fireheart?" Bluestar meowed as she came up. "It's time you had another apprentice. You did good work with Brackenfur, even though he wasn't yours."

"Thank you," meowed Fireheart, dipping his head to

acknowledge her praise. He couldn't help thinking sadly of Cinderpaw. He would never lose the feeling that he had been partly responsible for her accident, and he resolved to do better with Cloudkit.

"I'll work harder than any cat!" Cloudkit promised, his eyes wide. "I'll be the best apprentice there ever was!"

"We'll see about that," Bluestar mewed, while Brindleface purred with amusement.

"He's been pestering me day and night," she meowed fondly. "I know he'll do his best. He's strong and intelligent."

Cloudkit's eyes gleamed at her praise. *He seems to have gotten over finding out he was a kittypet,* Fireheart thought. *But he's arrogant, and he barely knows what the warrior code is, let alone respects it. Did I do the right thing, to bring him here?* he wondered yet again. Mentoring him wouldn't be easy, he knew.

"I'll call the meeting," Bluestar meowed, heading for the Highrock. With a glance at Fireheart, Cloudkit bounced after her, and the rest of the kits tumbled along behind.

"Fireheart," meowed Brindleface, "there's something I want to ask you."

Fireheart suppressed a sigh. "What is it?" Obviously he wasn't going to have time to eat his vole before Cloudkit's ceremony.

"It's about Graystripe. I know what he's been through, but he's never out of the nursery, watching over those two kits. It's as if he thinks Goldenflower can't look after them properly. He's getting in the way of all of us."

"Have you told him?"

"We've tried dropping hints. Speckletail even asked him if he thought he was expecting kits himself. He doesn't take any notice."

Fireheart gave the vole a last regretful glance. "I'll talk to him, Brindleface. Is he there now?"

"Yes, he's been there all morning."

"I'll fetch him out for the meeting." Fireheart padded across the clearing; as he reached the nursery he heard Bluestar summoning the Clan from the top of the Highrock.

As he entered the nursery he felt a jolt of surprise to meet Tigerclaw coming out. He stepped aside to let the deputy pass him, wondering what he had been doing in the nursery, until he remembered that one of Goldenflower's kits was a dark tabby; Tigerclaw must be their father.

The nursery was warm, and full of comforting milky smells. Goldenflower lay in her nest with Graystripe crouching over her, sniffing at the bundle of kits.

"Are they getting enough milk?" he meowed anxiously. "They're so small."

"That's because they're young," Goldenflower replied patiently. "They'll grow."

Fireheart went over to watch the four kits suckling busily in the warmth of their mother's body. The little dark tabby certainly looked just like Tigerclaw. Graystripe's two were smaller, but now that their coats had dried and fluffed out they looked just like any other healthy kits. One was the same dark gray as Graystripe, while the other had their mother's silvery coat.

"They're beautiful," Fireheart whispered.

"Better than he deserves," snorted Speckletail, pushing past on her way to answer Bluestar's summons.

"Don't listen to Speckletail," mewed Goldenflower when the older queen had gone. She bent over the kits and touched the silvery one with her nose. "She'll be as beautiful as her mother, Graystripe."

"But what if they die?" Graystripe blurted out.

"They're not going to die," Fireheart insisted. "Goldenflower is looking after them."

Goldenflower was gazing at all four kits with equal love and admiration, but Fireheart couldn't help thinking that she was looking tired and strained. Perhaps four kits were too much for her to manage. He pushed the thought away. The bond between a mother and her own kits was strong, he reflected, but Clan loyalty was strong too, and Goldenflower would give the best she could to these kits because they were half ThunderClan, and she had a kind heart.

"Come on." Fireheart gave Graystripe a nudge. "Bluestar has called a meeting. She's going to make Cloudkit an apprentice."

For a heartbeat Graystripe hesitated, and Fireheart thought he was going to refuse to come. Then he pushed himself up and let Fireheart herd him toward the entrance, looking back all the while at his kits.

Outside in the clearing the rest of the Clan had already gathered. Fireheart heard Willowpelt announce happily to Mousefur and Runningwind, "I'll have to move into the nursery soon. I'm expecting kits."

Runningwind murmured his congratulations, while Mousefur gave her friend's ears a joyful lick. Fireheart couldn't help wondering who had fathered these kits, and as he glanced around he noticed Whitestorm watching proudly from a distance. The news of Willowpelt's kits reassured Fireheart. No matter what disasters they had to face, Clan life went on.

With Graystripe at his side, he made his way to the front of the crowd, just below the Highrock. Cloudkit was there, sitting up very straight and importantly beside Brindleface. Tigerclaw was seated close by, a thundercloud of disapproval on his face. Fireheart wondered what had happened now to send the deputy back into his usual bad temper.

"Cats of ThunderClan," Bluestar began from on top of the Highrock. "I've called you here for two reasons, one good and one bad. To begin with the bad, you all know what happened a few days ago, when Silverstream of RiverClan died, and we gave shelter to her kits by Graystripe."

A hostile mutter swept through the crowd of cats. Graystripe crouched down, flinching, and Fireheart pressed comfortingly against him.

"Many cats have asked me what Graystripe's punishment will be," Bluestar went on. "I have thought carefully on this, and I have decided that Silverstream's death is punishment enough. What could any cat do to him that is worse than what he has already suffered?"

Her challenge led to outraged meows of protest. Longtail called out, "We don't want him in the Clan! He's a traitor!"

"If you become Clan leader, Longtail, these decisions will be yours," Bluestar meowed coldly. "Until then, you will respect mine. I say there will be no punishment. However, Graystripe, for three moons you will not attend Gatherings. This is not to punish you, but to make sure there is no risk to you from angry RiverClan cats who might be tempted to break the truce because of what you have done."

Graystripe bowed his head. "I understand, Bluestar. Thank you."

"Don't thank me," meowed the Clan leader. "But work hard and fight well for your Clan from now on. One day you will be a fine mentor for those kits."

Fireheart saw that Graystripe brightened a little at that, as if he suddenly saw something to hope for. Tigerclaw, however, scowled even more fiercely, and Fireheart guessed that he had wanted a harsh punishment for the warrior.

"Now I can turn to a happier duty," meowed Bluestar. "Cloudkit has reached his sixth moon, and he is ready to become an apprentice." She leaped down from the rock and beckoned Cloudkit to her with a flick of her tail. Cloudkit bounced over to her. He was quivering with excitement, his tail stuck straight in the air and his whiskers twitching. His blue eyes sparkled like twin stars.

"Fireheart," Bluestar meowed, "you are ready for another apprentice, and Cloudpaw is your sister's kit. You will be his mentor."

Fireheart stood up, but before he could walk over to the

Highrock Cloudkit scampered to meet him and lifted his head to touch noses.

"*Not yet!*" Fireheart muttered to him through his teeth.

"Fireheart, you know what it is to be one of us, yet born outside the Clan," Bluestar continued, ignoring Cloudkit's impulsiveness. "I rely on you to pass on all you have learned to Cloudpaw, and help him to become a warrior the Clan will be proud of."

"Yes, Bluestar." Fireheart dipped his head respectfully, and at last allowed Cloudpaw to touch noses with him.

"Cloudpaw!" the new apprentice mewed triumphantly. "I'm Cloudpaw!"

"Cloudpaw!" Fireheart felt a surge of pride in his sister's kit as the members of the Clan pressed around to congratulate the new apprentice. The elders, Fireheart noticed, were making a special fuss over him.

But Fireheart also noticed that some of the Clan held back. Tigerclaw never moved from where he sat at the base of the rock, and Longtail stalked over to sit beside him. As Fireheart stood back to let the other cats reach his new apprentice, Darkstripe shouldered past him on his way to the warriors' den.

Fireheart heard his disgusted, deliberately loud meow. "Traitors and kittypets! Is there no decent cat left in this Clan?"

CHAPTER 25

Fireheart paused at the edge of the trees. "Wait," he warned Cloudpaw. "We're near Twolegplace, so we have to be careful. What can you smell?"

Cloudpaw raised his nose obediently and sniffed. He and Fireheart had just been on the first long expedition of his apprenticeship, tracing the Clan boundaries and renewing the scent marks. Now they were near Fireheart's old kittypet home, outside the garden where Cloudpaw's mother Princess lived.

"I can smell lots of cats," Cloudpaw mewed. "I don't recognize any of them, though."

"That's good," Fireheart told him. "They're mostly kittypets, and maybe a loner or two. Not Clan cats." He had caught a trace of Tigerclaw's scent, too, but he didn't draw Cloudpaw's attention to it. He remembered the day long ago, when snow was on the ground, when he had tracked Tigerclaw to this place, and found the deputy's scent mixed with the scents of many strange cats.

Now Tigerclaw's scent proved he had been here again. Fireheart still could not tell whether he had met the other cats, or whether their scents just happened to have crossed. But why should Tigerclaw come so close to the Twolegplace, when he despised Twolegs and everything to do with them?

"Fireheart, can we go and see my mother now?" Cloudpaw demanded.

"Can you smell dogs? Or fresh Twoleg scent?"

Cloudpaw sniffed again and shook his head.

"Then let's go," mewed Fireheart. Looking carefully around, he stepped out into the open. Cloudpaw followed him with exaggerated caution, as if he wanted to show Fireheart how quickly he could learn.

Since his apprentice ceremony the day before, Cloudpaw had been unusually quiet. He was obviously trying very hard to be a good apprentice, listening to everything Fireheart told him with wide-eyed seriousness. But Fireheart couldn't help asking himself how long this uncharacteristic humility would last. Instructing Cloudpaw to wait, he leaped onto the fence and looked down into the garden. Lurid-colored flowers grew against the fence, and in the center of the grass some Twoleg pelts hung on a spiky, leafless tree. "Princess?" he called softly. "Princess, are you there?"

Leaves quivered on a shrub close to the house, and the tabby-and-white figure of Princess stepped delicately onto the grass. When she saw him she let out a delighted meow. "Fireheart!"

Bounding over to the fence, she sprang up beside him and pressed her cheek against his. "Fireheart, it's been such a long time!" she purred. "It's good to see you."

"I've brought someone else, too," Fireheart told her. "Look down there."

Princess peered over the fence to where Cloudpaw sat on the ground below, looking up at her. "Fireheart!" she exclaimed. "That's couldn't be Cloudkit! He's grown so much!"

Without waiting to be told, Cloudpaw leaped for the top of the fence, paws scrabbling madly against the smooth wood. Fireheart leant over and fastened his teeth in his scruff to pull him up the last couple of mouse-lengths so that he could sit on the fence beside his mother.

Cloudpaw looked at Princess with wide blue eyes. "Are you really my mother?" he asked.

"I really am," Princess purred, looking her son up and down admiringly. "Oh, it's so good to see you again, Cloudkit."

"Actually, I'm not Cloudkit," the fluffy white tom announced proudly. "I'm Cloud*paw* now. I'm an apprentice."

"That's wonderful!" Princess began to cover her son with licks, purring so hard that she barely had breath enough for words. "Oh, you're so thin . . . do you get enough to eat? Have you made friends where you are? I hope you do what Fireheart tells you."

Cloudpaw didn't try to answer the flood of questions. He wriggled out from his mother's caresses and edged away from her along the fence. "I'll be a warrior soon," he boasted. "Fireheart's teaching me to fight."

Princess closed her eyes for a moment. "You will have to be so brave," she murmured. For a moment Fireheart thought she was regretting her decision to give her son to the Clan, but then she opened her eyes again and declared, "I'm so proud of both of you!"

Cloudpaw sat even taller as he lapped up her attention. He twisted his head to groom himself with rapid strokes of his small pink tongue, and while he was distracted Fireheart whispered, "Princess, do you ever see any strange cats around here?"

"Strange cats?" She looked puzzled, and Fireheart wondered if there was any point in asking the question. Princess wouldn't know rogues or loners from ordinary ThunderClan cats.

Then Princess shivered. "Yes, I've heard them yowling in the night. My Twoleg gets up and shouts at them."

"You haven't seen a big, dark tabby?" Fireheart asked, his heart starting to pound. "A tom with a scarred muzzle?"

Princess shook her head, eyes wide. "I've only heard them, not seen them."

"If you do see the dark tabby, stay away from him," Fireheart warned. He didn't know what Tigerclaw was up to so far from the camp, if it really *was* Tigerclaw, but he didn't want Princess going near the deputy, just in case.

This made Princess look so scared that he changed the subject, encouraging Cloudpaw to describe his apprentice ceremony, and the expedition they had made around the borders. Soon she was happy again, exclaiming admiringly at everything her son told her.

The sun was past its height when Fireheart meowed, "Cloudpaw, it's time we went home."

Cloudpaw opened his mouth as if he was going to protest,

but he remembered himself in time. "Yes, Fireheart," he mewed obediently. To Princess, he added, "Why don't you come with us? I'd catch mice for you, and you could sleep in my den."

Princess let out a purr of amusement. "I almost wish I could," she replied honestly. "But really I'm happier as a kitty-pet. I don't want to learn to fight, or sleep outdoors in the cold. You'll just have to come and visit me again soon."

"Yes, I will, I promise," Cloudpaw mewed.

"I'll bring him," Fireheart meowed. "And Princess . . ." he added as he prepared to spring to the ground. "If you do see anything . . . odd around here, please tell me about it."

Fireheart stopped on the way back so that they could hunt. By the time he and Cloudpaw reached the ravine, the sun was near to setting, bathing the forest in red light and casting long shadows on the ground.

Cloudpaw was proudly carrying a shrew, which he was going to take to the elders. At least it filled his jaws and put a stop to his endless chatter. Fireheart was feeling worn out after a whole day in his company, but he had to admit he was more impressed than he had expected. Cloudpaw's courage and quick wits promised that he would make an exceptional warrior. As they slipped down the shadowy ravine toward the tunnel, Fireheart paused. An unfamiliar scent tickled his nostrils, drifting to him on the breeze that swept through the forest.

Cloudpaw stopped too and put down the shrew. "Fireheart,

what's that?" He tasted the air, and drew in his breath in a gasp. "You showed me that this morning. It's RiverClan!"

"Very good," Fireheart mewed tensely. He had recognized it himself a heartbeat before Cloudpaw spoke. Looking up toward the top of the ravine, he could make out three cats picking their way slowly through the boulders. "RiverClan it is. And it seems they're on their way here. Now go back to the camp and tell Bluestar. Make sure she understands it's not an attack."

"But I want—" The young apprentice broke off as Fireheart frowned. "Sorry, Fireheart. I'm going." He padded off toward the tunnel entrance, not forgetting to pick up his shrew.

Fireheart stayed where he was. He drew himself up and waited while the three cats drew closer. He recognized Leopardfur, Mistyfoot, and Stonefur. When they were only a couple of tail-lengths away, he asked, "RiverClan, what do you want? Why are you on our land?" Though he had to challenge them for entering ThunderClan territory uninvited, he tried not to sound too hostile. He didn't want to add to any possible trouble with RiverClan.

Leopardfur stopped, with Mistyfoot and Stonefur just behind her. "We come in peace," she meowed. "There are matters to be settled between our Clans. Crookedstar has sent us to talk to your leader."

CHAPTER 26

Fireheart tried to hide his misgivings as he led the three RiverClan warriors down the tunnel and into the camp. Clan cats rarely visited each other's territory, and he wondered what was so urgent that it couldn't wait until the next Gathering.

Alerted by Cloudpaw, Bluestar was already seated at the foot of the Highrock, and Fireheart's apprehension increased when he saw Tigerclaw was beside her.

"Thank you, Cloudpaw." Bluestar dismissed the apprentice as Fireheart approached with the newcomers. "Take your fresh-kill to the elders."

Cloudpaw looked disappointed to be sent away, but he went without protest.

Leopardfur walked up to Bluestar and dipped her head respectfully. "Bluestar, we come to your camp in peace," she began. "There's something we must discuss."

Tigerclaw let out a low disbelieving growl, as if he would rather be ripping the fur off the intruding cats, but Bluestar ignored him. "I can guess what brings you here," she meowed. "But what is there to discuss? What's done is done. Any punishment for Graystripe will be handled by his own Clan."

While she spoke to Leopardfur, Fireheart noticed, her eyes kept straying to Mistyfoot and Stonefur. It was the first time Fireheart had seen his leader with the RiverClan warriors since she had admitted to him that they were her kits. He did not think he was imagining the wistfulness in her blue eyes as she looked at them.

"What you say is true," Leopardfur agreed. "The two young cats were foolish, but Silverstream is dead, and Graystripe's punishment is not for RiverClan to decide. We've come here about the kits."

"What about them?" asked Bluestar.

"They're RiverClan kits," meowed Leopardfur. "We've come to take them home."

"RiverClan kits?" Bluestar's eyes narrowed. "Why do you say that?"

"And how do you know about them?" Tigerclaw demanded, glaring in fury as he sprang to his paws. "Have you been spying? Or did some cat tell you?"

He turned on Fireheart as he spoke, but Fireheart stood his ground, and Mistyfoot kept quiet, not betraying him by so much as a glance. Tigerclaw couldn't know for sure that he had told Mistyfoot, and Fireheart refused to regret what he had done. RiverClan had the right to know.

"Sit down, Tigerclaw," murmured Bluestar. She flashed a look at Fireheart, and he realized that his leader guessed what he had done, as surely as if she had seen him cross the river. But she didn't intend to give him away. "Who knows, perhaps a RiverClan patrol saw what happened? Such things can't be hidden for long. But Leopardfur," she went on, turning back to the visiting deputy, "the kits are also half ThunderClan, and one of our queens is taking good care of them. Why should I give them to you?"

"Kits belong with their mother's Clan," Leopardfur explained. "RiverClan would have raised these kits if Silverstream had lived, without knowing who the father was, and that makes them ours by right."

"Bluestar, you can't send the kits away!" Fireheart couldn't stop himself from interrupting. "They're all Graystripe has to live for."

A growl rumbled once again in Tigerclaw's throat, but it was Bluestar who answered. "Fireheart, be quiet. This doesn't concern you."

"Yes, it does," Fireheart dared to meow. "Graystripe's my friend."

"Silence!" hissed Tigerclaw. "Does your leader have to tell you twice? Graystripe is a traitor to his Clan. He has no right to the kits, or anything else."

Rage flooded through Fireheart. Had Tigerclaw no respect for Graystripe's terrible grief? He whirled on the deputy, held back from springing at him only because cats of another Clan were looking on. Tigerclaw bared his teeth in a snarl.

Bluestar flicked her tail angrily at both of them. "Enough!" she ordered. "Leopardfur, I admit RiverClan has some right to the kits. But so does ThunderClan. Besides, the kits are small and weak. They can't travel yet, especially across the river. It's too dangerous."

Leopardfur's hackles began to rise and her eyes narrowed to slits. "You are just making excuses."

"No," Bluestar insisted. "Not excuses. Would you risk the kits' lives? I'll think about what you have said and discuss it with my warriors, and give you our answer at the next Gathering."

"Now get out of our camp," growled Tigerclaw.

Leopardfur hesitated, as if she would have liked to say more, but it was clear that Bluestar had dismissed her. After a few tense moments, she dipped her head again and turned to go, with Mistyfoot and Stonefur behind her. Tigerclaw stalked across the clearing with them as far as the tunnel.

Left alone with Bluestar, Fireheart felt his anger begin to fade, but he couldn't help renewing his pleas. "We can't let them take the kits! *You* know how Graystripe would feel."

The bleak look Bluestar gave him made him wonder if he had gone too far, but her voice was soft as she replied, "Yes, Fireheart, I know. And I would give much to keep these kits. But how far will RiverClan go to take them? Will they fight? How many ThunderClan warriors would risk their lives for kits that are half-RiverClan?"

Fireheart's fur prickled with fear of the picture she painted. Clans at war over mewling kits—or ThunderClan split against itself as warriors fought among themselves. Was that the fate that StarClan had decreed for his Clan when Spottedleaf warned that water could quench fire? Perhaps it wasn't the floodwater that could destroy ThunderClan, but the cats that came from the territory by the river.

"Have courage, Fireheart," urged Bluestar. "It hasn't come

to a battle just yet. I've won us time until the Gathering, and who knows what will happen before then?"

Fireheart couldn't share her confidence. The problem of the kits would not go away. But he could do nothing except bow his head respectfully and withdraw to the warriors' den.

And now, he thought despairingly, *what am I going to tell Graystripe?*

By the time Silverpelt stretched across the sky, the whole of ThunderClan seemed to know why the RiverClan cats had come. Fireheart guessed that Tigerclaw had told his favourite warriors, and they had spread the news to the rest of the Clan.

As Bluestar had predicted, opinions were divided. Many cats thought that the sooner the Clan was rid of these half-breed kits, the better. But there were still several who were prepared to fight, if only because to give up the kits would mean that RiverClan had won.

Through it all, Graystripe remained silent, brooding in the warriors' den. He left it only once to visit the nursery. When Fireheart brought him fresh-kill, he turned his head away. He hadn't eaten since Silverstream died, as far as Fireheart could tell, and he was looking gaunt and ill.

"Is there anything you can do for him?" Fireheart asked Yellowfang, going to her den as soon as he woke the following day. "He won't eat, he can't sleep. . . ."

The old medicine cat shook her head. "There's no herb to heal a broken heart," she murmured. "Only time will do that."

"I feel so helpless," Fireheart confessed.

"Your friendship helps," Yellowfang rasped. "He might not realize it now, but one day he—"

She broke off as Cinderpaw appeared and dropped a bunch of herbs at Yellowfang's feet. "Are these the right ones?" she asked.

Yellowfang gave the herbs a quick sniff. "Yes, that's right," she mewed. "You can't eat before the ceremony," she added, "but I will. I'm too old and creaky to get to Highstones and back without something to keep me going." She crouched in front of the herbs and began to gulp them down.

"Highstones?" Fireheart echoed. "Ceremony? Cinderpaw, what's going on?"

"It's the half moon tonight," Cinderpaw mewed happily. "Yellowfang and I are going to Mothermouth so I can be made a proper apprentice." She gave a joyful wriggle. Fireheart felt a wave of relief that she seemed to be over her despair after Silverstream's death, and was looking forward again to her new life as a medicine cat. Her eyes had recovered all their old sparkle, but there was a new wisdom and thoughtfulness in their blue depths now.

She was growing up, Fireheart thought, with an odd feeling of regret. His enthusiastic, sometimes scatterbrained apprentice was maturing into a cat of great inner strength and power. He knew he should rejoice in the path StarClan had chosen for her, but part of him wished that they could still go out together on the hunting trail. "I'll come with you tonight, if you like," he offered. "As far as Fourtrees, anyway."

"Oh, would you, Fireheart? Thank you!" Cinderpaw mewed.

"But no farther than Fourtrees," warned Yellowfang, getting to her paws and swiping her tongue around her mouth. "Tonight at Mothermouth is for medicine cats only." She gave herself a brisk shake and led the way through the ferns to the clearing.

As Fireheart followed behind Cinderpaw, he saw Cloudpaw washing himself by the tree stump outside the apprentices' den.

The white tom sprang up as soon as he saw Fireheart and raced across to him. "Where are you going?" he demanded. "Can I come?"

Fireheart glanced at Yellowfang, and when the old cat voiced no objection, he replied, "All right. It'll be a good exercise for you, and we can hunt on the way back." Trotting up the ravine behind the she-cats, he explained to Cloudpaw where they were going, and how Yellowfang and Cinderpaw would carry on alone to Highstones. Deep within the tunnel known as Mothermouth was the Moonstone, which glittered dazzling white when the moon shone upon it. Cinderpaw's ceremony would take place in its unearthly light.

"What happens then?" Cloudpaw asked curiously.

"The ceremonies are secret," growled Yellowfang. "So don't ask Cinderpaw when she comes back. She isn't allowed to tell you."

"But every cat knows that she'll receive special powers from StarClan," Fireheart added.

"Special powers!" Cloudpaw's eyes grew round, and he

gazed at Cinderpaw as if he expected her to start uttering prophecies there and then.

"Don't worry; I'll still be the same old Cinderpaw," she assured him with an amused purr. "That won't ever change."

The sun grew hot as the four cats made their way to Fourtrees. Fireheart was thankful for the deep shade under the trees and the cool freshness of long grass and clumps of fern as they brushed against his orange fur. All his senses were alert, and he kept Cloudpaw busy, scenting the air and reporting on what he could smell. Fireheart hadn't forgotten the attack from ShadowClan and WindClan. They had been defeated once, but that didn't mean they wouldn't try again to kill Brokentail. Besides that, Fireheart was half expecting trouble from RiverClan over Graystripe's kits. He sighed. On a beautiful morning like this, with fresh green on the trees and prey practically leaping out of the bushes and waiting to be caught, it was hard to be thinking of attacks and death.

In spite of his worries, the group of cats reached Fourtrees without trouble. As they slid through the bushes down into the hollow, Fireheart dropped back to match Cinderpaw's uneven steps. "Are you sure about what you're doing?" he asked quietly. "Is it what you really want?"

"Of course! Don't you see, Fireheart?" Cinderpaw's eyes searched his, suddenly serious. "I have to learn as much as I can so that no cat dies because I couldn't save them, like Silverstream."

Fireheart flinched. He longed for a way to persuade his friend that Silverstream's death was not her fault, but he knew he would be wasting his breath. "And will that make you happy? You know medicine cats can't ever have kits," he reminded her, thinking of how Yellowfang had been forced to give up Brokentail and keep her bond with him a secret.

Cinderpaw purred to comfort him. "The whole Clan will be my kits," she promised. "Even the warriors. Yellowfang says they have about as much sense as newborns sometimes!" She took a pace forward that brought her to Fireheart's side, and rubbed her face affectionately against his. "But you'll always be my best friend, Fireheart. I'll never forget you were my first mentor."

Fireheart licked her ear. "Good-bye, Cinderpaw," he mewed softly.

"I'm not going away forever," Cinderpaw protested. "I'll be back by sunset tomorrow."

But Fireheart knew that in some ways, Cinderpaw *was* going away forever. When she returned, she would have new powers and responsibilities, given to her not by a Clan leader, but by StarClan. Side by side, they crossed the hollow beneath the four massive oaks and climbed the far slope to where Yellowfang and Cloudpaw were already waiting. The vast open moor stretched in front of them, a cool wind bending the sturdy clumps of heather.

"Won't WindClan attack you if you go through their territory?" Cloudpaw mewed anxiously.

"All the Clans may pass through safely on the way to Highstones," Yellowfang told him. "And no warrior would dare to attack medicine cats. StarClan forbid!" Turning to

Cinderpaw, she asked, "Are you ready?"

"Yes, I'm coming." Cinderpaw gave Fireheart one final lick and followed the old cat out onto the springy moorland grass. The breeze ruffled her fur as she limped swiftly away without a backward glance.

Fireheart watched her go, his heart heavy. He knew his friend was at the beginning of a new and happier life, but all the same he could not stifle a pang of bittersweet regret for the life that could have been hers.

Fireheart watched the sun climbing the trees. "Tigerclaw wants me to send Cloudpaw on a solo hunting mission today," he meowed to Graystripe.

The big gray warrior looked up in surprise. "That's early, isn't it? He's barely been made apprentice."

Fireheart shrugged. "Tigerclaw thinks he's ready. He told me to follow him and see how he does, anyway. Would you like to come and help?"

It was the morning after Cinderpaw had returned from Mothermouth. Fireheart had met her as she slipped down the ravine in the twilight. Though she greeted him affectionately, they both knew she could not tell him what she had gone through. Her face still wore a look of rapture, and the moon itself seemed to shine from her eyes. Fireheart tried hard not to feel that he had lost her to an unknown path.

Now he sat beside the nettle patch, enjoying a juicy mouse. Graystripe, crouching nearby, had taken a magpie from the pile of fresh-kill but had barely touched it.

"No, thanks, Fireheart," he mewed. "I promised Goldenflower I'd look in on the kits. Their eyes are open now," he added with a touch of pride.

Fireheart guessed that Goldenflower would rather that Graystripe stayed away, but he knew Graystripe would never be persuaded to leave his kits. "Okay," he meowed. "I'll see you later." Swallowing the last morsel of mouse, he went to find Cloudpaw.

Tigerclaw had been busy that morning, sending out one patrol with Whitestorm to renew the scent markings along the RiverClan boundary, and another with Sandstorm to hunt around Snakerocks, so he had neglected to tell Fireheart where Cloudpaw should go for his hunting mission. Fireheart hadn't felt the need to remind him.

"You can make for Twolegplace," he meowed to Cloudpaw. "Then you won't get in the way of the other patrols. You won't see me, but I'll be watching you. I'll meet you by Princess's fence."

"Can I talk to her if she's there?" Cloudpaw asked.

"Okay, as long as you've caught plenty of fresh-kill by then. But you're *not* to go looking for her in the Twoleg gardens. Or their nests."

"I won't." Cloudpaw's eyes gleamed, and his snowy fur was fluffed up with excitement. Fireheart couldn't help remembering how nervous he had felt before his own first assessment; Cloudpaw, in contrast, was bursting with confidence.

"Off you go, then," Fireheart meowed. "Try to get there by sunhigh." He watched the young apprentice race off toward the tunnel. "Pace yourself!" he called after him. "You've a long way to go!"

But Cloudpaw didn't slow down as he disappeared into the gorse. Shrugging, more amused than annoyed, Fireheart glanced around at Graystripe, but his friend was nowhere to be seen. His half-eaten magpie was left beside the nettle patch. *He must be in the nursery already*, Fireheart thought, and turned to follow Cloudpaw out of the camp.

The apprentice's scent was strong, showing where the young cat had ranged back and forth through the woods in search of prey. A flurry of loose feathers told of a caught thrush, and specks of blood on the grass showed that a mouse had fallen to his claws. Not far from the edge of the Tallpines, Fireheart found the spot where Cloudpaw had buried his fresh-kill so he could return for it later.

Impressed that his apprentice was hunting well so early in his training, Fireheart put on speed, hoping to catch up and watch him stalking his prey. But before he reached Two-legplace he caught sight of Cloudpaw racing back along his own scent trail, his fur bristling and a wild light in his eyes.

"Cloudpaw!" Fireheart ran forward to meet him, his body tingling with sudden fear.

Cloudpaw skidded to a halt, his claws scattering pine needles, barely managing to avoid a collision with Fireheart. "Something's wrong!" he panted.

"What?" Icy claws clutched at Fireheart's belly. "Not Princess?"

"No, nothing like that. But I saw Tigerclaw, and there were

some strange cats with him."

"At Twolegplace?" Fireheart meowed sharply. "Where we smelled them the day we visited Princess?"

"That's right." Cloudpaw's whiskers twitched. "They were huddled together, just on the edge of the trees. I tried to get closer to hear what they were saying, but I was afraid they would see my white fur. So I came to find you."

"You did the right thing," Fireheart told him, his mind racing frantically. "What were these cats like? Did they have a Clan scent?"

"No." Cloudpaw wrinkled his nose. "They smelled of crowfood."

"And you didn't recognize them?"

Cloudpaw shook his head. "They were thin and hungry-looking. Their fur was all mangy. They were *horrible*, Fireheart!"

"And they were talking to Tigerclaw." Fireheart frowned. That was the detail that worried him. He could take a guess at who the strange cats were—the former ShadowClan warriors who had left their Clan with Brokentail when he had been driven out. They had caused trouble before, and there were no other rogues that Fireheart knew of in the forest now—but what Tigerclaw was doing with them was a mystery.

"All right," he mewed to Cloudpaw. "Follow me. And keep as quiet as if you were creeping up on a mouse." He headed cautiously toward Twolegplace, stalking from paw to paw over the softly cracking pine needles. Long before he reached the edge of the forest he picked up the strong reek of cats.

The only one he could identify was Tigerclaw, and as if the thought had summoned him the deputy came into sight at that moment, bounding through the trees in the direction of the camp.

There was no undergrowth to provide cover under the pine trees. All Fireheart and Cloudpaw could do was flatten themselves in one of the deep furrows carved out by the Treecut monster and pray to StarClan they wouldn't be seen.

A group of scrawny warriors poured after Tigerclaw. Their jaws were parted eagerly and their eyes blazed. All the cats were so intent on the trail that they never noticed Fireheart and Cloudpaw, crouching in their scant cover a few rabbit-hops away.

Fireheart lifted his head and watched them race out of sight. For a moment he was frozen with horror and disbelief. There were more of them, he realized, than the group who had left ShadowClan with Brokentail moons before. Tigerclaw must have recruited more loners from somewhere. And he was leading them straight toward the ThunderClan camp!

CHAPTER 27

"Run!" Fireheart ordered his apprentice. "Run like you've never run before!"

Already he was pelting through the trees, not waiting to see if Cloudpaw could keep up. There was just a faint hope that he could outpace Tigerclaw and the rogues, and warn the Clan.

He sent out all those patrols this morning, Fireheart thought, fighting back panic. *And he told me to follow Cloudpaw. He left the camp with barely a warrior to defend it. He's been planning this all along!*

Fireheart hurtled through the trees, his powerful muscles bunching and stretching as he drove himself on. But when he reached the ravine, he realized that he had not run fast enough. The hindquarters and tails of the last of the rogues were just vanishing into the gorse tunnel.

Launching himself down the steep side of the ravine, with Cloudpaw scrabbling down behind him, Fireheart let out a yowl. "ThunderClan! Enemies! Attack!" He hurled himself into the tunnel and at the same moment he heard another yowl from the camp ahead.

"To me, ThunderClan!"

It was the familiar battle cry, but the voice was Tigerclaw's. A thought flickered into Fireheart's shocked mind: What if he had made a mistake? What if the rogues had been *chasing* Tigerclaw, not following him?

He burst into the clearing just as Tigerclaw whirled on the band of rogues, who scattered, yowling, from his attack. The deputy certainly looked as if he were trying to drive enemies from the camp, but Fireheart was close enough to see that his claws were sheathed. His heart plummeted. Tigerclaw's brave defense was all a sham. He had brought these enemy cats here, but he was cunning enough to conceal his own treachery.

There was no time for any more thought. However they had come here, the rogue cats were now attacking the camp. Fireheart turned swiftly to Cloudpaw.

"Go and find the patrols and tell them to come back," he ordered. "Whitestorm is somewhere along the RiverClan boundary, and Sandstorm went to Snakerocks."

"Yes, Fireheart." Cloudpaw raced back into the tunnel.

Fireheart sprang at the nearest rogue, a dark mottled tabby, and raked his claws down his side. The rogue snarled and twisted toward him, paws splayed for attack. He tried to pin Fireheart down; Fireheart's hindpaws pummeled his belly, and the rogue broke away howling.

Fireheart scrambled to his paws and crouched with tail lashing and fur bristling as he looked around for another enemy. Outside the entrance to the nursery, Graystripe was wrestling a rogue with a pale coat, the two of them rolling over and over as they tried to get hold with teeth and claws. Brindleface and Speckletail were fighting against a warrior twice their size. Near the warriors' den, Mousefur dug her front claws into the shoulder of a huge tabby, while her back claws shredded his flank.

Then Fireheart froze with shock. At the other side of the clearing, Brokentail had pounced on his guard, Dustpelt, fastening his teeth in the younger cat's throat. Dustpelt was struggling furiously to free himself. Though Brokentail was blind, he was still a formidable fighter, and he hung on. Fireheart realized with dread that he was fighting on the side of his old rogue companions, the cats who had left ShadowClan with him—not for ThunderClan, who had risked so much to defend him when he was injured and alone.

A tiny picture flashed into Fireheart's mind, of Tigerclaw and Brokentail lying side by side, sharing tongues. That had not been evidence of the deputy's compassion. Tigerclaw had been planning this with the former ShadowClan tyrant!

There was no time to think about that now. Fireheart plunged across the clearing to help Dustpelt, but before he got halfway he was bowled over by a rogue cat. His flank stung as claws raked down it. Green eyes glared a mouse-length from his own. Fireheart bared his fangs and tried to bite down into the enemy's shoulder, but the rogue cat batted him away. Claws ripped into his ear. His belly was exposed and he couldn't twist free. Suddenly his attacker let out a wail and released him. Fireheart caught a glimpse of the young apprentice Thornpaw with his teeth fastened into the rogue's tail; the rogue dragged him through the dust until Thornpaw released him and the enemy fled.

Panting, Fireheart scrambled to his paws. "Thanks," he gasped. "Well done."

Thornpaw nodded briefly before racing off to where Graystripe still battled in front of the nursery. Fireheart looked around again. Dustpelt had vanished and Brokentail was stumbling farther into the clearing, letting out a weird wailing that struck a chill into Fireheart's heart. Even blind, the former ShadowClan leader possessed a terrifying power that seemed driven by something more than mortal.

The clearing heaved with struggling cats, but as Fireheart poised himself to rejoin the fray he realized something that sent an even colder pang of fear along his spine. Where was Bluestar?

In a heartbeat, Fireheart realized that he couldn't see Tigerclaw either. Every instinct told him that danger was looming. He dodged around Willowpelt, who was clinging to the back of a much bigger rogue, her teeth fastened in his ear, and made for Bluestar's den. To his relief, as he approached the entrance he heard Bluestar meow from inside, "We can worry about that later, Tigerclaw. The Clan needs us now."

For a few heartbeats there was no reply. Then Fireheart heard Bluestar's voice again, surprised. "Tigerclaw? What are you doing?"

An answering snarl. "Remember me to StarClan, Bluestar."

"Tigerclaw, what is this?" Bluestar's meow was sharper

now, edged with anger, not fear. "I'm the leader of your Clan, or have you forgotten that?"

"Not for much longer," Tigerclaw growled. "I'm going to kill you, and kill you again. As many times as it takes for you to join StarClan forever. It's time for *me* to lead this Clan!"

Bluestar's answering protest was suddenly cut short by the sound of paws thudding against the hard floor of the den, followed by a dreadful snarling.

CHAPTER 28

❧

Fireheart sprang forward and burst through the curtain of lichen. Tigerclaw and Bluestar were writhing on the floor of the den. Bluestar's claws scored again and again across Tigerclaw's shoulder, but the deputy's greater weight kept her pinned down in the soft sand. Tigerclaw's fangs were buried in her throat, and his powerful claws raked her back.

"Traitor!" Fireheart yowled. He flung himself at Tigerclaw, slashing at his eyes. The deputy reared back, forced to release his grip on Bluestar's throat. Fireheart felt his claws rip through the deputy's ear, spraying blood into the air.

Bluestar scrambled to the side of the den, looking half stunned. Fireheart could not tell how badly hurt she was. Pain lanced through him as Tigerclaw gashed his side with a blow from his powerful hindpaws. Fireheart's paws skidded in the sand and he lost his balance, hitting the ground with Tigerclaw on top of him.

The deputy's amber eyes blazed into his. "Mousedung!" he hissed. "I'll *flay* you, Fireheart. I've waited a long time for this."

Fireheart summoned every scrap of skill and strength he

possessed. He knew Tigerclaw could kill him, but in spite of that he felt strangely free. The lies and the need for deceit were over. The secrets—Bluestar's and Tigerclaw's—were all out in the open. There was only the clean danger of battle.

He aimed a blow at Tigerclaw's throat, but the deputy swung his head to one side and Fireheart's claws scraped harmlessly through thick tabby fur. But the blow had loosened Tigerclaw's grip on him. Fireheart rolled away, narrowly avoiding a killing bite to his neck.

"Kittypet!" Tigerclaw taunted, flexing his haunches to pounce again. "Come and find out how a *real* warrior fights." He threw himself at Fireheart, but at the last moment Fireheart darted aside. As Tigerclaw tried to turn in the narrow den, his paws slipped on a splash of blood and he crashed awkwardly onto one side.

At once Fireheart saw his chance. His claws sliced down to open a gash in Tigerclaw's belly. Blood welled up, soaking into the deputy's fur. He let out a high-pitched caterwaul. Fireheart pounced on him, raking claws across his belly again, and fastening his teeth into Tigerclaw's neck. The deputy struggled vainly to free himself, his thrashing growing weaker as the blood flowed.

Fireheart let go of his neck, planting one paw on Tigerclaw's outstretched foreleg, and the other on his chest. "Bluestar!" he called. "Help me hold him down!"

Bluestar was crouching behind him in her moss-lined nest. Blood trickled down her forehead, but that did not alarm Fireheart as much as the look in her eyes. They were a vague, cloudy blue, and she stared horror-struck in front of her as if she was witnessing the destruction of everything she had ever worked for.

When Fireheart spoke, she jumped like a cat woken suddenly from sleep. Moving with dreamlike slowness, she crossed the den and pinned herself across Tigerclaw's hindquarters, trapping him. Even with wounds that would have stunned a lesser cat, Tigerclaw still fought to free himself. His amber eyes burned with hatred as he spat curses at Fireheart and Bluestar.

A shadow fell across the entrance to the den and Fireheart heard hoarse, ragged breathing. He turned his head, expecting to see one of the invaders, but it was Graystripe. Dismay flooded over Fireheart at the sight of his friend. He was bleeding heavily from his flank and one foreleg, and blood bubbled from his mouth as he stammered, "Bluestar, we—" He broke off, staring. "Fireheart, what's happening?"

"Tigerclaw attacked Bluestar," Fireheart told him quickly. "We were right all along. He is a traitor. He brought the rogues to attack us."

Graystripe went on staring, and then shook himself as if he had just climbed out of deep water. "We're losing the fight," he meowed. "There are too many of them. Bluestar, we need your help."

The leader looked at him but did not reply. Fireheart could see that her eyes were still dull and unseeing, as if the discovery of the truth about Tigerclaw had bruised her spirit beyond repair.

"I'll come," Fireheart offered. "Graystripe, can you help Bluestar hold on to Tigerclaw? We'll deal with him when the battle's over."

"You can try, kittypet," Tigerclaw sneered through a mouthful of sand.

Graystripe limped across the den and took Fireheart's place, planting his claws on Tigerclaw's chest. For a heartbeat Fireheart hesitated, uncertain that wounded Graystripe and Bluestar in a state of shock would be a match for Tigerclaw. But the deputy was still losing blood, and his struggles were definitely getting weaker. Swiftly Fireheart turned and raced outside again.

At first glance the clearing seemed to be filled with rogues, as if all the ThunderClan warriors had been driven out. Then Fireheart caught a glimpse of familiar shapes here and there—Longtail squirming underneath a huge tabby tom; Patchpelt scrabbling just out of reach of a skinny gray outlaw, whirling around to rake his nose with outstretched claws before he hurled himself at the rogue's belly.

Fireheart tried to collect his strength. The fight with Tigerclaw had exhausted him, and the wounds where the deputy had clawed him burned like fire. He did not know how long he could keep on. He rolled over instinctively as a ginger she-cat tried to drive her claws into his back. Out of the corner of his eye, he saw a lithe, blue-gray body racing across the clearing, yowling a challenge.

Bluestar! he thought in astonishment, and wondered what had happened to Tigerclaw. Then he realized that the warrior he had seen was not Bluestar. It was Mistyfoot!

With a massive effort Fireheart tore free of the ginger cat and scrambled to his paws. RiverClan warriors were pouring out of the tunnel. Leopardfur, Stonefur, Blackclaw . . . After them came Whitestorm and the rest of his patrol. They were strong and full of energy, and they fell on the invaders with claws outstretched and tails lashing in fury.

Terrified by the sudden appearance of reinforcements, the rogue cats scattered. The ginger she-cat fled with a shocked howl. Others followed her. Fireheart staggered a few paces in pursuit, hissing and spitting to speed them on their way, but there was no need. Surprised when they thought their victory was certain, and leaderless now that Tigerclaw had been caught, the rogues had no fight left in them.

Within a few heartbeats, they were gone. The only enemy remaining was Brokentail, bleeding badly from head and shoulders. The blind cat scrabbled on the ground, mewling faintly like a sick kit.

The RiverClan cats were gathering together again with murmurs of concern as Fireheart limped across to them. "Thank you," he meowed. "I've never been so glad to see any cat in my life."

"I recognized some of the old ShadowClan warriors," Leopardfur told him gravely. "The ones who left with Brokenstar."

"Yes." Fireheart didn't want to say anything yet about Tigerclaw's involvement. "How did you know we needed help?" he asked, puzzled.

"We didn't," replied Mistyfoot. "We came to talk to Bluestar about—"

"Not now," Leopardfur interrupted, though Fireheart guessed that Mistyfoot was going to say, "about the kits." "ThunderClan needs time to recover." She dipped her head graciously toward Fireheart. "We are glad to have helped. Tell your leader we will return soon."

"Yes, I will," Fireheart promised. "And thanks again." He watched the RiverClan cats leave, then looked around, feeling his shoulders sag with tiredness. The clearing was littered with blood and fur. Yellowfang and Cinderpaw were beginning to examine the injured cats. Though Fireheart hadn't noticed them in the fighting, they both bore the marks of enemy claws.

He took a deep breath. It was time to deal with Tigerclaw, but he did not know if he could summon the strength. His wounds throbbed with pain, and every muscle in his body shrieked a protest with each step. As he limped toward Bluestar's den, a voice sounded behind him. "Fireheart! What happened?"

He turned to see Sandstorm, newly returned at the head of her hunting patrol, with Cloudpaw panting just behind her. She was staring around the clearing as if she couldn't believe what she saw.

Fireheart shook his head wearily. "Brokentail's outlaws," he grunted.

"*Again?*" Sandstorm spat with disgust. "Maybe Bluestar will think twice about sheltering Brokentail now."

"It's more complicated than that." Fireheart felt unable to explain right then. "Sandstorm, will you do something for me, and not ask questions?"

Sandstorm gave him a suspicious look. "Depends what it is."

"Go to Bluestar's den and deal with what you find there. Better take another warrior too—Brackenfur, will you go? Bluestar will tell you what to do."

At least, I hope so, Fireheart added to himself as Sandstorm, still frowning, jerked her head at Brackenfur and headed for the Highrock. Out of everything that had happened, what disturbed Fireheart most was how Bluestar seemed to have lost her will to lead her Clan.

Fireheart stood numbly in the center of the clearing, watching as Yellowfang examined Brokentail and then began half pushing, half dragging him toward her den. The former ShadowClan leader was barely conscious, and a trickle of blood ran from the corner of his mouth. *She obviously still cares for him*, Fireheart thought in confusion. *Even after all this, she can't forget he was once her kit.*

Turning away from Yellowfang, Fireheart saw Sandstorm emerging from the den beneath the Highrock. She was followed by Tigerclaw, who struggled forward with an odd, lurching gait. His fur was matted with dust and blood, and one eye was half closed. He stumbled to a halt and collapsed in front of the rock.

Brackenfur trailed him closely, alert for any sign that the deputy intended to attack or flee. Behind him came Bluestar.

Her head was drooping and her tail dragged in the dust. Fireheart's worst fears flooded back. The strong leader Fireheart had respected seemed to have vanished, leaving instead this frail, wounded cat.

Last of all, Graystripe limped out of the den and sank down on his side in the shade of the Highrock. Cinderpaw hurried over to him and began to inspect his wounds with an anxious frown.

Bluestar raised her head and looked around. "Come here, all of you," she rasped, beckoning with a flick of her tail. While the rest of the Clan were gathering, Fireheart padded over to Cinderpaw. "Can you give Tigerclaw anything for his wounds?" he asked. "Something to ease the pain?" He thought he had wanted to defeat Tigerclaw more than anything, but now he found he could not bear the sight of the once-great warrior bleeding to death in the dust.

Cinderpaw looked up from her examination of Graystripe. To Fireheart's relief, she didn't challenge his request for her to treat the treacherous deputy. "Sure," she meowed. "I'll fetch something for Graystripe as well." She limped away in the direction of Yellowfang's den.

The Clan cats had taken their places by the time she returned. Fireheart could see them looking at one another, uneasily wondering what all this might mean.

Cinderpaw limped over with a wad of herbs in her mouth. She dropped some of them beside Tigerclaw, and gave the rest to Graystripe. The deputy sniffed the leaves suspiciously and then began to chew them.

Bluestar watched him for a moment and then began to speak. "I present you with Tigerclaw, now a prisoner. He—"

A chorus of worried murmurs interrupted her. The Clan cats were looking at each other in shock and dismay. Fireheart could see they did not understand what was happening.

"A prisoner?" Darkstripe echoed. "Tigerclaw's your deputy. What has he done?"

"I'll tell you." Bluestar's voice sounded more even now, but Fireheart could see the effort it was costing her. "Just now, in my den, Tigerclaw attacked me. He would have killed me if Fireheart hadn't arrived in time."

The sounds of protest and disbelief swelled even louder. From the back of the crowd, an elder let out an eerie wailing. Darkstripe got to his paws. He was one of Tigerclaw's strongest supporters, Fireheart knew, but even he was looking uncertain. "There must be some mistake," he blustered.

Bluestar raised her chin. "Do you think I can't tell when a cat tries to murder me?" she enquired dryly.

"But Tigerclaw—"

Fireheart sprang up. "Tigerclaw is a traitor to the Clan!" he spat. "He brought the rogue cats here today."

Darkstripe rounded on him. "He'd never have done that. Prove it, kittypet!"

Fireheart glanced at Bluestar. She nodded and beckoned him forward. "Fireheart, tell the Clan what you know. Everything."

Fireheart padded slowly to her side. Now that the moment for revealing everything had come, he felt strangely reluctant.

It was as though he were pulling down the Highrock, and nothing would ever be the same again. "Cats of ThunderClan," he began. His voice squeaked like a kit's, and he paused to control it. "Cats of ThunderClan, do you remember when Redtail died? Tigerclaw told you that Oakheart killed him, but he was lying. It was Tigerclaw who killed Redtail!"

"How do you know?" That was Longtail, with the usual sneer on his face. "You weren't at the battle."

"I know because I talked to someone who was," Fireheart replied steadily. "Ravenpaw told me."

"Oh, very useful!" growled Darkstripe. "Ravenpaw's dead. You can tell us he said anything, and nobody can prove you wrong."

Fireheart hesitated. He had kept the truth about Ravenpaw's escape a secret to protect him from Tigerclaw, but now that Tigerclaw was a prisoner, there could be no more danger. And he needed to reveal everything. "Ravenpaw isn't dead," he explained quietly. "I took him away after Tigerclaw tried to kill him for knowing too much."

More uproar, as each cat yowled their questions and protests. While Fireheart waited for them to settle down again, he glanced at Tigerclaw. As Cinderpaw's herbs did their healing work, the huge tabby had begun to recover some of his strength. He pushed himself onto his haunches and sat staring out over the crowd with eyes like stones, as if he were challenging any cat to come too close. The news about Ravenpaw must have shocked him, but he did not show it by a single twitch of his whiskers.

When the turmoil showed no sign of dying down, Whitestorm raised his voice. "Quiet! Let Fireheart speak."

Fireheart dipped his head in thanks to the older warrior. "Ravenpaw told me that Oakheart died when rocks fell on him. Redtail fled from the rockfall, and ran straight into Tigerclaw. Tigerclaw pounced on him and killed him."

"It's true." Graystripe raised his head from where he still lay in the shade, with Cinderpaw pressing herbs to his wounds. "I was there when Ravenpaw told Fireheart all this."

"And I've spoken to cats from RiverClan," Fireheart added. "They tell the same story, that Oakheart died in a rockfall."

Fireheart expected more noise then, but it never came. An eerie hush had fallen on the Clan. Cats were staring at one another as if they could find a reason for these terrible revelations in the faces of their friends.

"Tigerclaw expected to be made deputy then," Fireheart went on. "But Bluestar chose Lionheart instead. Then Lionheart died fighting ShadowClan, and at last Tigerclaw achieved his ambition. But being deputy wasn't enough for him. I . . . I think that he even laid a trap for Bluestar beside the Thunderpath, but Cinderpaw was caught in it instead." He glanced at Cinderpaw as he spoke, to see her eyes widen and her jaws open in a gasp of surprise.

Bluestar too looked astonished. "Fireheart told me his suspicions," she murmured. Her voice shook. "I didn't—I couldn't—believe him. I trusted Tigerclaw." She bowed her head. "I was wrong."

"But how could he expect to be made leader if he killed

you?" asked Mousefur. "The Clan would never support him."

"I think that's why he planned this attack the way he did," Fireheart ventured. "I guess he meant us to think that one of the outlaws killed Bluestar. After all"—Fireheart's voice grew hard—"who would expect Tigerclaw, the loyal deputy, to lay a claw on his leader?" He fell silent. His whole body was quivering and he felt as limp as a newborn kit.

"Bluestar," Whitestorm spoke up. "What will happen to Tigerclaw now?"

His question set off a crescendo of furious yowling from the Clan.

"Kill him!"

"Blind him!"

"Drive him out of the forest!"

Bluestar sat motionless, her eyes closed. Fireheart could feel the pain coming off her in waves, the bitter shock of betrayal as she discovered that the deputy she had trusted for so long was black at heart. "Tigerclaw," she meowed at last, "have you anything to say in your defense?"

Tigerclaw swung his head around and fixed her with a yellow glare. "Defend myself to *you*, you gutless excuse for a warrior? What sort of a leader are you? Keeping the peace with other Clans. *Helping* them! You barely punished Fireheart and Graystripe for feeding RiverClan, and you sent them to fetch WindClan home! I would have never shown such kittypet softness. I would have brought back the days of TigerClan. *I* would have made ThunderClan great!"

"And how many cats would have died for it?" Bluestar

murmured, almost to herself. Fireheart wondered if she was thinking of Thistleclaw, the arrogant, bloodthirsty warrior she could not have let become deputy instead of her. "If you have nothing else to say, then I sentence you to exile," the leader announced, her voice cracking. Every word seemed to be dragged out of her. "You will leave ThunderClan territory now, and if any cat sees you here after sunrise tomorrow, they have my permission to kill you."

"Kill me?" Tigerclaw spoke now, snarling his defiance. "I'd like to see any of them try."

"Fireheart beat you," Graystripe called out.

"Fireheart." Tigerclaw turned his pale amber eyes on his enemy, and Fireheart felt his fur prickle at the look of unfettered hatred there. "Cross my path again, you stinking furball, and we'll see who's the stronger."

Fireheart leaped to his paws, anger lending him energy. "Anytime, Tigerclaw," he spat.

"No," Bluestar growled. "No more fighting. Tigerclaw, leave our sight."

Slowly Tigerclaw got up. His massive head swiveled back and forth as he scanned the crowd of cats. "Don't think I'm finished," he hissed. "I'll be a leader yet. And any cat who comes with me will be well looked after. Darkstripe?"

Fireheart craned his neck to see Tigerclaw's chief follower. He waited for Darkstripe to get up and go to Tigerclaw, but the sleek tabby remained in his place, his shoulders hunched wretchedly.

"I trusted you, Tigerclaw," he protested. "I thought you

were the finest warrior in the forest. But you plotted with that . . . that *tyrant*"—Fireheart knew he was speaking of Brokentail— "and you said nothing to me. And now you expect me to come with you?" He looked away deliberately.

Tigerclaw shrugged. "I needed Brokentail's help to make contact with the rogue cats. If you choose to take this personally, that's your problem," he growled. "Longtail?"

Longtail gave a nervous start. "Come with you, Tigerclaw? Into exile?" His voice shook. "I . . . no, I can't. I'm loyal to ThunderClan!"

And you're a coward, Fireheart added silently, catching the fear-scent as Longtail shrank back into the crowd of cats.

For the first time, a look of uncertainty flickered across Tigerclaw's face, as the few cats he had trusted turned him down. "What about you, Dustpelt?" he demanded. "You'll have richer pickings with me than ever you will in ThunderClan."

The young brown tabby got deliberately to his paws and picked his way through the surrounding cats until he stood in front of Tigerclaw. "I looked up to you," he meowed in a clear, level voice. "I wanted to be like you. But Redtail was my mentor. I owe him more than any cat. And you killed him." Grief and fury made his limbs shake, but he kept going. "You killed him and betrayed the Clan. I'd rather die than follow you." He turned and stalked away.

A murmur of appreciation rose from the listening cats, and Fireheart heard Whitestorm whisper, "Well said, youngster."

"Tigerclaw," Bluestar broke in. "No more of this. Go now."

Tigerclaw drew himself up to his full height, his eyes blazing in cold fury. "I'm going. But I'll be back; you can be sure of that. I'll be revenged on you all!" He padded unevenly away from the Highrock. As he drew close to Fireheart he paused, drawing his lips back in a snarl. "And as for you . . ." he hissed. "Keep your eyes open, Fireheart. Keep your ears pricked. Keep looking behind you. Because one day I'll find you, and then you'll be crowfood."

"You're crowfood now," Fireheart retorted, struggling to hide the fear that crawled along his spine.

Tigerclaw spat, then turned and walked away. The Clan cats parted to let him through, every eye tracking him as he went. The great warrior was not completely steady on his paws—his wounds must be bothering him in spite of Cinderpaw's herbs, Fireheart realized—but he did not stop or look back. The gorse tunnel swallowed him up and he was gone.

CHAPTER 29

As he watched his defeated enemy disappear, Fireheart could not summon up the least sense of triumph. Surprising himself, he even felt a pang of regret. Tigerclaw could have been a warrior whose deeds would have been told to generations of kits—if only he had chosen loyalty over ambition. Fireheart could almost wail aloud at the waste.

All around him talk was beginning to break out again, as cats mewed urgently to one another about the startling events. "Who'll be deputy now?" he heard Runningwind ask.

Fireheart glanced at Bluestar to see if she meant to make an announcement, but she was slipping around the side of the Highrock toward her den. Her head was down and her paws dragged as if she were ill. There would be no announcement yet.

"I think Fireheart should be deputy!" Cloudpaw declared, bouncing with excitement. "He'd do a great job!"

"Fireheart?" Darkstripe's eyes narrowed. "A kittypet?"

"And what's wrong with being a kittypet?" Cloudpaw bristled in front of the much bigger warrior.

Fireheart was about to haul himself to his paws and intervene when Whitestorm pushed between Darkstripe and the young apprentice. "That's enough," he growled. "Bluestar will tell us who she chooses before moonhigh. That's the tradition."

Fireheart let his shoulders relax as Cloudpaw scampered off to join the other apprentices. He could see that his apprentice didn't realize the seriousness of what had happened. The older warriors, the ones who had known Tigerclaw well, were looking at one another as if their world had just come to an end.

"Well now, Fireheart." Graystripe looked up as Fireheart walked over to join his friend and Cinderpaw. "Would you *want* to be deputy?" There was pain in his eyes, and blood still trickled from his mouth, yet he looked more alive than Fireheart had seen him since Silverstream's death, as if the battle and the exposing of Tigerclaw's villainy had taken his mind off his grief for a moment.

Fireheart couldn't prevent a faint prickle of excitement from creeping along his spine. Deputy of ThunderClan! Then he realized how hard a job it would be, to pull these shattered cats together and mold them into a Clan again. "No," he told Graystripe. "And Bluestar would never choose me." He got up, shaking his head as if to put these thoughts out of his mind. "How are you feeling?" he asked. "Are those wounds very bad?"

"He'll be fine," meowed Cinderpaw. "But his tongue was scratched, and it's still bleeding. I don't know what to do for a scratched tongue. Fireheart, would you fetch Yellowfang for me?"

"Sure."

The last Fireheart had seen of Yellowfang, she had been dragging Brokentail into her den; she had not reappeared for the condemning of Tigerclaw. He padded across the clearing and into the fern tunnel. As he pushed through the soft green fronds, he heard Yellowfang's voice. Something about it—perhaps its gentleness, so unusual for Yellowfang—made him stay in the shelter of the arching ferns for a moment longer.

"Lie still, Brokentail. You have lost a life," Yellowfang was murmuring. "You're going to be fine."

"What do you mean?" snarled Brokentail, his voice weak from loss of blood. "If I've got another life left, why do my wounds still hurt?"

"StarClan have healed the wound that killed you," Yellowfang explained, still in the same soft murmur that sent prickles along Fireheart's spine. "The others need the skill of a medicine cat."

"Then what are you waiting for, you scrawny old pest?" hissed Brokentail. "Get on with it. Give me something for this pain."

"All right, I will." Yellowfang's voice suddenly turned icy cold, and a ripple of fear coursed through Fireheart. "Here. Eat these berries, and the pain will go away for good."

Fireheart peered out of the ferns to see Yellowfang dabbing something with her paw. Carefully, deliberately, she rolled three bright red berries in front of the wounded Brokentail, guiding his paw until he could touch them. Suddenly Fireheart was transported back to a snowy day in leaf-bare. Cloudkit was staring at a small, dark-leaved bush that bore scarlet berries, and Cinderpaw was saying, "The berries are so poisonous we call them deathberries. Even one could kill you."

He drew breath to call out a warning, but Brokentail was already chewing the berries.

Yellowfang stood watching him with a face like stone. "You and my Clan cast me out and I came here," she hissed into his ear. "I was a prisoner, just like you. But ThunderClan treated me well, and at last they trusted me enough to be their medicine cat. You could have earned their trust, too. But now—will any cat trust you ever again?"

Brokentail let out a contemptuous hiss. "Do you think I care?"

Yellowfang crouched even closer to him, her eyes gleaming. "I know you care for nothing, Brokentail. Not your Clan, nor your honor, nor your own kin."

"I have no kin." Brokentail spat out the words.

"Wrong. Your kin has been closer to you than you ever dreamed. I'm your mother, Brokentail."

The blind warrior made a curious rasping noise in his throat, like a terrible attempt at laughter. "Spiders have spun webs in your brain, old one. Medicine cats never have kits."

"That's why I had to give you up," Yellowfang told him, seasons of bitterness dripping from each word. "But I never stopped caring . . . never. When you were a young warrior, I was so proud of you." Her voice dropped to a low snarl. "And then you murdered Raggedstar. Your own father. You killed kits of our Clan, and made me take the blame. You would have destroyed our Clan completely. So now it is time to put an end to all this treachery."

"An end? What do you mean, you old . . ." Brokentail tried to rise to his paws, but his legs gave way and he fell heavily onto his side. His voice rose to a thin screech that chilled Fireheart to the bone. "What have you done? I can't . . . can't feel my paws. Can't breathe . . ."

"I fed you deathberries." Yellowfang's eyes were mere slits as she gazed at him. "I know this is your last life, Brokentail. Medicine cats always know. Now no cat will ever be hurt again because of you."

Brokentail's jaws parted in a cry of shock and fear. Fireheart thought he could hear regret there, too, but the blind warrior was unable to put words to it. His limbs thrashed and his paws scrabbled in the dust; his chest heaved as he fought for air.

Unable to go on watching, Fireheart backed away and crouched at the other end of the fern tunnel, shivering, until the sounds of Brokentail's last struggle died away. Then, mindful of Cinderpaw's request, he forced himself to go back, making sure that Yellowfang could hear him pushing his way through the bracken this time.

Brokentail lay motionless in the center of the small clearing. The old medicine cat crouched beside him, her nose pressed to his side. As Fireheart padded up, she raised her head. Her eyes were filled with pain and she looked older and frailer than ever. But Fireheart knew how strong she was, that the sorrow she felt for Brokentail would not destroy her. "I did everything I could, but he died," she explained.

Fireheart could not tell the medicine cat that he knew she was lying. He would never tell any cat what he had just seen and heard. Trying to keep his voice steady, he meowed, "Cinderpaw sent me to ask you what to do for a scratched tongue."

Yellowfang struggled to her paws as if she too could feel the numbing touch of deathberries. "Tell her I'm coming," she rasped. "I just need to fetch the right herb."

Still unsteady, she staggered over to her den. She did not turn once to look back at Brokentail's unmoving body.

Fireheart thought he would be unable to sleep, but he was so exhausted that as soon as he curled up in his nest he sank at once into deep unconsciousness. He dreamed that he was standing in a high place, with wind ruffling his fur and the stars of Silverpelt blazing with icy fire above his head.

A warm, familiar scent drifted into his nostrils and he turned his head to see Spottedleaf. She padded up to him and touched her nose gently to his. "StarClan is calling you, Fireheart," she murmured. "Do not be afraid." Then she faded, leaving him with nothing but the wind and the stars.

StarClan calling me? Fireheart thought, puzzled. *Am I dying, then?*

Fear jerked him awake, and he gasped with relief when he found himself safe in the dim light of the den. His wounds from the battle still stung, and as he got up his limbs protested stiffly, but his strength was returning. Still, it was hard to control his shivering. Had Spottedleaf just prophesied his death?

Then he realized that the chill he felt was not just because of fear. The den, usually warm from sleeping bodies, was cold and empty. Outside he could hear the murmuring of many cats. When he pushed his way out to join them, he saw that nearly all the Clan was already assembled in the clearing, with the pale light of dawn just rising above the trees.

Sandstorm pushed her way through a group of cats. "Fireheart!" she mewed urgently. "Moonhigh has come and gone, and Bluestar hasn't named the new deputy!"

"What?" Fireheart stared at the pale ginger she-cat in alarm. The warrior code had been broken! "StarClan will be angry," he murmured.

"We *must* have a deputy," Sandstorm went on, lashing her tail in agitation. "But Bluestar won't even come out of her den. Whitestorm tried to talk to her, but she sent him away."

"She's still shocked about Tigerclaw," Fireheart pointed out.

"But she's the leader of this Clan," retorted Sandstorm. "She can't just curl up in her den and forget about the rest of us."

Fireheart knew she was right, but he could not stifle a pang of sympathy for Bluestar. He knew how much she had depended on Tigerclaw, loyally defending him against Fireheart's accusations. She had chosen him to be her deputy, and had trusted him to help her lead the Clan. She must be shattered to realize that she had been wrong all along, and that never again would she be able to count on Tigerclaw's strength and fighting skills.

"She won't forget—" he began, and broke off.

Bluestar was stumbling around the Highrock from her den. She looked old and weary as she sat down in front of the rock, making no attempt to climb it. "Cats of ThunderClan," she rasped, barely loud enough to be heard over the anxious muttering. "Listen and I will appoint the new deputy."

Every cat was already turning toward her, and the clearing fell chillingly silent.

"I say these words before StarClan, that the spirits of our ancestors may hear and approve my choice." Bluestar paused again, staring down at her paws for so long that Fireheart wondered if she had forgotten what she was going to say. Perhaps she had not even decided yet who the new deputy should be.

One or two cats had begun to whisper uneasily, but as Bluestar raised her head again they stopped.

"The new deputy will be Fireheart," she announced clearly. As soon as she had spoken she rose to her paws again and padded back around the rock on legs that seemed made of stone.

The whole Clan froze. Fireheart felt as though a thorn had pierced his heart. *He* was to be deputy? He wanted to call Bluestar back and tell her there must be some mistake. He was barely a warrior!

Then he heard Cloudpaw's shrill voice raised gleefully. "I knew it! Fireheart's the new deputy!"

Close by, Darkstripe snarled, "Oh, yes? Well, *I'm* not taking orders from a kittypet!"

A few of the cats padded over to Fireheart and congratulated him. Graystripe and Sandstorm were among the first, and Cinderpaw, purring enthusiastically and throwing herself at him to give his face a thorough licking.

But other cats, Fireheart noticed, slipped quietly away, and did not speak to him at all. It was clear that they were as startled by Bluestar's choice as Fireheart was himself. Was this what Spottedleaf had meant in his dream, when she told him that StarClan was calling him? Calling him to new responsibilities within his Clan? "Do not be afraid," she had told him.

Oh, Spottedleaf, Fireheart thought desperately, as fear and uncertainty flooded his mind. *How can I not be afraid?*

CHAPTER 30

❧

"*Well, Clan deputy,*" *Whitestorm meowed softly* in his ear. "*What* would you like me to do now?"

Fireheart realized his offer was genuine, and he flashed the great white warrior a grateful glance. He knew Whitestorm could have expected to become deputy himself, and his support would be valuable to Fireheart in the days to come. "Yes . . . now . . ." he began, frantically trying to think what the most urgent priorities would be. With a jolt, he realized that he was trying to imagine what Tigerclaw would have done. "Food. We all need to eat. Cloudpaw, start taking fresh-kill to the elders. Get the other apprentices to help the queens in the nursery." Cloudpaw shot off with a flick of his tail. "Mousefur, Darkstripe, find yourselves two or three warriors each and go out on a hunting patrol. Split the territory between you. We'll need more fresh-kill right away. And keep a lookout for those rogues or Tigerclaw while you're at it."

Mousefur moved away with a calm nod, collecting Brackenfur and Willowpelt as she went. But Darkstripe glared at Fireheart for so long that Fireheart began to wonder what he would do if the dark warrior really refused to obey him. He met the pale blue gaze steadily, and at last Darkstripe turned away, meowing to Longtail and Dustpelt to follow him.

"All Tigerclaw's sympathizers," Whitestorm observed as he watched them go. "You'll need to keep an eye on them."

"Yes, I know," Fireheart admitted. "But surely they've shown that they're more loyal to the Clan than to Tigerclaw? I hope they'll accept me if I don't tread on their tails."

Whitestorm gave a noncommittal grunt.

"Anything for me to do?" asked Graystripe.

"Yes." Fireheart gave his friend's ear a quick, friendly lick. "Go back to your nest and rest. You were badly wounded yesterday. I'll bring you a piece of fresh-kill."

"Oh, okay. Thanks, Fireheart." Graystripe returned the lick and vanished into the den.

Fireheart padded over to the pile of fresh-kill, where he found Cinderpaw clawing a magpie out of the dwindling heap. "I'll take this to Bluestar," she offered. "I need to check her wound. And then I'll take some prey for Yellowfang."

"Good idea," Fireheart meowed, beginning to feel more confident as his rapid orders seemed to be restoring things to normal. "Tell her if she needs any help to collect herbs, she can have Cloudpaw, once he's seen to the elders."

"Okay." Cinderpaw chuckled. "You certainly know how to make your apprentices work, Fireheart." She bit down into the magpie and dropped it at once with a retch of disgust. The flesh of the dead bird fell away from the bones to reveal a writhing mass of white maggots. A foul stench hit

Fireheart and he winced.

Cinderpaw backed away, passing her tongue around her mouth over and over again as she stared at the rotting carcass. Her dark gray fur was fluffed up and her blue eyes wide. "Crowfood," she whispered. "Crowfood among the fresh-kill. What does it mean?"

Fireheart couldn't imagine how the rotten magpie had gotten there. No cat would have brought it in; even the youngest apprentice knew better than that.

"What does it mean?" Cinderpaw repeated.

Fireheart suddenly realized she wasn't thinking about any practical reasons for how maggot-ridden prey had ended up in the pile. "Do you think it's an omen?" he croaked. "A message from StarClan?"

"It might be." Cinderpaw shivered, and stared at him with huge blue eyes. "StarClan haven't spoken to me yet, Fireheart, not since the ceremony at the Moonstone. I don't know if it's an omen or not, but if it is . . . "

"It must be for Bluestar," Fireheart finished. His fur prickled as he realized this was the first sign of Cinderpaw's new powers as an apprentice medicine cat. "You were going to take the magpie to her." He felt a thrill of horror at the thought of what the omen might mean. Was StarClan trying to say that Bluestar's leadership was rotting away from the *inside*, even though Tigerclaw's outer threat had gone? "No," he meowed firmly. "That can't be right. Bluestar's problems are *over*. Some cat's been careless, that's all, and brought crowfood back by mistake."

But he didn't believe his own words, and he could tell that Cinderpaw didn't, either. "I'll ask Yellowfang," she mewed, shaking her head in bewilderment. "She'll know." Cinderpaw quickly snatched a vole from the heap and began limping rapidly across the clearing.

Fireheart called after her, "Don't tell any cat except Yellowfang. The Clan mustn't know. I'll bury this."

She flicked her tail to show she had heard, and vanished among the ferns.

Fireheart glanced around to make sure that no other cat had overheard their conversation, or seen the decaying magpie. Bile rose in his throat as he gripped the bird by the tip of one wing and dragged it to the edge of the clearing. He didn't begin to relax until he had scraped up enough earth to cover the vile thing.

Even then, he could not get it out of his mind. If the rotting, maggot-filled crowfood was indeed an omen, what new disasters did StarClan have in store for ThunderClan and their leader now?

By sunhigh, the Clan had settled down again. The hunting patrols had returned, all the cats were full-fed, and Fireheart was beginning to think it was time he went to Bluestar's den to see if she would talk to him about leading the Clan.

He was distracted by movement in the gorse tunnel. Four RiverClan cats appeared, the same four who had joined in the battle the day before: Leopardfur, Mistyfoot, Stonefur, and Blackclaw.

Leopardfur bore a newly healed wound across one dappled shoulder, and Blackclaw's ear was torn at the tip, proof of how they had fought with ThunderClan to drive out the rogue cats. Fireheart wished he could believe that they had come only to find out if the ThunderClan warriors were all right. But deep down he knew their mission had to do with Graystripe's kits. Struggling to hide the heaviness in his heart, he padded across the clearing and dipped his head to Leopardfur—not the respectful signal from a warrior to a deputy, but a courteous greeting between equals.

"Greetings," meowed Leopardfur, her eyes registering surprise at Fireheart's new attitude. "We need to speak to your leader."

Fireheart hesitated, wondering how much to explain. It would take the rest of the day to tell the full story of Tigerclaw's treachery, and to describe how Fireheart himself had been named deputy. In a heartbeat's pause, he decided to tell the visiting patrol nothing. Even RiverClan, though they seemed friendly now, might be tempted to attack a Clan that seemed to be weak. The next Gathering would be soon enough for them to know. He bowed his head once more and went to look for Bluestar.

To his relief, the Clan leader was sitting in her den, finishing a piece of fresh-kill. She looked more like herself than Fireheart had seen her since Tigerclaw's attack. As he announced himself at the entrance to the den, Bluestar looked up, swallowing the last of her mouse. Her tongue swiped around her jaws and she meowed, "Fireheart? Come in. We have a great deal to discuss."

"Yes, Bluestar," Fireheart mewed, "but not now. The RiverClan warriors are here."

"Ah." Bluestar rose to her paws and stretched. "I was expecting them, although I had hoped they wouldn't come back quite so soon." She led the way out of her den to where the patrol was waiting. By now, Graystripe had appeared and seemed to be exchanging news with Mistyfoot. Fireheart hoped he was not telling her too much as he settled down a respectful distance from the RiverClan patrol.

Other cats too were gathering around, their faces revealing their curiosity about the reason for the RiverClan cats' visit.

When Bluestar had greeted the newcomers, Leopardfur began. "We've talked for a long time about Silverstream's kits, and we've decided that they belong in RiverClan. Two RiverClan kits died yesterday. They had been born too soon. Their mother, Greenflower, has agreed to suckle these newborns. We think it may be a sign from StarClan. The kits will be well cared for."

"They're well cared for here!" Fireheart exclaimed.

Leopardfur glanced at him but still spoke directly to Bluestar. "Crookedstar has sent us to fetch them." Her voice was calm but determined, showing that she genuinely believed in her Clan's right to take the kits.

"Besides," Mistyfoot added, "the kits are older now, and the river has gone down enough to allow a safe passage across. They will be able to cope with the journey to our camp."

"Yes," meowed Leopardfur, with an approving look at the

younger warrior. "We could have taken the kits before this, but we care just as much about their welfare as you do."

Bluestar drew herself up. Though she moved stiffly and she still looked exhausted, outwardly at least she had recovered the authority of a leader. "The kits are half ThunderClan," she reminded Leopardfur. "I've already told you, I'll give you my decision at the next Gathering."

"The decision is not yours to make." The RiverClan deputy's tone had an edge like ice.

At her words meows of protest rose from the assembled cats.

"Cheek!" spat Sandstorm, from where she sat close to Fireheart. "Who does she think she is, walking in here and telling us what to do?"

Fireheart padded over to Bluestar and murmured in her ear, "Bluestar, these are *Graystripe's* kits. You can't send them away."

Bluestar twitched her ears. "You can tell Crookedstar," she calmly addressed the visitors, "that ThunderClan will fight to keep these kits."

Leopardfur's lips drew back in the beginnings of a snarl, while the ThunderClan cats yowled their approval.

Then a louder meow rose above the rest. "No!"

Fireheart's fur began to prickle. It was Graystripe.

The big gray cat came to stand beside Bluestar. Fireheart winced when he saw the looks of suspicion that ThunderClan gave him, and how they drew back as he passed. But Graystripe seemed to have hardened himself against their hostility.

Glancing first at the RiverClan patrol and then at the cats of his own Clan, he meowed, "Leopardfur is right. Kits belong with their mother's Clan. I think we should let them go."

Fireheart froze. He wanted to protest, but could find no words. The rest of the Clan was just as silent, except for Yellowfang, who muttered, "He's mad."

"Graystripe, think again," Bluestar urged him. "If I let Leopardfur take these kits, they are lost to you forever. They will grow up in another Clan. They will not know you as their kin. One day you may even have to fight them." Fireheart heard the sorrow in her voice as she spoke, and saw her eyes straying to Mistyfoot and Stonefur. Her words were full of such bitter knowledge that he wondered how any cat could listen to her and not realize the truth about the kits their leader had lost so long ago.

"I understand, Bluestar," Graystripe agreed. "But I've caused enough trouble for this Clan. I won't ask them to fight for my kits." He paused and added to Leopardfur, "If Bluestar agrees, I'll bring the kits to the stepping-stones at sunset. I give you my word."

"Graystripe, don't . . ." Fireheart burst out.

Graystripe turned his yellow eyes to his friend. Fireheart saw pain there, and measureless unhappiness, but also a determination that made him realize there was something in his friend's mind that Fireheart himself did not yet understand.

"Don't . . ." he repeated softly, but Graystripe did not reply.

Sandstorm pushed her nose into Fireheart's fur and murmured a few words of comfort, but Fireheart felt too numb to respond. He was vaguely aware of Cinderpaw nudging Sandstorm on the other side and whispering, "Not now, Sandstorm. There's nothing we can say. Leave him be."

Bluestar bowed her head for several long moments. Fireheart could see how much of her hastily summoned strength was ebbing away in the confrontation, and how desperately she needed rest. At last she spoke. "Graystripe, are you sure?"

The gray warrior lifted his chin. "Quite sure."

"In that case," Bluestar went on, "I agree to your demands, Leopardfur. Graystripe will bring the kits to the stepping-stones at sunset."

Leopardfur looked startled to win an agreement so quickly. She exchanged a glance with Blackclaw, almost as if she were asking if there could be trickery here. "Then we will hold you to your word," she meowed, turning back to the ThunderClan leader. "In the name of StarClan, see that you keep it." She dipped her head to Bluestar and led her cats away. Fireheart watched them go and turned to plead once more with Graystripe, but his friend was already vanishing into the nursery.

As the sun slid down behind the trees, Fireheart waited by the gorse tunnel. Leaves rustled above his head, and the air was filled with the warm scents of late newleaf, but Fireheart was barely conscious of his surroundings. His mind was full of thoughts of Graystripe. There was no way he was going to let his friend give up his kits without making one last attempt to stop him.

At last Graystripe emerged from the nursery, herding the two kits on stumpy, unsteady legs in front of him. The small dark-gray tom already looked as if he would grow into a sturdy warrior, while the she-cat with her silvery coat was a copy of her mother, promising the same beauty and swiftness.

Goldenflower followed them out of the nursery and dipped her head to touch noses with both kits. "Farewell, my beloveds," she mewed sadly.

The two kits let out bewildered meows as Graystripe nudged them away, and Goldenflower's own kits nuzzled their mother's flank, as if they meant to comfort her.

"Graystripe—" Fireheart began, stepping forward as his friend approached with the kits.

"Don't say anything," Graystripe interrupted him. "You'll understand soon. Will you come with me to the stepping-stones? I . . . I need your help to carry the kits."

"Of course, if you want me to." Fireheart was ready to agree to anything that seemed to offer the smallest chance of persuading Graystripe to change his mind and keep the kits.

The two warriors padded together through the forest, as they had done so many times before. They each carried one of the kits; the tiny scraps mewed and wriggled as if they wanted to walk on their own paws. Fireheart did not know how his friend could bear to give them up. Had Bluestar felt like this, he wondered, when she looked on her own kits for the last time before letting Oakheart have them?

By the time they reached the stepping-stones, the red light of sunset was fading. The moon was beginning to rise, and the river was a silvery ribbon that reflected the pale sky. Its liquid murmur filled the air, and the long grass on the edge of the shore felt fresh and cool beneath Fireheart's paws.

Fireheart set down the kit he was carrying in a soft clump of grass, and Graystripe placed the other gently beside it. Then he moved away a pace or two, jerking his head for Fireheart to follow him. "You were right," he meowed. "I can't give up my kits."

Sudden joy flooded through Fireheart. Graystripe had changed his mind! They could take the kits home, and face up to the threat from RiverClan, whatever it might be. Then his heart froze as Graystripe went on.

"I'm going with them. They're all I have left of Silverstream, and she told me to take care of them. I'd die if I were parted from them."

Fireheart stared at him, his mouth dropping open. "What? You can't!" he gasped. "You belong to ThunderClan."

Graystripe shook his head. "Not anymore. They don't want me, not since they found out about me and Silverstream. They'll never trust me again. I don't even know if I *want* them to trust me anymore. I don't think I've got any Clan loyalty left."

His words clutched at Fireheart's belly like the claws of an enemy, trying to tear it into shreds. "Oh, Graystripe," he whispered. "What about me? *I* want you there. I'd trust you with my life, and I'd never betray you."

Graystripe's yellow eyes were brimming with sorrow. "I know," he murmured. "No cat ever had such a friend as you. I'd give my life for you; you know that."

"Then stay in ThunderClan!"

"I can't. That's the only thing I can't do for you. I belong with my kits, and they belong in RiverClan. Oh, Fireheart, Fireheart . . ." His voice trailed off into an anguished wail. "I'm being torn in two!"

Fireheart pressed close to him, licking his ear and feeling the trembling that racked his friend's powerful body. They had been through so much together. Graystripe had been the first Clan cat he had ever spoken to, as a kittypet lost in the woods. He had been his first friend in ThunderClan. They had trained together and been made warriors together. They had hunted in the hot days of greenleaf when the air was filled with scent and the murmuring of bees, and through a bitter leaf-bare when the whole world was frozen. Together they had discovered the truth about Tigerclaw, and risked Bluestar's anger to do it.

And now it was coming to an end.

But worst of all, Fireheart could not find the words to argue with his friend. It was true that ThunderClan still mistrusted the gray warrior for his love of Silverstream, and they showed no sign that they would ever fully accept his kits. If they had fought to keep them, it would have been only for the honor of the Clan. Fireheart could see no future for his friend or the kits in ThunderClan.

At last Graystripe moved away and went back to call the

kits. They stumbled up to him, mewling in tiny, high-pitched voices. "It's time," he meowed softly to Fireheart. "I'll see you at the next Gathering."

"It won't be the same."

Graystripe held his gaze for a long moment. "No, it won't be the same." Then he turned and carried one of the kits down the shore to the stepping-stones, leaping over the gaps with the kit gripped safely by the scruff. On the opposite bank, a gray shape slipped out of the reeds and stood waiting while Graystripe returned for the second kit.

Fireheart recognized Mistyfoot, Silverstream's best friend. He knew she would love these kits as much as her own. But no cat could feel more strongly for Graystripe than Fireheart had done, for four long seasons.

Never again, his heart was crying. *No more patrols, no more play-fights, or sharing tongues in the den after a day of hunting. No more laughter shared or dangers faced together. It's over.*

There was nothing he could do or say. He watched help-lessly as Graystripe and the second kit reached the far river-bank. Mistyfoot touched noses with the gray warrior, then bent to sniff the kits. With unspoken agreement, she and Graystripe each picked up a kit, and all four cats disappeared into the reeds.

Fireheart stayed there for a long time, watching the silver water as it slid past the shore. When the moon had risen above the trees, he forced himself to his paws, and padded back into the forest.

He felt a sadness and a loneliness greater than anything he

had ever felt before, but at the same time he could sense a surge of energy rising from deep inside himself. He had revealed the truth about Tigerclaw and stopped the deputy from causing any more destruction within the Clan. Bluestar had honored him beyond measure by choosing him to be her second in command. He could go on from this moment, guided by his leader, and with Spottedleaf and StarClan watching over him.

Unconsciously, his pace quickened, and by the time Fireheart reached the ravine he was running, his flame-colored pelt a blur in the lilac dusk, eager to return to ThunderClan and his new life as their deputy.

KEEP WATCH FOR

WARRIORS

BOOK 4:

RISING STORM

Warm shafts of sun shine streamed through the canopy of leaves and flickered over Fireheart's pelt. He crouched lower, aware that his coat would be glowing amber among the lush green undergrowth.

Paw by paw, he crept beneath a fern. He could smell a pigeon. He moved slowly toward the mouthwatering scent until he could see the plump bird pecking among the ferns.

Fireheart flexed his claws, his paws itching with anticipation. He was hungry after leading the dawn patrol and hunting all morning. This was the high season for prey, a time for the Clan to grow fat on the forest's bounty. And although there had been little rain since the newleaf floods, the woods were rich with food. After stocking the fresh-kill pile back at camp, it was time for Fireheart to hunt for himself. He tensed his muscles, ready to leap.

Suddenly a second scent wafted toward him on the dry breeze. Fireheart opened his mouth, tipping his head to one side. The pigeon must have smelled it too, for its head shot up and it began to unfold its wings, but it was too late. A rush of white fur shot out from under some brambles. Fireheart stared in surprise as the cat pounced on the startled bird, pinning it to the ground with his front paws before finishing it off with a swift bite to the neck.

The delicious smell of fresh-kill filled Fireheart's nostrils. He stood up and padded out of the undergrowth toward the fluffy white tom. "Well caught, Cloudpaw," he meowed. "I didn't see you coming until it was too late."

"Nor did this stupid bird," crowed Cloudpaw, flicking his tail smugly.

Fireheart felt his shoulders tense. Cloudpaw was his apprentice as well as his sister's son. It was Fireheart's responsibility to teach him the skills of a Clan warrior and how to respect the warrior code. The young tom was undeniably a good hunter, but Fireheart couldn't help wishing that he would learn a little humility. Deep down, he sometimes wondered if Cloudpaw would ever understand the importance of the warrior code, the moons-old traditions of loyalty and ritual that had been passed down through generations of cats in the forest.

But Cloudpaw had been born in Twolegplace to Fireheart's kittypet sister, Princess, and brought to ThunderClan by Fireheart as a tiny kit. Fireheart knew from his own bitter experience that Clan cats had no respect for kittypets. Fireheart had spent his first six moons living with Twolegs, and there were cats in his Clan that would never let him forget the fact that he was not forest-born. He twitched his ears impatiently. He knew he did everything he could to prove his loyalty to the Clan, but his stubborn apprentice was a different matter. If Cloudpaw was going to win any sympathy from his Clanmates, he was going to have to lose some of his arrogance.

"It's just as well you're so quick," Fireheart pointed out. "You were upwind. I could *smell* you, even if I couldn't see you. And so could the bird."

Cloudpaw's long snowy fur bristled and he snapped back, "I *know* I was upwind! But I could tell this dumb dove wasn't going to be hard to catch whether he smelled me or not."

The young cat stared defiantly into Fireheart's eyes, and Fireheart felt his annoyance turning to anger. "It's a pigeon, not a dove!" he spat. "And a true warrior shows more respect for the prey that feeds his Clan."

"Yeah, right!" retorted Cloudpaw. "I didn't see Thornpaw show much respect for that squirrel he dragged back to camp yesterday. He said it was so dopey, a kit could have caught it."

"Thornpaw is just an apprentice," Fireheart growled. "Like you, he still has a lot to learn."

"Well, I caught it, didn't I?" grumbled Cloudpaw, prodding the pigeon with a sullen paw.

"There's more to being a warrior than catching pigeons!"

"I'm faster than Brightpaw and stronger than Thornpaw," Cloudpaw spat back. "What more do you want?"

"Your denmates would know that a warrior never attacks

with the wind behind him!" Fireheart knew he shouldn't let himself be drawn into an argument, but his apprentice's stubbornness infuriated him like a tick on his ear.

"Big deal. You might have been downwind like a good warrior, but *I* got to the pigeon first!" Cloudpaw raised his voice in an angry yowl.

"Be quiet," Fireheart hissed, suddenly distracted. He lifted his head and sniffed the air. The forest seemed strangely silent, and Cloudpaw's loud meows were echoing too loudly through the trees.

"What's the matter?" Cloudpaw glanced around. "I can't smell anything."

"Neither can I," Fireheart admitted.

"So what are you worried about?"

"Tigerclaw," Fireheart answered bluntly. The dark warrior had been prowling through his dreams since Bluestar had banished him from the Clan a quarter moon ago. Tigerclaw had tried to kill the ThunderClan leader, but Fireheart had stopped him and exposed his long-hidden treachery to the whole Clan. There had been no sign of Tigerclaw since, but Fireheart felt icy claws of fear pricking at his heart now as he listened to the stillness of the forest. It seemed to be listening too, holding its breath, and Tigerclaw's parting words echoed in Fireheart's mind: *Keep your eyes open, Fireheart. Keep your ears pricked. Keep looking behind you. Because one day I'll find you, and then you'll be crowfood.*